ORPHAN COWBOY

ALSO BY ROBERT VAUGHAN

The Tenderfoot

On the Oregon Trail

Cold Revenge

Iron Horse

Outlaw Justice

Western Fiction Ten Pack

The Founders Series

The Western Adventures of Cade McCall

Faraday Series

Lucas Cain Series

Chaney Brothers Westerns

Arrow and Saber Series

The Crocketts Series

Remington Series

...and many more

ORPHAN COWBOY

ROBERT VAUGHAN

WOLFPACK PUBLISHING
— EST 2013 —

ORPHAN COWBOY

ONE

WHEN THE YOUNG WOMAN LEFT THE HANSOM CAB, SHE walked three blocks down Avenue C, carrying a bundle in her arms. She stopped when she reached the address she was looking for. The sign read Our Lady of Mercy Orphanage.

Steeling herself with a deep breath, she walked up to the front door and rang the bell. A woman in a nun's habit opened the door, a beatific smile on her face.

"May I help you?" the nun asked.

The young woman thrust the blanket-covered bundle into the nun's arms.

"He's one week old. I can't keep him," the woman said as tears ran down her cheeks.

"What are you doing? You can't..." the nun started, but before she could finish her sentence, the young woman turned and ran down the cobbled walkway.

After the woman was out of sight, the startled nun took the baby to the office of the Mother Superior.

"What have you there, Sister Maria?"

"It's a baby."

"I can see that, but whose baby is it?"

"Some lady rang the bell, and when I opened the door, she thrust him in my arms."

"And where is she now?"

"She left," Sister Maria said.

"Left? With no explanation or information about the baby? She just left?"

"Yes. What will we do with him, Mother Superior?"

"Did she give you his name?"

"She did not."

Mother Superior looked at the baby.

"Well, then we shall give him a name until someone comes to retrieve the infant."

"Do you think she will come back?"

"It's hard to say what circumstance has caused this woman to give up a child," Mother Superior said. "What was her demeanor when she left? Do you think the child was hers, or do you think the baby belonged to someone else?"

"She seemed to be distraught when she ran down the walkway. I believe the baby is hers."

Mother Superior's expression changed to one of concern. "Sister Maria, I will charge you to see to the child's wellbeing until such time as he is surrendered to his natural mother or he is chosen for adoption by loving parents. In the meantime, you choose the name he will have while he is with us."

Sister Maria smiled. "I will name him Lee Edward Holt. That was my father's name, and he was a good and decent God-fearing man."

"Then Lee Edward Holt it is."

* * *

THE TALL MAN LIT A PIPE, then walked over to look out the window. He took a few puffs from his pipe so that the smoke curled around his head. "Where did she go?"

The question was directed to the man who had just come into the room.

"She's still in San Antonio," the second man answered.

"What did she do with the baby?"

"She left him at Our Lady of Mercy in San Antonio."

"So, it's a boy."

"Yes, sir."

"What kind of orphanage is it? How does it treat its wards?"

"From what I have learned, the children in their care are treated with love and respect."

"That's good to know. I want you to do whatever it takes to keep abreast of his upbringing. I want to be kept informed, but I don't want him, or anyone at the orphanage, to know what you are doing."

"Yes, sir, I understand."

* * *

OUR LADY OF MERCY ORPHANAGE—1864

Lee Edward was with Sister Maria when a new resident, a six-year-old boy, arrived.

"Lee Edward, do you see that new boy?" Sister Maria asked. "His name is Timothy, and he has come to live with us, so I want you to be nice to him."

"Yes, ma'am, I will, but why is he crying?"

"He's crying because his parents have died, so he didn't have anyone to take care of him."

"What is a parents?"

"Your mother and father are parents."

"You mean Mother Superior and Father Tuttle are parents?"

Sister Maria looked shocked by Lee Edward's question, then she hugged him. "Oh, bless your heart, child, it never dawned on me that you wouldn't know what parents are, but then you never knew your parents."

* * *

DURING THE NEXT EIGHT YEARS, Lee Edward was educated, not only in school, but in life. He knew about a mother and father and understood that, like everyone else, he had had parents, though nobody knew who his parents were. He also learned that the normal person had been named by their parents and that their last name was their father's name. His name, he now knew, had been given to him by Sister Maria. He also knew that his mother had given him away because she didn't want him.

"Oh, Lee Edward, please don't be upset with her. She loved you and wanted the best for you, but she was unable to care for you. That's why she brought you to us," Sister Maria had explained.

But where was his father, Lee Edward wondered. Why didn't anyone know anything about him?

Even though Lee Edward had had such thoughts while he was a resident of the orphanage, he sometimes felt guilty when he wondered about it. This had been the only home he had ever known, and he had been well treated. He knew Sister Maria loved him and he was certain he couldn't love his birth mother more than he loved Sister Maria.

* * *

OVER THE NEXT FEW YEARS, Lee Edward grew in size and wisdom. He made many friends and enjoyed the games they played. The orphanage had its own school and Lee Edward did exceptionally well with his studies.

Lee noticed that there was one thing different about him, from all the other boys in the orphanage, and that was his relationship with Sister Maria. Although Sister Maria treated everyone with kindness, she seemed to show even more warmness when she dealt with Lee Edward. And though Lee Edward had respect for all the sisters, he actually felt love for Sister Maria.

By the time he was fourteen, Lee Edward had grown tall, with wide shoulders and muscular arms. Because of his size, nobody, not even the older boys, ever picked on him. Some of the younger boys weren't so lucky though, and one day, Lee Edward saw two fifteen-year-olds picking on a boy who had just arrived. The boy was still saddened that his mother had so recently died.

"You know why you don't have a daddy?" one of the bigger boys challenged. "It's 'cause your mama was a whore, 'n she didn't even know who your daddy was."

"Please, leave me alone," the boy said.

"You're a crybaby," the other of the two bigger boys said.

"Tyler, you and Sheldon leave Tony alone," Lee Edward said.

"Well, if it ain't Sister Maria's boy," Tyler said.

"You're goin' to take care of this crybaby, are you?" Sheldon asked.

"No," Lee Edward answered. "I'm going to take care of you."

"Are you, now?" Sheldon asked. "I'm sure you noticed that there are two of us, 'n there's only one of you."

"One of me is all I need."

"Thank you," Tony said as he moved closer to Lee Edward.

"Don't thank him yet," Tyler said. "You can thank him after we leave his ass lyin' on the floor."

Tyler nodded at Sheldon, and with broad, confident smiles, the two boys advanced toward Lee Edward. Lee Edward took Tyler down with a right hook and Sheldon down with a left.

By now, several of the other orphans had gathered around, and they laughed at the two bullies as Tyler and Sheldon regained their feet. Looking at Lee Edward in obvious fear, they turned and hurried from the cafeteria as they heard the mocking laughter of the others.

Shortly after the incident in the cafeteria, Lee Edward was summoned to the Mother Superior's office. She looked at him with an expression of displeasure, and Lee Edward was made uneasy by her reproachful glare.

Sister Maria was there as well, and Lee Edward was shamed that his misbehavior had involved Sister Maria.

"Lee, you have been here longer than anyone," Mother Superior said. "You know that violence is not to be tolerated."

"Yes, ma'am," Lee Edward replied quietly,

"Mother Superior, if I may," Sister Maria interjected. "Sheldon and Tyler were bullying young Tony Kern. As you know, Tony only recently came to be with us. His mother was lost in a house fire and he hasn't gotten over that terrible sorrow. Lee Edward came to the boy's defense."

"While I don't condone any kind of violence, I can see that your heart was in the right place," Mother Superior said, the reproving glare gone. "But please, Lee Edward, try to restrain yourself from any future such episodes. You must set an example for the others."

"Yes, Mother Superior," Lee Edward said quietly.

As Lee Edward and Sister Maria left Mother Superior's office, Sister Maria reached out to put her hand on Lee Edward's shoulder.

"I'm like Mother Superior, in that I don't appreciate violence," Sister Maria said. Then, she smiled at him. "On the other hand, I'm proud of you for coming to the aid of young Tony."

* * *

By the time Lee Edward was sixteen years old, it was already apparent that he was going to be a larger-than-average man. Despite his youth, his shoulders were broad and his arms muscular. He stood just under six feet tall, and it was fairly obvious that he would continue growing. It was also obvious that Lee Edward was going to be a handsome man. His hair was chestnut brown, his eyes were hazel, and he had a squared jaw and brilliant white teeth when he smiled.

This morning, he was standing before the Mother Superior's desk, holding a twenty-dollar bill he had just been given.

"We aren't exactly sure of your birthday, but we do know that you have reached the age of sixteen because you have lived with us for that long," Mother Superior said as she took a deep breath.

Lee Edward thought he saw a tear roll down Mother Superior's face.

She quickly looked away as she wiped her eye. "You have to know that you have been a favorite here at Our Lady of Mercy, but at sixteen, you are a man. It is time for you to leave us."

"Yes, ma'am," Lee Edward said as he looked down at the floor.

Mother Superior smiled at him. "I know it will be hard to leave us, but we won't be turning you out on your own. We have arrangements with good people who are prepared to offer honest employment to our young men as they leave us." She picked up a sheaf of papers and handed them to him.

"Here are ten people who have jobs to offer. Look through them, then decide which job you would like to take. You can stay here one more night, but tomorrow, you are on your own. Do you think you are ready to be on your own?"

"Yes, ma'am," Lee Edward replied with a big smile.

The next morning, even before breakfast, Lee Edward sought out Sister Maria.

"You are leaving today, aren't you?" Sister Maria asked.

"Yes, ma'am." Lee Edward saw that Sister Maria was crying, and seeing that, he choked up as well.

"You'll come see me from time to time?" Sister Maria asked.

"Yes, ma'am, I'll come see you. That I will promise."

"I know that you will, but carry all that you have learned from me and this place close to your heart. Remember the teachings of the Lord and be a just and worthy man. I feel you will be rewarded in this life." Sister Maria pulled him into her embrace, and for the first time, gave him a kiss on his cheek.

He returned the embrace, then turned and walked down the cobblestone path. He couldn't look back, but he knew Sister Maria was watching him. He vowed to himself he would make her proud of him.

* * *

THE TWENTY-DOLLAR BILL Lee Edward had been given was the most money he had ever had. He was carrying a cloth bag with one change of clothes. He had outgrown his coat, so he left it at the orphanage, but as it was August, no coat was needed.

Lee had his breakfast in the Sunrise Café. It wasn't the first time he had ever been there, but it was the first time he had ever been there alone. As he ate, he examined the job offers. Eight were from San Antonio merchants and none of those appealed to him. There were two jobs that he considered more seriously. One was working at the stage depot where he would be changing teams and keeping the stalls clean. The other job was at Marathon Ranch.

The idea of working on a cattle ranch appealed to him, so that was the offer he decided to take. Marathon Ranch, the offer said, was located just outside the town of Selma. Selma was eighteen miles from San Antonio, which meant he would have to take a stagecoach.

After breakfast, Lee Edward walked down to the stage depot. He felt a sense of freedom, but that feeling was somewhat dampened by anxiousness. He was on his own for the first time in his life, without guidance or restrictions other than those which were self-applied.

He thought of an expression. This was the first day of the rest of his life. He smiled at that thought.

He stepped into the depot, then walked up to the counter.

"What can I do for you, young man?" the ticket agent asked.

"How much does it cost to get a ticket for Selma?" Lee Edward asked.

"That'll be one dollar and fifty cents."

"Oh. That's a lot," Lee Edward said. This would be the most money Lee Edward had ever spent at one time.

"It may be, but that's what it's going to cost you, if you want to go to Selma."

"I've got to go to Selma. I have a job there," Lee Edward said.

The ticket agent smiled. "Well, look at it this way. If you have a job there, you'll earn enough money to replace this."

Now it was Lee Edward's time to smile. "Yeah, that's right, isn't it? All right, give me a ticket to Selma." He put two dollars on the counter and waited for the change.

There were three others in the waiting room, an overweight man wearing a jacket that pulled at the buttons. He was carrying a small case of some sort. There was also a woman and a little girl.

"Are you going to Selma?" the little girl asked Lee Edward.

"Yes, ma'am."

The little girl laughed, then looked up at her mother. "Mama, he said 'yes ma'am' to me. He's not supposed to say that to me."

"Maybe he's just being nice," her mother said.

"Are you being nice to me?" the little girl asked.

"Yes, ma'am, I suppose I am." Lee Edward chuckled. The orphanage had only boys in residence. Over the years, he had seen girls and had talked to them, but he had no idea how to talk to a girl child this young. He had so much to learn.

A bearded man stepped in through the front door. "Folks, the coach is ready for you to climb aboard."

Lee picked up his cloth bag and stepped outside with the others. The overweight man crowded in front of the woman to get on the coach first.

"Mama, I can't climb up," the little girl said as she tried to put her foot on the step.

"Here, let me help you," Lee Edward said, picking up the little girl and setting her inside the coach. He then stepped back to let the woman board.

"I'm glad there's at least one gentleman on this coach," she said as she glared at the man who had taken up one entire seat.

Lee, the woman, and the child sat on the other seat. He had never ridden on a stagecoach before, and he could feel the excitement as the coach pulled away from San Antonio. He stared out the window, watching what he thought was the world rolling by. And he, Lee Edward Holt, was a part of it.

Two

It was a little after noon when the stage reached Selma. Lee Edward said goodbye to the woman and the little girl, then stepped out of the coach. He stood there for a minute, wondering what he should do next. Looking across the street, he saw a building with the sign "City Marshal" on the front. Thinking to start there, he crossed the street and stepped inside.

There was a man leaning back in his chair with his feet up on the desk. Lee saw that he was wearing a badge.

"What do you need, kid?"

"I'm looking for the Marathon Ranch."

"Why?"

The blunt, one-word response surprised Lee Edward, and to be honest, aggravated him somewhat.

"Because I have a job there."

"You have a job there, but you don't know where the ranch is?"

"I have a job there, but this will be my first day. I've never been there, and all I know is that it is near Selma."

The marshal chuckled. "Don't mind me, I'm just

foolin' with you. Go back outside on the road you were just on and turn to your right. That will be north, and Marathon Ranch is just about three miles north. You can't miss it; you'll see a big sign out on the road when you reach the turnoff."

"Thanks," Lee Edward said. Then, stepping back outside and clutching his bag, he started down the road in the direction the marshal had indicated.

Lee Edward had been walking no more than an hour when he saw a long entry road that went off at a right angle to the road. There was a sign at the junction that read:

MARATHON RANCH
ANDREW MATTHEWS OWNER

Lee started up the road with his bag tossed over his shoulder. He saw a good-sized house in front of him, with several other buildings and structures close by. As this was the first ranch he had ever seen, he had no idea what any of the other buildings were, so he stepped up onto the porch and knocked on the door.

The woman who answered the door was slender, with gray hair. Lee Edward had been around a lot more women than he had been men, so he was able to make a pretty good estimate of the woman's age, putting it at about fifty.

"Yes? May I help you?" the woman asked.

"I came here to work. My name is Lee Edward Holt."

"I beg your pardon?"

"I came here to work," Lee Edward said again. Then when he saw the puzzled expression on the woman's face, he was afraid that he had made a mistake.

"Young man, I have no idea what you're talking about."

Lee reached down into his clothes bag and pulled out the paper that had the job offer.

"They gave me this at the orphanage and said that I could get a job here."

The confused expression on the woman's face was replaced by a big smile.

"Yes, indeed! Do come in!" The woman stepped back to let Lee Edward enter, then she turned her head to call out. "Andy, won't you come here, please? I want you to meet Lee Edward Holt."

Andy Matthews was nearly as tall as Lee Edward. He had gray hair, a neatly trimmed gray mustache, and a friendly smile.

"So, you chose me, did you?" Matthews said when he saw the paper in Lee's hand. "I left my offer at the orphanage some time ago. Are you just now leaving the place?"

"Yes, sir."

"All right, come with me. I'll introduce you to our foreman, Ray Dockins. He'll get you settled into the bunkhouse, then tell you what's expected from you."

Lee followed Matthews from the house that he would later learn was called the Big House, to the bunkhouse where all the hands who worked for Mathews lived.

They were greeted by a man who was about five inches shorter than Lee Edward, but he was the kind of man that Lee Edward realized had a wiry toughness about him.

"Mr. Dockins, this is Lee Edward Holt. He just left the orphanage and will be our newest hand," Matthews said.

"So, this young man is going to ride for the brand, is he?" Dockins asked.

"He is indeed," Matthews replied.

"Ride for the brand?" Lee Edward asked, with a quizzical look on his face.

"It means you are working for the Marathon brand," Dockins explained.

After being shown around the ranch, meeting all the other cowboys, and having a very welcome supper, he returned to the bunkhouse where the others were engaged in conversation and a lot of teasing with one another. Lee Edward came under some of the teasing as well, and rather than being put off by it, he felt, and rightly so, that it was just the other men letting him know that he was being welcomed into the group.

As he lay in his bunk that night, he had mixed feelings about leaving the orphanage. It was the only home he had ever known, but he was equally excited about starting a new undertaking that was so foreign to him. He thought he had made a wise choice.

* * *

LONG TRAIL RANCH

The Long Trail was just over seventy-five miles northwest of Marathon Ranch. At 85,000 acres, Long Trail was one of the larger ranches in Kerr County, Texas. Jacob Austin, owner of Long Trail, was mounted, and looking out over a gather of cattle. His foreman and longtime friend, Linus Walker, was sitting on his horse beside him.

"It looks like you've got everything ready to take them to the railhead," Jake said.

"I figure on leaving right after sunrise tomorrow—

that'll put us in San Antonio by late afternoon the next day, and we'll have them on the train east by the third day."

Jake chuckled. "I'd say you've got it all planned. If I didn't know better, I'd say you've been around ranching for a long time."

"I guess if you count the time I was born on your father's ranch until now, that would be thirty-eight years so, yeah, I've been around ranching for a while."

"Wait a minute, are you talking about that little kid that was always following me around getting into trouble?"

"You were the leader, Jake, so if there was any trouble, you were always there first."

"Yeah, now that you mention it, I suppose I was. But, you know, it's good to still have you around."

The two men were quiet for a moment longer, then Jake took leave of Linus and headed back to headquarters. He was met by his fourteen-year-old stepdaughter.

"Hello, Papa Jake," the pretty young girl greeted.

"Mary Beth," Jake said as he jumped down and handed the reins of his horse to the girl. "Is your mother in the house?"

"When I snuck out, she and Abe were in the parlor."

"Hmm, does that mean Abe is in Dutch again?"

"A little, I think. But it wasn't anything bad, or Mama would be mad at him, and she's not."

"You're always a good girl. Maybe you should take Abe under your wing."

"Ha, I'm afraid Abe wouldn't cotton to that—not even a little bit."

Jake stepped into the parlor and saw Hannah sitting on the sofa. Abe was sitting in the big chair.

"Hello, dear," Hannah said as she rose to greet her

husband. "Has Linus got everything ready for the drive tomorrow?"

"You know Linus."

Hannah chuckled. "Then everything is ready."

"Can I go, too?" Abe asked.

"Not this year. You're still a little young for that," Jake said.

"I'm not too young. I can ride as well as any cowboy you have working for you."

"You're not going, Abe, and that's it," Hannah said.

Abe stomped out of the room and went outside, slamming the door behind him.

"How long 'til supper?" Jake asked. "I'm hungry."

Hannah laughed. "When are you not hungry? I'll check with Alenada. It shouldn't be much longer."

* * *

MARATHON RANCH

Within six months of arriving at Marathon, Lee Edward had learned many of the skills needed to be a cowboy. He was a quick learner and a good worker who was well-liked by all the other men. And one of the hands, Hank Everson, soon became his best friend.

There was one hand, however, who was particularly bothersome. His name was Dan Willard. He was two years older than Hank and four years older than Lee Edward. Because Willard was older, he assumed a position of authority over Lee Edward that he didn't have.

One afternoon Lee Edward, Hank, James McCoy, and Willard were repairing a fence. Although nobody had been put in charge, Willard assumed the role.

"Dammit, Holt, can't you do anything right?" Willard

said, and coming over to the post where Lee Edward had just attached some wire, Willard used a wire snip to cut through the wire.

"Now, string it again," he ordered.

"What the hell, Willard? There wasn't anything wrong with that wire," Hank said. Hank was at the other post from Lee Edward, and when Willard cut the wire, that meant Hank would have to restring his end as well.

"You're lazy, and Holt doesn't know what the hell he's doin'. Dockins picked a fine crew for me to work with today," Willard said.

"Who put you in charge?" one of the other cowboys asked.

"Well, look at 'em, McCoy. We can't go back in until this job is done, and the way these two are workin', we'll prob'ly wind up missin' our supper tonight."

"I wouldn't worry about it if I were you," Lee Edward said. "You've snitched enough food that you're not likely to starve."

"What the hell? Are you callin' me a thief?"

"Yeah, I guess that word would fit. Unless you can come up with another one," Lee Edward replied.

"You'd better watch your step, Mister. You don't want to tangle with me."

Lee put the hammer down and turned to face Willard. "Yeah, I think maybe I do."

Willard looked at Lee Edward and took the measure of him. Lee Edward was over six feet tall, with broad shoulders, well-muscled arms, and with an expression that was almost anxious for a fight.

"Well, I'm goin' to let it go this time, but you 'n Hank hurry up, lessen' you want a cold supper."

Lee Edward and Hank continued, with no further input from Willard.

THREE

THE OWNER OF DOUBLE DIAMOND RANCH, RUBEN Pugh and two of his men, Bull Travers and Scooter Condon, were negotiating with Elmer Watson. Watson owned a small farm that was adjacent to the Double Diamond.

The reason for the negotiation was that Pugh had recently purchased a thousand acres from Morley Patterson, but because of Watson's farm, the Patterson acquisition was not contiguous with the Double Diamond.

"I really don't want to sell, Mr. Pugh," Watson said. "I've got more 'n a hunert acres of cotton in, 'n when I get that crop out, why, I'll be able to pay off ever' thing I owe."

"I'm offering you enough money to pay off all your debts now," Pugh said.

"Yes, sir, that's true, but if I take your money to pay off all my debts, I won't have nothin' left, 'n no farm to work. How'm I s'posed to make a livin' then? But iffin I pay off my debts with the money I'll make from the cotton, I'll still have the farm left. No, sir, I ain't in no mood to sell."

"Well, just remember, you were given your opportunity," Pugh said.

* * *

DOUBLE DIAMOND RANCH

Later that day, Pugh and Travers were discussing the Watson farm.

"I've got to have that land," Pugh said. "Without it, the Patterson land is useless to me."

"If you give me free rein, I might be able to come up with something that would convince him to sell," Travers said.

"Do what you have to," Pugh said. "If we can get this taken care of, then we might be able to use the same tactics for Long Trail."

* * *

LONG TRAIL RANCH

Jake Austin and his foreman, Linus Walker, had ridden out to the northernmost pasture of the Long Trail Ranch, then dismounted and walked through the pasture, looking at the fifteen dead cows that were lying there. All fifteen had been shot.

"Who the hell would do something like this?" Jake asked.

"Pugh," Linus answered. "He is exactly the kind of son of a bitch who would do this."

"I know we've had a disagreement as to where the boundaries of the LT and the Double Diamond are, but I never thought he would do something like this."

"What if we were to take fifteen Double Diamond cows?" Linus suggested.

"Let me go talk to Pugh first," Jake suggested.

"If you're going into enemy territory, I'm going with you," Linus said.

Jake laughed. "Enemy territory?"

"Well, what else would you call it?"

"I don't know. Enemy territory may be as good a way of describing Pugh's empire as any, I suppose."

"All right, let's go see him," Linus said. He started toward the Double Diamond.

"No, Linus, not that way," Jake called out to him. "If one of those crazies that ride for him sees us on Double Diamond land, they would as likely as not take a shot at us."

"Yeah, you may be right. Probably would be better to go around by the road, but it'll take us a half hour longer."

"Better half an hour than an eternity."

The two men rode back from the north pasture, by the headquarters of the Long Trail Ranch, then out onto the road that would take them to the Double Diamond, the bordering ranch just to the north of the LT. They were met by Ron Ferrell, one of Pugh's riders.

"What do you two want?" Ferrell asked, the tone of his voice reflecting his belligerence.

"We're here to speak to your boss," Linus said.

Ferrell stared at the two men for a moment, then with a shrug, turned his horse around. "All right, follow me."

The road leading from the gate to the main house was

about a quarter mile from the main road. When they got there, Pugh was standing out on the front porch.

Pugh was a thin man with a beak-like nose, a prominent Adam's apple, and a blotchy red face.

"What do you want, Austin?" Pugh asked gruffly.

"I found fifteen cows killed in my north pasture. I was wondering if you knew anything about that."

"I don't know anything about fifteen cows dead in *your* pasture, but I do know that about that many cows strayed over on my land, and I figured since you let them come onto my land, you didn't want them anymore, so I had them shot, and left 'em lying there, so you could see that they were on my land."

"We've been through this before, Ruben. That is my property."

"So you say, but I have a bill of sale for it. I bought it from Swayne Bird."

"Bird was renting that property from me. It wasn't his to sell."

"That's not my problem. That was between you and Bird. I've got a bill of sale for the property, and it's mine."

"We can take it to court and see how it turns out," Jake suggested.

"No need to do that. Like I said, I've got a bill of sale for it, and in my book, that's all I need. Now, as for your cows, I'll give you fifteen dollars apiece for them. That comes to two hundred and twenty-five dollars."

"That's sixty dollars a head, less than they're worth," Jake said.

"If you think you can get seventy-five dollars a head for dead cows, well, you just take 'em away and see if you can sell 'em."

Jake ran his hand through his hair. "All right, give me the two hundred twenty-five dollars."

"How about it, Jake?" Pugh said in a more conciliatory tone of voice. "None of this needs to happen. We don't need to be enemies. If you would just sell your ranch to me, you'd have enough money to live the rest of your life in ease, and I would have one of the biggest ranches in Texas. We'd both come out ahead that way."

"I'm not interested in selling Long Trail. Just give me the two hundred twenty-five dollars, and I'll be on my way."

"You do know, don't you, boss? Pugh isn't going to stop trying to buy Long Trail. He's buying out every small rancher he can buffalo into selling to him."

"He can try all he wants. I'm not selling."

"There's likely to be more things like this happening to us."

"We'll deal with it," Jake said in a way that let Linus know that he didn't want to discuss the issue any further.

* * *

MARATHON RANCH

Lee Edward was both intelligent and a hard worker, so it didn't take long for him to find his way around the ranch. Within the first year of Lee Edward coming to work at Marathon, Dockins made the observation to Matthews that Lee Edward and Hank Everson were the two best hands.

"I see that everyone is wearing a gun belt," Lee Edward said. "Why do we need to carry a pistol?"

"Well, for one thing, to guard against any rustlers," Dockins said. "And also, for self-protection. You're a cowboy now, and being a cowboy can sometimes, through no fault of your own, lead you into trouble. It has been my observation that innocent people are sometimes drawn into a shooting contest, and when they do, they need to be able to handle a gun well enough to defend themselves."

"Will you teach me?" Lee Edward asked.

"What makes you think I can teach you?"

"It's just some things I've heard about you," Lee Edward said.

"Oh?" Ray said. He cocked an eye as he studied Lee Edward. "And just what have you heard?"

Lee Edward hesitated a moment before he replied. He was aware that he may have overstepped his bounds by a bit, but he had opened the line of conversation, and he couldn't just leave it unsaid now.

"I heard that you were a gunfighter and that you...uh, that you sometimes sold your gun to the highest bidder."

Ray glared at Lee Edward for a long moment, and Lee Edward found himself wishing he had never opened this conversation.

"You're wrong," Ray Dockins said rather sharply. "I was a gunfighter, and I did sell my gun, but not to the highest bidder. I always had a sense of right and wrong, so I made my gun available, not to the highest bidder, but to the person who was in the right."

"Why did you stop being a gunfighter?" Lee Edward asked.

"How old are you?" Ray Dockins asked.

"I'm seventeen."

"Seventeen," Ray said. He stared at Lee Edward for a long moment, long enough to make Lee Edward feel uncomfortable. "It was something that happened."

"What happened?" Lee Edward asked.

"You don't want to know."

"Well, I think I do want to know, but if you don't want to tell it, I'll respect your privacy."

"You will?"

"Yes, sir."

Ray Dockins sighed. "You're a good man, Lee Edward."

Ray began to tell the story then, telling it in such detail and with such feeling that Lee Edward could believe he was there, not just watching the event unfold, but actually living through it.

* * *

RAY DOCKINS' STORY

Ray was in a bar in Dodge City, Kansas. He had just completed a job for Lou Blanton, a client, who had paid him to bring in the killers of the client's brother. Ray had done so, bringing in all three of the killers, but only one of them was alive.

He was in the bar having a drink and a quiet conversation with Blanton.

"I want to thank you, Mr. Dockins," Blanton said. "This didn't bring Bernie back, but taking care of the men who killed him will help bring some peace to the family."

"I hope it does," Ray said.

The quiet conversation between the two men was interrupted by a woman's scream, and when they looked toward the source, they saw that someone had grabbed one of the bar girls. Her assailant had his arm around her neck. He was holding his pistol to her head, but he was yelling at three men who were sitting at a card table.

"You been cheatin', mister! You been cheatin' from

the moment I sat down here. And this here woman's been helpin' you."

"What are you talking about? I haven't done anything!" the woman said, her voice breaking with fear.

"The hell you ain't. Do you think I don't know how you been sneakin' around behind me, tellin' him what cards I was holdin'? Now all of you, get up from the table and leave the money on it. I aim to get back what I was cheated out of."

Ray pulled his pistol and stood up.

"What are you doing, Dockins?" Blanton hissed. "That son of a bitch is crazy. Don't get him any more riled than he already is."

Ray raised his pistol and aimed it at the man who was holding the bar girl, then started walking toward him. The man didn't even notice him approaching until Ray was within ten feet of him, then he jerked around, still holding his gun to the girl's head.

"Stop right there, mister!" he called out angrily. "What do you think you're about to do?"

"I think I'm about to kill you," Ray said, his voice flat and completely emotionless.

"What do you mean you're about to kill me? Are you blind? Don't you see that I got a gun pointed at this woman's head?"

"Yes, and that's your problem. Your gun is pointed toward her—my gun is pointed toward you."

"Drop the gun, mister. Drop it now, or I'll kill the girl."

"Go ahead," Ray said easily.

"What?" the man asked, shocked by Ray's response. "Look, you don't understand. If you don't drop the gun now, I'm going to kill her!"

"Let the girl go. You may as well hold the gun to your own head, because if you kill her, I'll kill you."

The man who was holding the girl looked at Ray and saw the black hole of the end of Ray's pistol pointing straight at him. His eyes grew wide in fear, and small beads of perspiration popped out on his forehead and on his upper lip.

"I'll give you to the count of three to make up your mind," Ray said. "One."

"You're crazy!"

"Two."

To Ray's shock, the man pulled the trigger, blasting blood and splinters of bone from the young woman's head. Ray pulled the trigger immediately after, killing the man with a bullet between his eyes.

* * *

RAY WAS silent for a long moment after he finished the story. Lee Edward looked on, so startled by the story that he couldn't speak.

"I killed that woman, same as if I had shot her myself," Ray said.

"No," Lee Edward said, shaking his head. "You didn't kill her, that man killed her."

"Yes, the court decided that I wasn't the one who killed her, so I wasn't found guilty. I might not have been the one that pulled the trigger, but that didn't mean I was innocent regardless of what the court said. I was as responsible for that girl's death as if I had actually pulled the trigger. I haven't sold my gun one time since then."

FOUR

LEE EDWARD BOUGHT A PISTOL, SELECTING A COLT Army .44 caliber, single-action revolver. His choice of a pistol was suggested by Hank Everson, who, a few years earlier, had bought the same weapon.

He showed his pistol to Ray.

"It's a good one, all right," Ray said. "But remember, it's a single action, and that means it won't shoot unless you pull the hammer back first."

Lee Edward put the pistol back in his holster, then tried a fast draw. Just as the gun cleared the holster, it went off, shooting a hole in the ground less than an inch from Lee Edward's foot.

"No, no, you do it like that, you're going to shoot a toe off, or worse," Ray said, waving his arms. "I tell you what, let's break this down into two things: learn to shoot, then learn to draw your gun. Remember, it doesn't matter how fast you draw your pistol if you can't hit what you're shooting at. Then, when you start learning the fast draw, begin with an empty gun."

"All right," Lee Edward said. "So, what's the first thing?"

"Like I said, the first thing is to learn how to shoot. Get some empty tin cans from the cook, then set them up as targets."

Excited to be learning how to shoot, Lee Edward got half a dozen empty cans, then lined them up on the top rail of the fence.

"All right, let's see what you can do," Ray said.

Lee Edward fired six rounds without hitting a single can. Holding the smoking gun in his hand, he looked at Ray with a sheepish expression on his face.

"I missed," he said.

"I expected you to miss. Load your gun and try again."

Lee Edward tried six more times and missed every shot. It was not until his fifteenth shot that he hit one of the cans, and he let out a little shout of victory. "I hit it!"

"That's not bad, but you're already dead," Ray said.

"What do you mean I'm already dead?"

"Tin cans can't shoot back," Ray said. "Men can, so if you'd been shooting at someone who was trying to kill you, they'd have had fourteen chances to do it."

"Oh," Lee Edward said, "I see what you mean."

"I tell you what, over the next few days, anytime you're free of chores, you start practice shooting. When I think you're ready, I'll work with you some more."

* * *

OVER THE NEXT MONTH, Lee Edward spent every free moment practicing his shooting. The .44 caliber bullets cost fifty cents a box, and each box held fifty rounds. By the time Lee Edward had fired off a thousand rounds, he took great satisfaction in knowing that he could shoot his pistol until it was empty and score a hit with every round he fired.

It was with a sense of satisfaction and self-pride that Lee Edward approached Ray Dockens to show his boss and former gunfighter what he could do.

"Watch this," Lee Edward said. He put six cans on the fence, then extended his arm, closed his left eye, and aimed. He shot six times and was rewarded for each shot with a tin can being knocked off the top rung of the fence.

"What do you think of that?" Lee Edward asked with a smug expression on his face.

"It's pretty good," Ray said. "Good enough that I think we can move on to the next lesson."

"I'm going to learn the fast draw!" Lee Edward said excitedly.

"No, you're going to learn to shoot."

"Learn to shoot? What are you talking about? I just showed you six hits from six bullets."

"Uh, huh, and that would be pretty good if all you had to do was shoot at a target. But it was my understanding that you wanted to learn how to shoot well enough so that you could defend yourself," Ray said.

"Yes, and I just showed you that I can put six bullets on target with six shots."

"Six shots that you had your arm stretched out in front of you, and you took very careful aim."

"Well, isn't that the idea?" Lee Edward asked.

"It would be if you were target shooting at a county fair. But aren't you doing this so you can learn to protect yourself?"

"I am."

"Then you have to learn to hit your target without aiming at it."

"What? Come on, Ray, what are you talking about? How do you hit something without aiming at it?"

"Put the cans back on the fence," Ray said.

Lee Edward did as he was told.

"Now, step back here out of the way."

After Lee Edward set out the cans, he returned to stand beside Ray. Ray drew his gun and began firing. He wasn't aiming, his arm wasn't straight out. It was bent at the elbow, and he fired every shot in what was almost one sustained roar. All six cans flew off the top rung of the fence.

"How did you do that?" Lee Edward asked, amazed by what he had just seen.

"I thought the bullets to the targets," Ray said.

"That doesn't make any sense."

"Where is the cook shack?" Ray asked.

"What do you mean? You know where it is."

"Point it out to me."

"Why, it's right over there." Lee Edward pointed toward the building.

"All right, hold everything you've got right now. Don't move a muscle," Ray said.

"What are you talking about?"

"Why isn't your arm stretched out straight in front of you?" Ray asked.

"Because I don't need to do that, just to show you where..." Lee Edward stopped in mid-sentence. "Wait a minute. I think I know what you're saying."

"Use the next few days to learn how to shoot the tin cans without stretching your arm out in front of you."

* * *

OVER THE NEXT SIX WEEKS, Lee Edward and the other Marathon men were engaged in all the chores associated with ranching, from feeding to medicating, to calving, tending to horses and cattle, moving the cattle from pasture to pasture, cleaning stalls, maintaining wagons and other equipment, and keeping fencing in good repair. Much of the work was dawn to dusk, which prevented Lee Edward from practicing his shooting as much as he would have liked.

Lee Edward didn't resent the work though, because since he had made the commitment to be a cowboy, he wanted to be the best he could be.

"You know what?" Lee Edward said to Hank as the two of them were working on one of the fences. "I'd like to own a ranch someday."

Hank laughed. "Yeah, you can do that right after you sprout wings and fly."

Lee Edward laughed as well. "That wouldn't be a bad idea. If I could do that, I'd be able to keep an eye on all my hands just to make sure they're working like they're supposed to."

"Ha! I don't think you could make Dan Willard work, even if you could hover right over the top of him."

Hank's observation about Willard was pretty accurate. Willard was a big man who used his size to dominate all the other ranch hands. He was known as someone who avoided work as much as he could.

"I wouldn't even try to hover over him," Lee Edward said. "If I really did own a ranch and he worked for me, I would fire his ass in the first week."

"Whooee, you're goin' to be a hard one to work for," Hank teased.

"Nope. If somebody holds up his end of the work, I'm goin' to be a good boss."

"I tell you what. You buy that ranch, and I'll come work for you," Hank said. "Somebody's goin' to have to keep you straight."

Lee Edward did manage to find some time to practice his shooting, gradually getting better and better until he could shoot six times and hit six cans without stretching his arm out in front of him.

One day, just as Lee Edward finished practicing his shooting, he heard someone clapping softly behind him. When he turned, he saw Ray Dockins standing there.

"That's pretty fair shootin'," Ray said. "I'd say you're about ready to learn the fast draw."

A broad smile spread across Lee Edward's face. "I've been hoping you'd work with me again."

"You want to know the reason why I'm willin' to mess with you?" Ray asked.

"Because I've gotten good at shooting?"

"No, that's not it. You've proven to be a good worker, Lee Edward. You've learned to shoot by putting in a lot of practice, but, and this is the most important part, you haven't lost a minute of work. We don't need another gun hand around here—what we need are good workers. But, as it so happens, you've turned out to be both a good gun hand, and even more importantly, a good worker. Now, let me show you how to learn the quick draw."

Ray went to the horse barn and retrieved a bucket. He set it on the ground and then picked up a rock.

"Hold your hand out, palm down over this bucket."

Lee Edward did that and was surprised when Ray put the rock on the back of his hand.

"Here's what you do. You turn your hand so the rock will fall in the bucket, but you draw and shoot before you hear the rock hits. Do you think you can do that?"

"I'm damn well going to try," Lee Edward said.

* * *

ONE DAY RAY asked Lee Edward to take a walk with him. They started out across one of the pastures.

"I've gone as far as I can go with you, Lee Edward. Your speed and accuracy are as good as anyone I've ever known. There's only one thing left, and this I can't teach you. This, you have to decide for yourself."

"And what's that?"

"You have to learn not to think."

"What?" Lee Edward had a puzzled look on his face. "What do you mean?"

"If you have two gunmen facing each other down, and one is as fast as the other, and one is as good a shot as the other, there's only one thing remaining. By learning to shoot as well as you have, you've taken on quite a responsibility.

"If two men of equal skill face each other, do you know which one will win?"

"I don't know if you say one is as good as the other."

"Most men won't be able to draw and shoot without thought. They know that if they pull the trigger, they are likely to kill the other man. The average person will think about that, and he will hesitate for just an instant, even if he is facing the most despicable opponent. And when that happens, the one who hesitates is the one who'll be killed."

"Yeah," Lee Edward said thoughtfully. "I hadn't thought of that."

"You'll have to walk a fine line here, my friend. If it ever comes to where you find yourself in a life-and-death moment, you must be ready to kill the other man. Don't think, just shoot."

FIVE

LEE EDWARD HAD BEEN WORKING AT MARATHON FOR six years when they began making plans to take five hundred head of cattle to the rail head in San Antonio. It would be an easy two-day drive.

"You fellers should 'a been around when they was real cattle drives," Moe Rollins said. Rollins was forty-seven and the oldest of any of the cowboys.

"We had us one hell of a time goin' up, 'n keepin' twenty-five hunnert, to maybe three thousand cows a' goin'. 'N there warn't nothin' easy about it neither, I'm a' tellin' you."

"I think one of those real long drives would be a great adventure," Lee Edward said.

"Yeah, well, you'd see what kind of adventure it'd be if it was you in the saddle for twelve hours, burnin' up in the sun, 'n eatin' dust," Rollins said.

"Moe, if it's all that bad, why are you still cowboying?" Lee Edward asked.

Rollins paused for a moment, then he smiled. "I'm

still a' cowboyin' on account of it's the best job any feller would ever be a' wantin'."

Lee Edward chuckled. "I think so too. That's why I'm looking forward to this drive."

"Well, we'll get underway first thing in the mornin'," Rollins said. "So make sure you get some shut-eye tonight."

* * *

KERR COUNTY, THE WATSON FARM

"Janey, my girl, if we make as much cotton as I think we're gonna, we'll be out of debt with enough left over to last us a whole year," Elmer Watson said to his wife over supper that night.

"So, then you could say we're going to be in tall cotton?" Janey answered with a smile.

Elmer laughed. "Oh, that's a good one, but yes, darlin', you could say that."

"It's taken us a long time to get here."

"It has at that, but that's why we'll enjoy it all the more," Elmer said.

* * *

JANEY DIDN'T KNOW why she woke up, she didn't need to use the chamber pot, but something had definitely awakened her.

As she lay in bed for a moment, she finally decided it wasn't anything to worry about, so she rolled over to her other side to go back to sleep. That's when she saw it. Yellow light was flashing against the wall. Curious, and a little apprehensive, Janey got out of bed and walked over to the window to look outside. She saw then where the light was coming from. The barn was completely enveloped in flames.

"Elmer!" she screamed loudly.

Elmer was awake instantly. "What's wrong?"

"The barn's on fire!"

Jumping out of bed, Elmer hurried over to the window. "The mules!"

Elmer didn't even bother to put on clothes. Instead, he ran out of the house heading for the barn. He could hear his two mules, Harry and Rhoda, screaming out in panic.

Elmer tried to get to them, but he couldn't as the fire pushed him back.

The mules quieted, and all Elmer could hear was the cracking of the flames as the barn continued to burn.

By now Janey was outside. She had dressed and brought Elmer's shoes with her. Elmer sat on the grass, putting on his shoes as he watched the barn burn. The front wall collapsed from the flames causing the roof to fall as well.

"Poor Harry and Rhoda," Janey said as tears ran down her cheeks. "They didn't deserve to die like this."

Elmer had no words as a knot formed in his throat. He put his arm around Janey and pulled her close.

* * *

DOUBLE DIAMOND RANCH

"I don't think Watson is goin' to give us any more trouble 'bout sellin' his farm," Bull Travers said.

"What makes you think that?" Ruben Pugh asked.

"Somehow or the other, his barn caught on fire 'n

burn't down," Travers said with a chuckle. "And what happened was both of his mules got kilt in the fire, so he ain't goin' to have no way to take care of his cotton field."

"That's too bad," Pugh said. "I'll make him another offer for his farm, but without a barn, it won't be worth as much as it was. He should have taken my first offer."

"People like Watson don't learn none too easy," Travers said.

"Apparently not," Pugh replied. "I'll do what I can to be a good neighbor for him."

* * *

THE WATSON FARM

Neither Elmer nor Janey Watson felt like eating the next morning after the fire, so they just sat at the table drinking coffee and fighting back the tears. And it wasn't only Janey who was struggling with their emotions.

"What are we going to do now, Elmer?"

"I don't know, darlin'. God help us, I don't know."

"What do you think caused the fire?" Janey asked.

"I know it didn't come from a lantern or anything because we didn't have a lantern out there," Elmer said.

"Are we going to have to sell out?"

"We might have to," Elmer replied. "Without the mules, we can't take care of the crops."

"And just when everything was looking so good for us," Janey said.

"Yeah," Elmer said, with bitterness in his one-word reply.

"Do you think we can find someone to buy it?" Janey asked.

"Oh, yeah, there's one person that very much wants to buy it."

"You're talking about Ruben Pugh, aren't you?"

"Yeah, I'm talking about Pugh."

"Oh, I hate selling our farm to him. He is such an awful man. Don't you think we can find someone else who will buy it?"

Elmer shook his head. "If someone did buy it, he'd find himself in the same position we're in now. Pugh's bound to get this land, one way or the other."

Janey reached across the table and put her hand on Elmer's. "Do what you have to do."

* * *

WITHOUT HIS MULES, Elmer was unable to work the fields. He tried to chop the cotton, but even with Janey's help, the weeds overtook most of the crop. When he applied for a bank loan, he was turned down because he had already borrowed money against the crop, and the farm had been put up for collateral. As he had predicted, he couldn't find anyone who would buy the farm.

"What are we going to do now?" Janey asked.

"There's only one thing we can do," Elmer replied.

"Oh, Elmer, surely we aren't going to sell out to Pugh," Janey said. "He's such a despicable man."

"I agree with you, darlin', but I don't see as we have any choice. We only have fifty-six dollars to our name, and that won't pay the taxes and the interest on our loan, let alone get us through the winter."

"All right, but when we get the money, let's go back to Sikeston," Janey said, speaking of the small town in Missouri where they had come from. "You can go back to working for Daddy in his blacksmith shop, and I can get a job as a clerk at the mercantile."

Elmer nodded. "Seems to me like that's about the only thing we can do."

* * *

MARATHON RANCH

The five hundred head of cattle that had been selected for the drive stayed in the near pasture, and night riders watched over the gather to keep them from straying back to the main herd.

The next morning, they had a cold breakfast from the chuck wagon and then got underway. The men were given jerked beef and a canteen of water to eat on the trail. The chuck wagon left before the herd, so Pedro could find a good place for a bedding ground and a place to cook supper. It was not an easy task because he had to estimate how far he thought the herd would be able to get by the end of the day.

As the foreman, Ray Dockins rode with the cowboys. In addition to Ray, Hank, and Lee Edward, there were four more men from Marathon who were making the drive. That gave them six drovers, plus Ray, who would sometimes ride at the head of the herd, or on each side or behind, wherever he was needed.

There was a bit of excitement when a steer broke away from the rest of the herd soon after they were underway.

"Stop 'im, Lee Edward!" Dockins shouted. "Get 'im back."

Lee Edward jerked his horse around and started after the escaping steer. He caught up with the animal rather quickly, then taking his lariat from the saddle horn, he twirled it over his head, making a large loop. Closing in on the steer, he dropped the loop over the steer's head, then quickly returned the now docile steer to the herd.

When they camped for the night, they enjoyed a plate of chili con carne that Pedro had prepared and then sat around telling jokes and sharing stories.

"So, how are you a' liken your first cattle drive so far, Lee Edward?" Hank asked. "Et enough dust yet?"

"Uhmm," Lee Edward said, holding out his mess kit. "Why, that dust on my chili is like putting salt and pepper on a boiled egg. It spices it up."

The others laughed at Lee Edward's rejoinder.

* * *

THEY WOULD BE DELIVERING the cattle to the buyers the next day, but tonight they would camp just short of San Antonio. Lee was one of the night riders and his turn was from ten to twelve. It was a perfect shift for him, because he would be able to go to bed at twelve and sleep uninterrupted for the rest of the night.

It was quiet and the stars were so bright that it was almost as if he could reach up and grab one. He was alone, and that was a condition that was rare for him. He had slept in a dormitory room in the orphanage, and now he slept in the bunkhouse with the others at the ranch. He found that he was much enjoying the solitude.

Being alone gave him the opportunity to think, and he thought about some of those he had left at the orphanage.

He also thought about Sister Maria. She was nice to everyone, but she had been particularly nice to him. He had no idea who his mother was, and sometimes he wondered if Sister Maria was actually his mother. On the one hand, he knew that was very unlikely because she was a nun. But it was for that same reason that if she had been his mother, no one would be able to tell him.

Lee decided that it didn't matter whether she was his mother or not. He knew he couldn't love a real mother any more than he loved Sister Maria.

* * *

DOUBLE DIAMOND RANCH

Early in the afternoon of the next day, Elmer Watson visited Ruben Pugh, and was now sitting in his office.

"I'll give you one hundred dollars for your farm," Pugh said.

"One hundred dol..." Elmer gasped, unable to finish the sentence. "But you offered me seven hundred fifty dollars."

"And you should have taken the offer. Your farm's worth a lot less now with no barn and a poor crop."

"But you weren't going to use my land as farmland. You said you wanted it because it connected your land with the other property you'd bought."

"Like I said, you should have taken my offer when I first made it."

"But what you're offering won't even pay off my debt. I owe the bank a hundred-twenty-five dollars."

"I'll tell you what I'll do," Pugh said. "I'll raise my offer to a hundred twenty-five. That'll be enough to pay off the bank."

"Could you raise your offer by ten dollars?" Elmer asked. "My wife and I want to go back to Missouri. We have enough money for train fare, but we don't have enough for vittles along the way."

Pugh smiled. "All right, good neighbor that I am, I'll do that for you. But I want you out by the end of the week."

"What about the furniture in my house? I was going to try and sell it," Elmer said.

"It's not yours to sell. I just bought it. Now, like I told you, be out by the end of the week."

Elmer nodded without speaking, then turned and walked out of the house. He fought the emotions of anger, fright, and sadness as he rode home to tell Janey how it would have to be.

Six

WITH THE CATTLE DRIVE

THE MARATHON HERD REACHED THE RAIL HEAD BY early afternoon the second day. After the buyer had looked them over and dickered with Ray Dockins over the price, the drovers began pushing the cattle into holding pens. After the gates were secured, Dockins announced that the men were on their own as long as they were back to the ranch by noon the next day.

"Come on, Lee Edward, let's go get drunk," Hank invited.

"You go on without me, Hank. I have somewhere else I need to go."

"Yeah? Well, we're goin' to have us some good whiskey and some fine women. I sure don't know how you could miss out on somethin' like that."

"Huh, a real woman would scare him to death," Willard said derisively.

"How are you going to do it, Willard?" Hank asked.

"How'm I goin' to do what?"

"Convince a blind woman that you're not as ugly as a fence post. 'Cause a blind woman is about the only kind you can get."

The others laughed.

Saying goodbye to everyone, Lee Edward rode away from the railroad depot, knowing exactly where he planned to go. About fifteen minutes later, he came to a building that was as familiar to him as the bunkhouse where he had spent every night since he came to Marathon Ranch. Actually, this building was more familiar to him, because here is where he had spent every night of his first sixteen years.

The sign out front read: OUR LADY OF MERCY ORPHANAGE.

* * *

LEE TIED his horse off to the hitching rail and then followed the walkway to the door. He was about to push it open and go in as he had always done. But, as it had been three years since his last visit, he was afraid he would frighten anyone who may not know him. So, he rang the bell.

As soon as the door was opened, Lee Edward knew he had made the right decision. It was answered by a new nun, one that Lee Edward had never before seen.

"Yes, sir, may I help you?" she asked.

"Yes, I would like to speak with Sister Maria."

"All right, I will fetch her, and what is your name, sir?"

Lee Edward smiled. "No, please, don't tell her my name. I want to surprise her."

"I don't know that I should do that."

"I used to live here, Sister. Sister Mary Frances, Sister Kathleen, Sister Blandina, Sister Mary Elizabeth, who is the Mother Superior, and Father Tuttle were all here when I was here. Will that convince you that it's safe to get Sister Maria?"

The young nun smiled. "I'm Sister Margaret and I've only been here three months. Oh, and Father Tuttle isn't here anymore. Now it's Father Pyron. Wait here while I get Sister Maria for you."

Lee Edward stood in the entrance hall, looking at all the religious icons while he waited. Everything was so familiar.

"You wished to see me, sir?" Sister Maria asked as she approached him.

He turned to face her.

As soon as she saw Lee Edward, her expression of concern turned to a huge smile.

"Oh, Lee Edward!" she said as she hurried across the entry foyer with her arms spread wide.

Lee met her halfway, and they embraced one another. As he held her, he knew that no one who had a mother could love her more than he loved Sister Maria.

"Come into the kitchen," Sister Maria invited. "We'll have coffee."

Lee laughed. "Now you'll let me drink coffee. You never would, before."

"Well, you were a little boy then, and I've always heard that coffee will stunt your growth," Sister Maria said. Then she added, with a smile, "And I see my keeping you from coffee paid off. You're so tall now."

"No doubt the lack of coffee is what did it," Lee Edward agreed with a little laugh. "Come on, let's have that coffee."

As the two walked toward the kitchen, they encountered several other nuns who had been in residence when Lee Edward was there. The word passed quickly that he was visiting, and all came to greet him to include Mother Superior.

"Have you hit anyone lately?" Mother Superior asked with a smile.

"No, ma'am, but there's one I would like to hit," Lee Edward answered, thinking of Willard.

"Remember, the Lord likes a man with patience," she said.

"Yes, ma'am." Lee Edward lowered his gaze, just as he had countless times before when he was addressed by the Mother Superior.

After all greetings were done, the sisters left Lee Edward and Sister Maria alone. "Come, let's sit in the dining room."

Lee Edward carried both cups of coffee as Sister Maria chose a table near a window.

"Let me look at you, my son," she said as she placed her hand on his cheek. "When you left us, you chose to work on a ranch, I believe. Are you still there?"

"Yes ma'am, and I love it," Lee Edward said. "I have made friends—good friends. But we all work hard. In fact, the reason I am in San Antonio is because I helped bring a herd of cattle to the shipping yards."

"Oh, I'm so glad you did," Sister Maria said, reaching across the table to lay her hand on his.

"Sister Maria, may I ask you a question?"

"Of course you may. I hope I can answer your question."

"On the way here, we were sleeping under the stars. It was like I could reach up and touch the heavens." Lee

Edward stopped and then continued. "I was thinking about you, and I was wondering..."

"I think I know what you want to ask."

"Who is my mother?"

Sister Maria took a deep breath. "Before I answer, may I ask you why you never asked me this question before?"

"Because when I lived here, you were my mother as far as I was concerned. And in my boyish mind, I thought that if I asked you, you might consider me ungrateful for all the love and care you were giving me."

Tears came to Sister Maria's eyes then, and she squeezed Lee Edward's hand. "What a sweet thing for you to say. But I'm afraid I don't have an answer for you. Your mother, or at least the woman I assumed was your mother, brought you here when you were a week old. She didn't tell me her name, though I did see her a few more times. Or at least, I thought I did. A woman, whom I thought resembled the one who brought you to our door, visited a couple of times, but she never approached me or asked about you specifically, so I don't know if it was the same woman or not. You have to remember, when she left you, the whole experience was so overwhelming to her and to me that I'm not sure I would have recognized her at all. She placed you in my arms. Mother Superior said at the time that God had chosen me to be your shepherd." She withdrew her hand. "And that is what I've tried to be—your shepherd."

"But my name, Lee Edward Holt. Shouldn't that have given you a clue as to who she was?"

"Bless your heart, child, I've never told you. I gave you that name," Sister Maria said. "That was my father's name."

"Then I shall take pride in bearing the name, for it

was given to me by the woman I have always considered my mother." Lee Edward took her hand once again. "And I always will."

Tears came down Sister Maria's cheeks. "And you are the child my chosen calling would never let me have."

SEVEN

LONG TRAIL RANCH

MARY BETH HUNTER RODE HER HORSE, DAN, AT A trot as she came back to the house from the eastern range of the Long Trail. From a distance, one might think she was a boy—she was wearing pants and riding astride. But when one got closer, anyone could see she was very much a girl and a very pretty one at that.

Dismounting in front of the Big House, Mary Beth tied her horse off at the hitching rail. Then, taking off her hat and shaking her head to let the long tresses of blond hair tumble down her back, she climbed the steps and went into the house.

"Where've you been?" Hannah Austin asked.

"I was out in the east pasture."

"And pray tell, what were doing out there?"

"I told you this morning, Mama. Mr. Walker said he would be moving some of the cattle to another pasture, so I was helping out."

"I remember, you did say that, but go get cleaned up

because it will soon be suppertime," Hannah said as she headed for the kitchen.

"So, you're working for Walker now, are you?" Mary Beth's brother Abe asked after Hannah left the room. Abe was only slightly taller than Mary Beth, and like Mary Beth, had blond hair and pale blue eyes.

"Yes, I was helping move some cows."

"You don't work for Walker. He works for us," Abe pointed out.

"No, brother dear, he doesn't work for us—he works for Papa Jake."

"Why do you call him Papa? He's our mother's husband, and that's all."

"I've always called him Papa Jake, and I think he likes it."

"I do indeed, darlin'," Jake Austin said, coming into the room at that precise moment.

"Well then, hello, Papa Jake," Mary Beth said with a bit of laughter in her voice.

"Did Linus get all the cows moved?"

"Yes, sir, we didn't run into any kind of problem."

"I wouldn't think so," Jake answered. "To my way of thinking, Linus is the best ranch foreman in the country."

"You and Mr. Walker go back a long way, don't you?"

Jake chuckled. "I don't know. I was ten, and he was twelve when we met. Is that a long way back?"

"I'll just bet that you two were a couple of terrors then," Mary Beth said.

"Hellions is more like it," Jake replied. "By the way, your mama sent me to get the two of you for supper."

"Oh, no, Mama said to get cleaned up," Mary Beth said.

"You look fine the way you are," Jake said as he moved toward the dining room.

"I'm surprised you didn't eat with the cowboys," Abe said as they followed Jake.

"I've eaten with them before," Mary Beth said, "and Mr. Jones is a good cook."

"Yes, Edna used to say she wished she could cook as well as Max," Jake said.

Jake's comment was followed by a moment of silence. Edna had been Jake's first wife, who died after suffering from dementia.

"I'm sorry, I uh..."

"That's nonsense, Jake. You have no need to apologize," Hannah said, reaching out to touch her husband. "I know you loved her as you love me."

Jake smiled. "As I love my whole family," he said, taking in Mary Beth and Abe with a wave of his hand.

Mary Beth came over to stand for moment with Jake and her mother. Abe took his seat at the dinner table.

"I have so many things to be thankful for that if nobody minds, I would like to say a blessing," Hannah said as the others found their seats as well.

"Now, just who would mind?" Jake asked.

The four of them bowed their heads as Hannah gave the blessing.

"Bless us, Oh Lord, and these thy gifts, which we are about to receive, from thy bounty, through Christ, Our Lord. Amen."

"Amen," both Mary Beth and Jake added. Abe remained quiet.

* * *

MARATHON RANCH—1884

Lee Edward Holt was now twenty-four years old, but work and exposure to the sun made him look even older, so there was little left of the youth who eight years ago, had left the orphanage. Since reconnecting with Sister Maria, he had gone to San Antonio several times to see her. None of the current residents of the orphanage had been there when Lee Edward was, but they all knew him because he was such a frequent visitor.

Just returning from a visit, he put his horse away, then stepped into the chow hall where four men were eating. One of them was Hank Everson. He was Lee Edward's closest friend, and he knew Lee Edward's history from the time he had been left at Our Lady of Mercy Orphanage. He also knew about Sister Maria, and he had gone with Lee Edward to the orphanage on one of his visits.

"So, how's Sister Maria doing?" Hank asked.

"She's doing well. She asked about you," Lee Edward said.

Hank smiled. "Yeah, it's 'cause I made such a good impression on her."

"You must've done something right, though Lord knows what it could have been," Lee Edward teased.

"Yeah, I just bet he did something right," Dan Willard said with a snicker.

Of all the men who rode for the Marathon brand, Willard was the only one Lee Edward couldn't get along with. He had no idea what had caused the initial animosity between them, but as time passed, it seemed to get worse.

"What do you mean?" Lee Edward asked.

"He probably learned from you. You think nobody knows why you go see that nun all the time? You know, nuns don't get out much, so if she wants to have a good time, why men have to come to her. And I'll just bet..."

That was as far as Willard got before Lee Edward slapped him so hard that Willard's ears rang.

"Why you..." Willard shouted, then he waded into Lee Edward and threw a right cross that sent Lee Edward staggering back several steps. When Willard charged in, trying to follow up, Lee Edward leaned back so Willard's attempt found only air.

Willard's missed swing caused him to be off balance, and Lee Edward took advantage of it by a straight punch of his right hand into Willard's mouth. A tooth fell out, followed by a gush of blood that streamed down Willard's chin.

Willard connected with a left hook, but he wasn't set well when he threw the punch, so though Lee Edward felt it, the punch had little effect. Throwing the punch left Willard open, and Lee Edward, taking advantage of Willard's exposure, stepped in and ended the fight with a crushing uppercut to Willard's chin.

Willard fell flat on his back, his arms spread out to either side, and his eyes closed.

At the time of the fight, there had been only four others in the chow room, including Hank, who stepped up to stare down at the prostrate Willard.

"I'll bet that keeps him quiet for a while," Hank said.

"I hope you're right, but I wouldn't count on it," Lee Edward said.

When Willard came to, Lee Edward leaned over and held down his hand. "Here," Lee Edward said, "let me help you up."

Willard grabbed Lee Edward's hand and let himself be pulled up from the floor.

"What do you say we have a truce between us?" Lee Edward asked.

Willard glared at Lee Edward but said nothing. He put his hand to his chin and then pulled it away to look at the blood on his palm. He walked over to the wash basin and got a towel. He wet it and held it to his face.

There was an uneasy truce between the two men for the next three months. They spoke to each other, but only when their work required it.

* * *

LEE EDWARD CONTINUED his practice of drawing and shooting and had reached the level that Ray Dockins declared Lee Edward to be better than he was.

"I'm not better than you," Lee Edward said. "I learned everything I know from you."

Ray chuckled. "And you have overtaken the teacher."

Not long after that discussion, Ray came to Lee Edward with a simple request.

"Here's a bank draft from Mr. Matthews. He wants you to go into town, and get enough money for the payroll," Ray said.

"When does he want me to go?"

Ray smiled. "Now would be a good time."

The bank draft was for five hundred dollars which Lee Edward knew was more than was needed to make the payroll. Lee Edward didn't think much about it though. It was Mr. Matthews' money.

It was a short ride into Selma, so it was less than an hour later that Lee Edward walked into the bank.

"Hello, Mr. Holt," the teller said when Lee Edward stepped up to the teller's cage. "What can I do for you today?"

"Hello, Mr. Sidwell. Mr. Matthews wants me to pick up the payroll for him," Lee Edward said. "Here's the draft," he added, sliding the piece of paper across the counter.

"Five hundred dollars," Sidwell said as he examined the draft. "Tens and twenties all right?"

"Yes, I'm sure it is."

* * *

A MAN NAMED Corey Mason was in the bank at the same time. Mason was not quite as tall as Lee Edward, and his face was disfigured by a scar that had practically eliminated his left eyelid. Mason had come to the bank for one reason. He needed money and banks had money. It just so happened that none of the money the Bank of Selma had belonged to Mason.

Mason had been standing at the table in the lobby for the last few minutes, planning to rob the bank. But when he heard that the man who had just come in would be leaving with five hundred dollars in cash, he decided it would be a lot easier to take the money from one person than it would be to attempt a bank robbery.

Mason had heard the teller address the man as Holt. And while Holt wouldn't have as much money as was in the bank, five hundred dollars was enough money to meet his needs right now. Mason went out to stand in front of the bank, intending to take the money from Holt as soon as he came outside.

* * *

LEE EDWARD HAD JUST STUCK the money down into the inside pocket of his vest when he saw Fred Stone, owner of the leather goods shop, coming toward the bank.

"Lee Edward," Stone said. "I've got that new pair of boots that you ordered."

"Great, I'll come down and pick them up before I head back to the ranch."

"Let me take care of my banking and we can go together. It'll only take a minute."

"There ain't neither one of you a' goin' nowhere 'till I take that five hunnert dollars offen you," a third voice said.

Both Lee Edward and Fred Stone turned to look at the man who had just spoken. He was holding a pistol, and it was pointed toward the two men.

At that moment, facing what could be a life-and-death situation, Lee Edward recalled what Ray Dockins had told him was the most critical thing to learn.

"Most men won't be able to draw and shoot without thought. They know that if they pull the trigger, they are likely to kill the other man. The average person will think about that, and he will hesitate for just an instant, even if he's facing the most despicable opponent. And when that happens, the one who hesitates is the one who'll be killed."

"If you'll put your gun back in your holster and walk away, I won't kill you," Lee Edward said.

Mason laughed, then raised his pistol and pulled the hammer back.

Lee Edward's response was instantaneous. To the surprise of both Stone and Mason, the gun appeared in Lee Edward's hand and he pulled the trigger before Mason could. Mason got a look of shock on his face as the bullet punched into his chest.

Mason put his hand over the wound, then looked

down at the blood streaming through his fingers. That was Mason's last conscious thought as his eyes rolled up and he collapsed before them.

* * *

BECAUSE LEE EDWARD had Fred Stone and two others who happened to be on the street at the time as his witnesses, Merlin Morris, the Selma city marshal, declared that Lee Edward faced no legal problems for the shooting. On the contrary, word spread around quickly and several began thinking of Lee Edward as a hero.

"I'm not a hero," Lee Edward said to Hank. "And I don't mind telling you that all this hero talk bothers me."

Hank smiled. "You're a reluctant hero, and that's even better."

EIGHT

LONG TRAIL RANCH

ABE HUNTER STEPPED INTO THE BUNKHOUSE WHERE fourteen of the ranch's employees were sleeping.

"Everybody up, everybody up!" he yelled, banging the dipper against the water bucket. "Everybody up!"

There were groans from some of the men, all of whom were still in bed.

"What time is it?" someone asked.

"It's four o'clock," Abe said.

"Four o'clock? In the morning?"

"No, four o'clock in the afternoon," Abe replied cynically. "Get up!"

"Come on, Hunter, Moses don't even serve breakfast 'til six."

"What did you call me?" Hunter asked.

"I'm sorry, I meant Mr. Hunter. I just forgot, is all."

"Yeah, well, don't forget again."

Hunter turned then and left a bunkhouse full of disgruntled and complaining men.

"There ain't a damn thing we have to do before seven o'clock," Porter, one of the cowboys, said.

"It don't matter whether there is or not, Hunter got us up," Atkins said.

"I'd like to get that son of a bitch behind my horse," Porter replied. "You know I can make him kick anytime I want."

"Wouldn't do no good. As hard as that son of a bitch's head is, your horse is liable to break his foot," Atkins said.

Linus Walker, the ranch foreman, came into the bunkhouse. Linus was a big man, but his size and weight were muscular, not flab. He was fifty-six years old, but someone just seeing him would think he was ten years younger. He wore a full mustache that was the same color gray as his hair. "Well, I see you boys are all up early, ready and raring to go."

"Linus, you're the foreman. Will you tell that son of a bitchin' Hunter to stay the hell out of our bunkhouse? He ain't got no business comin' in here like that," Porter said.

"Hate to tell you this," Linus said, "but he does have the right to come in here, now, doesn't he? He'll more 'n likely own the ranch one day."

"Yeah, well, when he gets it, that's the day I'll be quittin'."

"No, you won't, Porter," Linus said soothingly. "You're too good a man to run off and leave the rest of us to deal with Hunter."

"I'll stay as long as you take care of us," Porter said.

Linus chuckled. "I'll do what I can."

"You can start by havin' Moses get breakfast started early this morning," Atkins said.

"You don't have to worry about Moses," Linus said.

"He's already got the biscuits in the oven, and I could smell the coffee when I went by."

"Yeah, coffee," Tanner said. "That's what I need."

Linus stood by and watched the men leave the bunkhouse and head for the chow hall, where they would take their breakfast. Looking around, he saw Abe Hunter out by the horse barn, so he went to talk to him.

* * *

ABE HUNTER WAS twenty-two years old. He was about eight inches over five feet tall, slender, with a narrow face and pale blue eyes. But it wasn't as much his looks that described him as it was his attitude. He had an arrogance about him that was as noticeable as the clothes he wore.

"Abe, did you think you needed to go into the bunkhouse at four o'clock and wake all the men?"

"Yeah. You got somethin' to say about it?"

"These men do hard, physical, tiring work every day. They have a right to a good night's uninterrupted sleep. Why did you wake them up at four in the morning? Breakfast isn't until six."

"Breakfast is when I say it is, and this morning, I told Moses to have it ready by five."

"Why?"

"Because I said so, that's why. When I take over this ranch, I'm going to get a full day's work out of these bastards. And you'll either go along with me on this, or I'll toss you out on your ass."

Linus glared at him for a moment, then turned and walked away. Abe Hunter's time would come. Linus smiled at the thought.

* * *

KERRVILLE, TEXAS

The two men were sitting at a table in the back of the Saddle and Bit Saloon. Half a bottle of whiskey sat on the table between them, and a nearly full glass sat in front of each one.

One of the men had a beard, not a well-trimmed beard, but just a scruffy patch of black hair. The other man was much larger, and he was clean-shaven, except for a well-tended mustache.

"Five hunnert dollars," the man with the scruffy beard said.

"Impossible. You've more than doubled what we offered you," the big man said.

"You're asking a lot from me for a lousy two hundred dollars," the bearded man said.

"If you won't do it, we'll find someone else."

"I don't think so."

The big man stroked his chin. "Two hundred fifty dollars and that's it."

"I'll do it for three hundred dollars and not a penny less."

The man with the mustache pondered the last offer, then nodded. "You're holding us up, but we'll go three hundred."

In fact, the big man felt a sense of victory. He had been given five hundred dollars to close the deal, and now he would come out two hundred dollars ahead of the game. It was all he could do to hold back a smile.

"When do you want it done?"

"I would say as soon as possible, but it's in your hands now. Do it whenever you can."

* * *

LONG TRAIL RANCH

The scruffy-bearded man's name was Roscoe, and he knew that in order to get everything set up, he was going to have to do something to give himself the maximum advantage. Seeing a bull standing near the boundary fence of Long Trail Ranch, he shot it.

The animal fell in place, then Roscoe moved back about three hundred yards from the opposite side of the fence. Shielded by a growth of shrubbery, he put a bullet into his Sharps Buffalo Gun, lay down, and sighted in on the bull. Now, all he had to do was wait. He knew his target had a habit of riding the fence line, and he knew that seeing the downed bull would draw him to it.

* * *

JAKE HAD LEFT the house mid-morning, telling Hannah that he intended to ride the fence all the way around the perimeter of the Long Trail property line.

"Jake, you ride the fence line every day. We have fourteen men working on this ranch, and you know that any one of them would ride the fence line for you."

Jake smiled. "Yeah, but what if I told you I do this just because I like to ride the fence line?"

"I know, to see how big the ranch is." Hannah laughed. "I swear you're like King Midas, counting his gold."

"The difference is, my gold is all on four legs," Jake said.

"What about lunch?" Hannah asked.

"If I'm not back by dinner, just go ahead without me."

"All right, I'll keep it warm for you, though I'm not sure you're worth it," Hannah added with a smile.

"Ha. You love me so much that if I asked you to cook me an all new dinner, you'd push Alenada out of her kitchen and whip up something just for me."

Hannah laughed. "All right, what can I say? Yes, I do love you that much."

"I knew you did," Jake said, giving Hannah a kiss before he left.

* * *

Jake had been riding for about half an hour when he saw a cow lying on the ground. Because it was lying on its side, he knew that it was dead. He didn't know why, but he figured the worst, so urging his horse into a rapid trot, he approached the downed animal.

"Damn!" he said aloud.

It wasn't just a cow, it was a prized bull, and the cause of death was easy to see. It had been shot through the head.

But why? He wondered. This wasn't like the previous episode of slain cows. This bull was nowhere close to land claimed by the Double Diamond. And who would kill a bull for no reason?

* * *

Three hundred yards away, Roscoe wet his finger, then held it up to check for wind. Feeling no movement of the air, he pulled the hammer back on the Sharps, set up a site picture, then slowly squeezed the trigger.

Jake didn't even hear the shot that killed him. The bullet entered the temple on the left side of his head and exited the right temple. He fell across the downed bull.

Roscoe waited for a few minutes to see if anyone was

close enough to have heard the shot and would be coming to investigate. He waited for almost fifteen minutes, and when no one showed up, he rode down to the fence to get a closer look at the man he had just shot. There was a big hole just above the left ear. Blood, bone detritus, and brain matter exuded from the exit hole on the right side of his head. Roscoe smiled, then rode away. He had earned his three hundred dollars.

"I got 'im," Roscoe said. "I'll take my three hundred dollars now."

"Are you sure he's dead?"

"Yeah, I'm sure. Unless he can live with a hole in his head, big enough to drive your fist into it."

"All right, here's your money."

Roscoe watched as the three hundred dollars were counted out in twenty-dollar bills.

"This is going to be a big help in..."

Roscoe held up his hand to interrupt the explanation. "You don't understand," Roscoe said. "I don't give a damn why you wanted him killed. All I care about is the money."

"How many men have you killed, Roscoe?"

"That depends."

"What do you mean, that depends?"

"That depends on whether you're talking about facing somebody down with a pistol or a stand-off killing like with Austin, when the son of a bitch don't even know I'm there."

"All right. Both ways. How many have you killed?"

"I've killed eleven men in a face-to-face showdown where I was faster than they were. And this makes the fourth one I've killed like I did this one."

"We may need you a few more times, before all this is done. I take it that three hundred dollars is acceptable?"

"If I kill 'em the way I killed Austin, three hundred dollars will be enough. It'll cost you more, if I have to face 'em down."

"How much more?"

"It depends on who I'm facin'."

"I'll keep that in mind."

* * *

WHEN JAKE HADN'T RETURNED by late afternoon, Hannah began to worry about him, and when she saw Linus, she called out to him.

"Yes, ma'am?" Linus asked, starting toward her.

"Linus, I'm worried," Hannah said. "Jake went out this morning. He said he was going to ride the fence line, but he isn't back yet. How long should it take?"

"He should be able to do it in an hour, no more than an hour and a half if there aren't any breaks. Even if he had to mark some spots, it shouldn't take more than a couple of hours. How long has he been out?"

"It's been much longer than that," Hannah said with an anxious tone.

"Well, that is a little long," Linus agreed.

"I'm afraid something's happened to him. He rode out on Smokey, and you know how skittish that horse is."

"I wouldn't worry about it too much. You know how Jake is. If he sees something that needs fixing, he'd just as soon do it himself as call on someone else."

"I do hope you're right," Hannah said. "It's just..."

"I know. I'll go find him for you if that will make you feel better," Linus offered.

"Thank you, I appreciate that. I just can't get over the feeling that something's wrong. I'd hate to think that he's been lying out there all this time and he's hurt."

Linus saddled his horse, then started riding the perimeter fence. He didn't tell Hannah, because she was already worried enough, but even though he tried to reassure her that everything was all right, he shared her concern.

He was about halfway around the fence line when he saw Jake's horse. For just a second, he felt a sense of relief, then he saw the downed cow. Almost immediately, he saw a body lying across the cow. And even though he was too far away to make out the features, he knew, without a doubt, that it would be Jake.

Linus urged his horse into a gallop then. Reaching the site, he swung down from the saddle.

"Oh, no, no, no, no," he said aloud.

Linus kneeled beside Jake and saw both the entry and the exit wound in Jake's head.

Linus stood up and pinched the bridge of his nose as his eyes filled with tears. He stood there for a long moment.

"Well, Jake, my old friend, I can't go see Hannah like this. I've got to pull myself together and be strong for your family."

Linus lifted Jake up and lay his body across the horse.

IT WAS Mary Beth who first saw Linus. He was leading a horse, and Mary Beth thought that was strange. Then she saw a body draped across the horse and she knew what it was. She recognized that it was the horse Jake had ridden out that morning, and she gasped as her eyes began to burn with tears.

Mary Beth hurried out to meet Linus, but he stopped her before she got to him.

"Oh," Mary Beth said. "It's Papa Jake! What happened? Did Smokey throw him?"

"No." Linus bit his lip before he continued. "He was shot."

"Shot?" she asked in disbelief. "He couldn't be shot!" She started running toward the horse and then she saw the awful sight. She threw herself against the body as she began to sob uncontrollably.

Linus took her in his arms, and not knowing how to comfort her, he began patting her head.

"Who would do this?" she managed to get out between sobs. "Papa Jake was the kindest man I've ever known—everybody liked him."

"I know," Linus said, "but now I need you to do something for me and for Papa Jake. I need to tell your mama, and I think it'll be easier if you are with me."

Mary Beth stepped back, taking one more look at Papa Jake. "I'll go with you, but it's going to be hard."

"Of course it is child, it's going to be hard for both of us, but it has to be done."

When Linus and Mary Beth went into the house, they were greeted by a smiling Hannah.

"Thank goodness you found him," Hannah said. "I'll go have Alenada fry up another batch of salt pork. He never would eat that cold. Oh, and tell him I made him a buttermilk pie myself. That should put a..." She stopped in mid-sentence as she saw their expressions. The smile left her face as she put her trembling hand over her mouth.

"Jake?" she said in a quaking voice.

"I'm sorry, Hannah," Linus said.

"Nooooo!" Hannah wailed as she began crying. Mary Beth wrapped her arms around her mother, weeping with her.

Linus stood nearby, fighting his own tears. He had just lost his best friend.

Abe came into the room and saw his mother and sister crying in each other's arms. Linus was standing beside them with his eyes red-rimmed.

"What happened?" Abe asked.

"Oh, Abe, it's Papa Jake," Mary Beth said. "He's dead."

Abe stood there, looking at all three of them crying. He stepped over to put his arms around his mother and sister. Jake had been a part of his life from childhood to adult, so though he didn't feel as intense a sorrow as Hannah or Mary Beth, he did feel sadness.

But then he had a thought that was even stronger than his grief. With Jake dead, the ranch would belong to him. He fought back the urge to smile.

NINE

LEE EDWARD DISMOUNTED IN FRONT OF THE EASY Pickins Saloon, tied his horse off at the hitch rail, then went inside.

He studied the saloon for a moment until he saw the man he was looking for.

Hank Everson was sitting at a table, sharing a drink with one of the girls who worked in the saloon. Lee Edward crossed over to the table, and Hank looked up.

"Lee Edward," Hank greeted.

"Let me get Addie, and you can join us," the girl said.

"Thank you, Loreen, but I can't stay. Hank can't either," Lee Edward said.

"What do you mean, I can't stay?"

"Ray wants everyone back at the ranch. The hundred and fifty head of cattle we had gathered in the alfalfa pasture are gone."

"Gone, what do you mean, gone?"

"I mean gone, as in they aren't there anymore."

"What the hell? Did someone rustle them?"

"That's what it looks like."

"Well, damn, I didn't do it. What does Ray want with me?"

"Not just you, he's gathering every hand that works on the Marathon. Ray's just doin' what Mr. Matthews asked him to do."

"All right, sorry, Loreen, but if I want to keep my job, I guess I'd better go with this ugly feller here," Hank said.

"What do you mean, ugly? Why, Lee Edward is the best looking of all of you Marathon boys," Loreen replied with a teasing smile.

"Damn, Loreen, does Lee Edward pay you to say such things?"

"I'll never tell," Loreen said.

After leaving the saloon, Lee Edward and Hank started back toward the ranch. Lee Edward had come to the Marathon right after he left the orphanage, and this was the only place he had ever worked. He had been with the Marathon for nine years now, and only Ray Dockins, Hank Everson, and Dan Willard, with whom the adversarial relationship continued, had been on the ranch longer.

When they arrived, they saw a gathering of some of the other hands who also rode for the Marathon brand. The Marathon crew had grown from the original seven and now there were twelve who worked for Andy Matthews. Lee Edward did a quick count and saw those five men, including Dan Willard, had not yet assembled.

Ray Dockins, who had been in the Big House talking to Mr. Matthews, came outside to talk to the hands who had gathered for this called conference. News of the missing cattle had already spread around, and there were looks of confusion and concern on everyone's face.

Dockins held up his hands to get everyone's attention.

"Who knows when the cows were still in the alfalfa patch?"

"I saw them this morning when I was checking the windmill," James McCoy said. "That was right after breakfast, so it must have been around seven."

"Was everyone at breakfast, or was anybody missing?" Ray asked.

"The same ones missing right now," McCoy said.

Lee Edward had already noticed that Dan Willard wasn't present. It took a moment or two while everyone looked around, then they came up with the other names of the missing.

"Lee Edward, Hank, would you two join me in my office? The rest of you, get back to work. Wilson?"

"Yeah, boss?"

"I want you and Jenkins to keep watch on the far edge of the herd."

"All right," Wilson replied. He looked around. "Jenkins?"

"I'm right here," Jenkins answered.

"You heard the man. Let's get saddled and get out there."

Lee watched the gathering as it disbursed, then he and Hank joined Dockins in the foreman's office.

"Willard, Gilbert, Sanchez, Carter, and Lewis are missing," Dockins said. "What does that say to you?"

"I'd say that it's a pretty good chance that they are either the ones who took the cattle, or else they know who did," Lee Edward said.

"Good guess," Dockins replied. "I want you two to go after them."

"Boss, there's five of them, there's only two of us," Hank said.

"All I want you to do is find them, then report back to me."

"We'll find 'em," Lee Edward promised.

"Where do you think we should start?" Hank asked as the two men walked back toward their horses.

"Well, the cows were in the west alfalfa field, so I suggest we go west. More specifically, southwest," Lee Edward answered.

"Southwest?"

"They're going to want to turn the cows into money, and San Antonio's the nearest place they can do that."

"Yeah, but the cattle agent there will recognize them as Long Trail cattle, won't he?"

"He will, but he'll also recognize Willard as someone who has worked for Mr. Matthews for a long time, and that's what Willard's counting on. He'll just tell the agent he's representing Long Trail. He'll get paid for the cows, then they'll split the money and be gone."

"Damn, I wonder how much they'll get?"

"Well, a hundred fifty cows at twenty-five dollars a head would be thirty-seven hundred and fifty dollars."

"Dayum!" Hank said. "That's a lot of money."

"Yeah, it is."

"What are we going to do when we find them?" Hank asked.

"We'll follow them, then we'll tell the purchasing agent that the cattle are stolen."

"Do you think the agent will believe us?"

"He's handled Marathon cattle before, so if he doesn't believe us right away, I think we'll at least be able to talk him into holding the cattle until he can get word from

Mr. Matthews that he hadn't authorized the shipment," Lee Edward said.

It didn't take long before the two men picked up the trail of the cattle.

"Looks like this is them," Hank said.

"Yes, it does. McCoy said the last time he saw the cattle was around seven this morning, so figuring Willard and the others left shortly thereafter, they've got a good start on us."

"We'll catch 'em when they stop for the night."

"Huh, uh, they won't stop," Lee Edward said.

"What do you mean they won't stop? Every time we take any cows to San Antonio, it's a two-day trip."

"That's because we've no need to push them," Lee Edward said. "Willard has to get them there as fast as he can, so what he's probably planning on, is getting there in the middle of the night, then holding them 'til tomorrow, when he can make the sale. But the chances are very good we'll catch up with them before they get there."

"Ha! Then we'll have 'em right where we want 'em," Hank said.

"Yeah," Lee Edward answered. He paused for a moment. "Unless they see us first, then they'll have us right where they want us."

"Oh, damn, what if they do see us first?" Hank asked, concern showing in his voice.

"Then we'll just have to deal with it," Lee Edward said.

At this precise moment, Dan Willard and the others were about five miles ahead of Lee Edward and Hank. Willard called Lewis over to him.

"Why don't you go back a little way and see if anyone is coming after us?" Willard suggested.

"What if I see someone?"

"It depends on how many you see. If there are several of them, we'll turn the cattle around and tell 'em the cattle wandered off and we're bringing them back. But if there's only one or two, we'll take care of 'em."

"What do you mean, take care of 'em?" Lewis asked.

"We'll ambush 'em, 'n kill 'em."

"Wait a minute, Willard. Some of them boys is friends of mine," Lewis said.

"Lewis, when you agreed to do this, you gave up all your friends except for the ones that's ridin' with us," Willard said. "Do you understand that?"

"Yeah," Lewis said. "Yeah, I guess you're right."

Leaving Willard and the herd behind him, Lewis had gone no farther than half a mile when he saw Lee Edward Holt and Hank Everson. He knew he hadn't been seen, so he turned and galloped back to the herd.

"What is it?" Willard asked when he saw how quickly Lewis had returned.

"You're right, we're being followed," Lewis reported.

"How many?"

"There's only two of 'em. Holt and Everson."

"Holt," Willard said with an evil smile. "Yeah, this couldn't be better."

"What do you mean? I told you, there's a couple of men followin' us."

"Round up the others," Willard ordered.

A few minutes later, Lewis returned with the other three men.

"What's up?" Gilbert asked.

"We've got company," Willard replied. "We're being followed."

"Oh, damn," Sanchez said.

Willard chuckled. "No, it's good. I was concerned

that Dockins might send ever'one after us. But the dumb son of a bitch only sent two men."

"What are we goin' to do?" Carter asked.

"You're going to stay here with the herd," Willard said. "The rest of us are goin' to ambush them two 'n kill 'em."

Willard and the others started back down the trail. If there were only two following them, he would have no trouble in getting them out of the way. And the fact that one of them was Lee Edward Holt made it even better. Damn, how he didn't like that son of a bitch, and if this really was Holt and Everson trailing the herd, it couldn't be sweeter.

Five minutes later, Willard saw the two men approaching him. Smiling, he raised the Winchester to his shoulder, aimed, then pulled the trigger. "Goodbye, Holt," he said quietly.

* * *

AT THAT EXACT MOMENT, Lee Edward had leaned forward to make an adjustment to the harness. He was startled by the loud popping sound of a bullet passing but inches from his head. Looking up, he saw the smoke from a rifle.

"Dismount!" he shouted, leaping down from his horse and grabbing his rifle.

A second shot was fired.

"I'm hit!" Hank called.

"Can you move?"

"Yeah, it's in my shoulder."

"Get over there, get down."

Lee Edward pointed to a nearby depression, and the

two ran to it as other shots were fired. Luckily, none of them found their target.

As soon as Lee and Hank dismounted, their horses turned and headed back to the ranch.

Now, with the protection of the depression, Lee Edward took a look at Hank's shoulder.

"It doesn't look too bad," Lee Edward said. "It's just a graze."

"Yeah, well, it hurts like hell."

Lee tore the shirt arm off.

"What are you doing?"

"I'm going to tie this around the wound to stop the bleeding."

With the bandage in place, the two men moved up to look over the edge of the shallow hole.

Lee Edward was sighting down his rifle, when one of the men rose up to take a shot. Lee Edward pulled the trigger, and the shooter fell backward.

"You just kilt Lewis, you son of a bitch!" someone shouted. Lee Edward recognized Willard's voice.

"Willard, if you'll bring the cattle back now, probably the worst that will happen to you is you'll get fired," Lee Edward called back.

"The hell I will. I plan to get these here cows sold."

"They aren't yours to sell."

"Yeah? Well, I'm the one that's got 'em," Willard called back. He followed his shout with another shot, and this bullet was so close that it kicked dirt into Lee Edward's eyes.

He heard Hank shoot, and looking up, he saw Sanchez pitch forward.

"I got 'im," Hank said.

"We're thinning you out, Willard," Lee Edward said. "Are you sure you don't want to give yourself up now?"

Willard's answer was another shot. Both Lee Edward and Hank returned fire.

"Hold it, hold it, don't shoot no more!" Gilbert shouted. "I'm givin' up!"

Lee saw Gilbert leave the protection of the trees, then start toward them with both hands in the air.

"Gilbert, you cowardly son of a bitch!" Willard shouted. Lee Edward heard a shot, then saw Gilbert fall forward. A puff of gun smoke drifted up from the trees.

"Damn, Willard shot 'im!" Hank said.

"I'd say—what a sorry human being."

A moment later, they heard the sound of a galloping horse.

"It's Willard. He's getting away," Hank said.

"Let's go after 'im."

"How are we goin' to do that? Our horses are long gone."

"I only heard one horse leavin'. I'll bet the others are still tethered somewhere," Lee Edward said.

"Let's go find out."

"Keep your eyes open, just in case anyone is still alive."

As the two men crossed the open area between the shallow dip in the ground and the growth of trees where Willard and the others had been hiding, they passed Gilbert. Lee Edward squatted down to check on him. Gilbert was still breathing, but it was in short, gasping breaths.

"Gilbert?" Lee Edward said.

"Kill Willard for me, Lee Edward," Gilbert said. "Kill the son of a bitch."

"We'll have to let him go for now," Lee Edward said. "We need to get you to a doctor."

"I ain't goin' to live long enough to get to a doctor, 'n you know it. I'm thirsty, get me some water."

"Our canteens are on our horses, and the horses ran away. Is your horse tethered, and do you have a canteen?"

Gilbert gave a couple more gasping breaths, then he was silent.

"He don't need no water now," Hank said. "I think he's dead."

Lee felt for a pulse. "You're right, he's dead."

"What are we goin' do with 'im?"

"First thing we have to do is see if we can find some horses, then we'll go after Willard and the cattle, and we'll pick the bodies up on the way back."

"All right."

There were three tethered horses and because the horses belonged to Marathon, they knew them.

"What'll we do with the third horse?"

"Turn 'im loose, he'll go back home."

* * *

THEY FOUND the herd within less than a mile, and Willard and Carter were waiting at the back of the herd. When Lee Edward and Hank approached, the two opened fire. They missed. Lee Edward and Hank returned fire. They didn't miss.

"Come on," Lee Edward said. "We have to get ahead of the herd before they stampede."

The shooting had startled the herd, and the cows began moving around nervously. But when Hank and Lee Edward got in front of the herd, they were able to turn them, and with only a hundred fifty cows, there were able to start moving the cows back toward the ranch.

It was well after dark by the time they reached the

Marathon Ranch, but the cattle, sensing familiar ground, were easy to push.

* * *

ANDY MATTHEWS and Ray Dockins were waiting for the herd, opening the gate to allow them into the small holding pasture. When they saw Lee Edward and Hank, there were smiles on both men's faces.

"I don't mind tellin' you, you two boys done a hell of a good job," Ray said.

"Where are Willard and the others?" Matthews asked. "I don't cotton to cattle rustlers, and I intend to turn them in to the law. Hands can't get away with this kind of shenanigan without being punished."

"They're all dead," Lee Edward said. "We didn't plan to kill them, but they opened up on us."

"Did you leave the bodies out there?"

"We had no choice if we were going to get the cattle back."

"You did the right thing," Matthews said. He turned to his foreman. "Ray, send a couple of men out in a wagon to bring back the bodies."

"Yes, sir," Dockins replied.

Matthews turned his attention back to Lee Edward and Hank. "As far as you two are concerned, you did such a good a job that I think you deserve a little bonus."

Matthews gave Lee Edward and Hank a hundred dollars apiece.

"Woohee!" Hank said. "All them girls at Easy Pickins are goin' to fall in love with me, now!"

"We should get you to a doctor first thing tomorrow," Lee Edward said.

"Bullet didn't do nothin' but graze me. The doctor ain't goin' to do more doctorin' than you already done."

"We're goin' to see him anyway," Lee Edward insisted.

* * *

THE NEXT MORNING the doctor cleaned and dressed Hank's wound, then let Hank go his own way. Hank went to the saloon. Lee Edward rode into San Antonio.

* * *

"OH, Lee Edward, this is so much money," Sister Maria said. "We can't take this from you."

"Sister Maria, I lived here for sixteen years. I'm sure I cost the orphanage more than six dollars and twenty-five cents per year, which is how this one hundred dollars would break down. Please take it. I want to do something for my family, and Our Lady of Mercy is the only family I've ever known."

Sister Maria smiled. "Even as a child, you were always generous. All right, come with me, and we'll give the money to Mother Superior to use as she sees fit."

* * *

"OH, what a wonderful thing for you to do, Lee Edward," Mother Superior said happily. "We'll find some way to use it for the children. Do you have any suggestions?"

"Yes, maybe some new playground equipment, a seesaw, a swing set, a croquet set, maybe even a football," Lee Edward suggested.

Sister Maria smiled. "I knew you could come up with

suggestions. You always were such a clever and sweet little boy."

Lee Edward chuckled. "Even if your 'little boy' is over six feet tall now?"

Sister Maria put her hand on Lee Edward's arm. "Lee Edward, you always were clever and sweet, and you will always be my little boy—no matter how big you get."

Lee put his hands on Sister Maria's cheeks. "God didn't send me to you, He had you there for me."

TEN

THE COFFIN WAS BEING DISPLAYED IN THE DRAWING room at the Big House, and the lid was raised so that the body of Jacob Randolph Austin, the man who had built Long Trail Ranch, could lie in repose.

Hannah Austin was sitting in the front row of the chairs that had been assembled. Abe Hunter was sitting beside her.

At the moment Linus Walker was standing at the coffin, looking down upon the man who had been so much a part of his life.

Mary Beth joined him at the casket.

"You didn't just work for Papa Jake," Mary Beth said. "You cared for him deeply."

"I couldn't have loved him more if he had been my own brother," Linus said.

Mary Beth put her hand on Linus's arm. "I know what you mean. He wasn't my birth father, but I couldn't have loved him more if he had been."

"And you know he loved you like a daughter."

"He was such a good man. How could this have happened to him?"

Linus shook his head. "I don't know, but I know I'll do everything I can to find out who did this to him."

Everyone who rode for the Long Trail brand filed in to take seats behind Hannah and Abe. Next came the owners of some of the neighboring ranches, along with their wives. Also present was Ruben Pugh and his foreman, Bull Travers. As a result, the drawing room, though quite large, was full of mourners.

Linus and Mary Beth stood by the open casket until they saw Reverend Fielding Pike come into the room. They took the two vacant seats beside Hannah as the preacher took his place. It wasn't necessary for everyone to grow quiet, as they already were.

Pike stood between the coffin and those who had come for the funeral.

"Dear Lord, we the family and friends of Jacob Austin, have come to bid him a final goodbye," the preacher said.

"I would like to share with you, Jake's favorite passage of the Bible. It is not unusual that this is Jake's favorite, for many have drawn solace from this verse for over two thousand years. It is the twenty-third Psalm.

"The Lord is my shepherd; I shall not want. He maketh me to lie down in green pastures, He leadeth me beside the still waters, He restoreth my soul. He leadeth me in the paths of righteousness for his name's sake. Yea, though I walk through the valley of the shadow of death, I will fear no evil, for Thou art with me; Thy rod and Thy staff, they comfort me. Thou preparest a table before me in the presence of mine enemies. Thou anointest my head with oil; my cup runneth over. Surely goodness and mercy shall follow

me all the days of my life, and I will dwell in the house of the Lord for ever."

Following the reading of scripture, Reverend Pike gave a homily of no more than five minutes, then invited everyone to process to the gravesite for the committal of Jake Austin's last remains. The gravesite was under a spreading Alamo tree about fifty yards from the house. The grave of Edna, Jake's first wife, was beside the open hole where Jake's casket would be.

After the coffin was lowered into the grave, Father Pike stepped up to give the prayer.

"For as much as it has pleased our Heavenly Father in His wise providence to take unto Himself our beloved husband, step-father and friend, Jacob Randolph Austin, we therefore commit his body to the ground, earth to earth, ashes to ashes, dust to dust, looking for the blessed hope and the glorious appearing of the great God in our Savior Jesus Christ who shall change the body of our humiliation and fashion it anew in the likeness of His own body of glory according to the working of His mighty power wherewith He is able even to subdue all things unto Himself."

Father Pike then dropped a handful of dirt onto the coffin. "Remember that we are dust, and to dust we shall return." He then said a dismissal prayer and everyone began walking back toward the house for a reception.

Alenada had prepared plates of sandwiches, as well as cookies and lemonade.

Ruben Pugh came forward to express his condolences to Hannah.

"Mrs. Austin, it's no secret that Jacob and I had our differences, but those differences were clearly about business. Despite all that, I've always had the greatest respect for him, for what he had done. He built an 85,000 acre ranch—one of the finest in Texas, and he built it from nothing. I not only admired the man, I considered him a friend."

"Thank you for your kind words, Mr. Pugh," Hannah replied.

"I want you or your son to know that if I can be of any assistance to you either now or in the future, please don't hesitate to call on me."

"I'll keep that in mind," Hannah said as she looked around to see where her children were. Mary Beth was mingling with the other people, and Abe was speaking to Linus Walker. The two men were standing in the front hall.

* * *

"WALKER, I thought you might like to know that I'll be keeping you on as foreman. I hadn't intended to," Abe said. "I wanted to fire you, but my mother convinced me to keep you because she said you could be of some help to me. But I want it well understood by you and all the hands, that I am the boss."

"And why are you the boss?" Linus asked.

"Why am I the boss? That's a dumb ass question. I'm the boss because I have just inherited this ranch."

"Oh? I wasn't aware that the will had been read."

"Well, use your head for once. Austin was married to my mother, and he has no other heirs. Who else would he leave the ranch to?"

"You never can tell," Linus said.

"Good Lord, I should fire you for pure stupidity!" Abe stomped out of the house, slamming the door behind him.

* * *

AFTER THE FUNERAL, Linus went into Kerrville to take care of some business. Then, with business taken care of, he went to the Saddle and Bit Saloon where some of the Long Trail hands had gathered to share memories of Jake Austin.

"Let me tell you what's botherin' me the most," Hal Crader said. "What's botherin' me most is thinkin' about that sorry bastard, Abe Hunter, bein' our boss."

"Hell, it won't be all that bad for us," Clem Porter said. "We've been takin' orders all along." He looked over at their foreman, who had come into the saloon to be with the men on this sad occasion. "It's Linus I'm thinkin' about. If I was Linus, I'd quit."

"Good Lord no, please don't have Linus quit," Bobby Wilson said. "Him being here is the only protection we've got against Abe Hunter."

"Yeah, I see what you mean," Buck Adams said.

"He's right over there. Why don't you ask him?" Wilson said.

"All right, I will," Davy replied. He walked over to talk to Linus, who was standing at the bar all alone. He was staring into his mug of beer with one of the saddest expressions Davy had ever seen. He was hesitant to approach him, but he really wanted to be assured that Linus wasn't about to abandon them.

"Are you goin' to quit, Linus?" Davy Adams asked.

"What are you boys tryin' to do, turn me out to pasture?"

"You mean you're a' plannin' on stayin' on?" Clem Porter asked.

"I thought I might."

"Good!" Porter replied with an enthusiastic smile.

"What the hell, Porter?" Wilson said. "Are you a'

wantin' Linus to be browbeat all the time? You know if he stays, he's goin' to be Hunter's special target."

"Yeah, but I think he's strong enough to take it. And I figure if he stays around, he can keep a lot of it off of us."

"So, I'm to be your shield, am I?" Linus asked with a chuckle.

"Yeah. Well, no but...come on, Linus, you know what I'm talkin' about," Porter said.

"I'll tell you what I'll do. I'll do everything I can to keep him off all your asses," Linus said.

"Linus, you are a damn good man, and I don't mind tellin' you, that you are the best foreman I ever worked for," Hal Crader said.

"Well, Loomis, I might really appreciate that, if you'd ever worked for any other foreman," Linus said with a smile. "But I know for a fact, this is the first job you've ever had."

"Oh, yeah, well, I mean it anyway," Crader said.

The others laughed.

Linus signaled one of the bar girls, and she came to him with the flirtatious grin of her trade.

"What can I do for you, honey? Are you looking for some company?"

"What's your name, darlin'?" Linus asked.

"Abby."

"Well, Abby, as you can see, I've already got quite a bit of company," Linus said, taking in all the others with a wave of his hand. "But I'd like for you to bring all these boys another drink, then get a drink for yourself and a couple of your friends, and join us."

"All right, honey, I'll be right back," Abby said.

A few minutes later, Abby and two other girls came back to the table, carrying enough drinks for everyone.

There were laughs around the table and some suggestive teasing, then Linus called out, "Gentlemen?"

His rather loud call got everyone's attention, and the table got quiet as the men and the three young women looked at him.

Linus held up his glass. "Ladies," he said, "and gentlemen," he added. "I propose that we drink a toast to Jake Austin, one of the finest men I ever had the privilege to know."

"To Mr. Austin," Crader replied.

All held their drinks toward the middle of the table for a moment, then tossed them down.

* * *

THE NEXT DAY, Linus saw an article in the newspaper that caught his attention.

MURDER TRIAL

On Monday next, Lee Edward Holt and Henry (Hank) Everson will be tried for murder. Holt and Everson, employees of Marathon Ranch, were given instructions by Andrew Matthews to recover some cattle that he suspected had been illegally taken by five other hands of the ranch. During the act of recovering the purloined cattle, all five of the cattle rustlers were killed.

ELEVEN

SHERIFF LEROY PATTERSON, THE OVER-ACTIVE SHERIFF of Bexar County charged Lee Edward Holt and Hank Everson with murder because of the shooting death of Daniel Willard, Claude Gilbert, Juan Sanchez, Ralph Carter, and Herbert Lewis who were suspected of stealing cows from the Marathon Ranch. The trial would be held in San Antonio, and Andrew Matthews hired Robert Norton as defense attorney for the two men. Norton was considered by many, to be the premier lawyer in Bexar County.

The trial opened with the bailiff reading the charges.

"Your Honor, there comes before this court Lee Edward Holt and Henry R. Everson to be tried for murder on the Seventh of May, in this Year of Our Lord, 1886."

Norton told the two men that their biggest problem was that they had no witnesses to validate their claim that they had shot the robbers in self-defense.

"But we didn't have any choice, Mr. Norton. They shot at us first."

"I'm not suggesting we change our plea. I'm just saying that, without a witness, it could cause us some trouble."

Although neither Lee Edward nor Hank were required to take the stand, Norton convinced them that without any witnesses, the only way they could support the claim was to testify on their own behalf. Lee Edward was the first one to testify.

After he was sworn in, he took his seat in the witness chair.

"Would you please say for the court, your name?" Norton asked.

"My name is Lee Edward Holt."

"Mr. Holt, you are being charged with the unlawful deaths of Daniel Willard and..." Norton took out a piece of paper and read the other names. "...Claude Gilbert, Juan Sanchez, Ralph Carter, and Herbert Lewis. Would you please stipulate that these are the names of the men who worked on the Marathon Ranch and were in possession of one-hundred fifty cows at the time of their deaths?"

"Those are the men," Lee Edward said.

"Would you please tell the court how it happened that these five men were shot and killed?"

Lee proceeded to tell the court how Willard and the four others had stolen one hundred fifty head of cattle from Marathon Ranch. He told also how he and Hank were recruited to find the men and bring the cattle back.

"We followed the tracks of the cattle, but before we reached the herd, Dan Willard and the others began shooting at us. We shot back."

"And, in the engagement that they had precipitated, they were killed," Norton said. "Is that correct?"

"Yes, sir, that is correct," Lee Edward said.

"No further questions. Your witness, counselor," Norton said. He glanced toward the prosecutor's table.

After Norton returned to his seat behind the defense table, the prosecutor, Foss Meyer, rose and approached Lee Edward.

"When you were sworn in a moment ago, you swore to tell the truth and nothing but the truth, but even in that statement, you lied, didn't you?"

"Lied? No, I didn't lie. What are you talking about?"

"What name did you give the court?"

"Lee Edward Holt."

"Ah, but that isn't your birth-given name, is it?"

"What?" Lee Edward asked, surprised by the question.

"Is it, or is it not true, that in September of the year of our Lord, 1860, you were brought to the Our Lady of Mercy Orphanage as an unwanted foundling, and there abandoned by the woman who gave you birth, who left without identifying you, herself, or the man who impregnated her. You are, sir, in the biblical definition of the word, a bastard. If you would, sir, tell the court how you came by your name."

"Sister Maria named me."

"So then, you agree that you have gone your entire life without a real name," Meyer stated.

"Objection, Your Honor!"

"What is the nature of your objection?" Judge Bartlett asked.

"Your Honor, none of us name ourselves. We all use names given to us by others. The fact that Mr. Holt was named by Sister Maria does neither negate nor invalidate his name," Norton said.

"But we know that Holt is not the name of his father," Meyers said. "Therefore, his name is not valid."

"You are married, are you not, Mr. Meyer?" Norton asked.

"I am, sir, but I fail to see the relevance of that question."

"What is your wife's last name?"

"Why, it's Meyer, of course."

"Is that the name of her father?"

"You know that it is not. Why would you think it would be?"

"Then, even though Meyer is not the name of her father, the name she bears is legitimate, is it not?"

Meyer stared at Norton for a moment, unable to come up with a response.

"Objection sustained," the judge said.

"Mr. Holt, Dan Willard isn't the first man you've killed, is he?"

"Uh," Lee Edward said, then he continued. "No."

"It is a fact, is it not, that you also killed Corey Mason?"

"Yes, that is true."

"And you claim that killing, too, was in self-defense."

"It was in self-defense, but I didn't have to make the claim. No charges were filed against me."

"Holt, do you deny that you and your co-defendant killed Dan Willard, Claude Gilbert, Juan Sanchez, Ralph Carter, and Herbert Lewis?"

"We didn't kill Gilbert. Willard killed him."

"Are you trying to convince this court that Willard killed one of his own men?"

"I don't know whether or not I'm convincing anyone,

but it is true that Dan Willard shot Claude Gilbert."

"All right, we will put that aside. Even if Willard did kill Gilbert, that leaves you and Mister Everson guilty of murdering the other four men, does it not?"

"We didn't murder them."

"You do admit that you and Mr. Everson killed them though, do you not? All but Mister Gilbert?"

"Yes, but we killed them in self-defense."

"How would you describe your relationship with Dan Willard?"

"We both rode for the same brand."

"I don't mean that, Mr. Holt. What I am asking is what was your personal relationship with Willard? Would you say that you were friends?"

"No, sir, I don't believe I would say that."

"The truth is, you and Willard once had a difference of opinion that developed into a fight. Is that true?"

"Yes."

Foss Meyer spent the next several minutes, trying to break down Lee Edward's self-defense plea. He pointed out that it was known that there was bad blood between Lee Edward and Willard.

Lee stuck to his story until a disgusted Meyer withdrew any further questioning.

When it came time to present the defense, Norton called Ray Dockins to the stand. Ray testified that he had personally chosen Lee Edward Holt and Henry Everson to attempt to return the stolen cattle, because they were longtime employees known to be good workers and dependable men.

"Mr. Dockins. Ray Dockins. Were you, at one time in your life, referred to as Deadly Dockins?"

Ray was silent as he looked toward Lee Edward and Hank. He took a deep breath and answered the question.

"That was a long time ago," Ray replied.

"Long ago or not, you were known as quite an accomplished gunfighter, were you not?"

"Yes," Ray answered without elaboration.

"And did you instruct Lee Edward Holt on how to be an efficient gunfighter."

"Yes," Ray replied, again in a flat, one-word response.

"Do you believe it is possible that using the skills you taught him, Lee Edward Holt, along with Henry Everson, murdered Willard and the others who stole the cattle?" Norton asked.

"Not even for a minute. I am totally convinced that it all went down exactly the way Lee Edward and Hank testified."

Andrew Matthews and half a dozen of the other hands also testified, and to a man, they declared their belief that the shootings of Willard and those with him, were an act of self-defense on the part of Lee Edward and Hank.

Defense and prosecution gave their closing arguments, then the jury retired for their deliberation.

Matthews and Dockins remained in the courtroom with Lee Edward, Hank, and Norton.

"They aren't really going to find these men guilty of murder, are they?" Matthews asked. "I sent them out to recover my cattle, and they did exactly as I asked. I know damn well they are innocent, and if they're found guilty, I'll feel responsible."

"I think we made a pretty good case," Norton said. "But if we do get a guilty verdict, we'll appeal."

The jury returned within half an hour, and Judge Bartlett called the court to order.

"Has the jury selected a foreman?" Judge Bartlett asked.

One of the men of the jury stood.

"We have, Your Honor. I'm Frank Edmonston and I have been elected foreman."

"Have you reached a verdict?"

"Yes, sir, we have, Your Honor."

"Are they individual verdicts, or will the verdict apply to both defendants?" Judge Bartlett asked.

"The verdict will apply to both defendants."

"Very well, if you would, please publish your verdict."

"We find the defendants, Lee Edward Holt and Henry J. Everson..."

The foreman paused for a moment, and Lee Edward held his breath, waiting for the verdict.

"Not guilty."

Lee Edward let out his breath, then looked over at Hank with a broad smile on his face. His smile was mirrored by Hank.

There were cheers from the other Marathon hands who were present in the courtroom.

Judge Bartlett slapped the hammer against the bench to restore order. Then he addressed the court.

"The jury, having found Lee Edward Holt and Henry Everson not guilty, they are hereby released."

Lee reached over to shake Norton's hand, as did Hank.

Foss Meyer came over to the defense table, wearing a smile. He reached out to shake hands with Lee Edward and Hank.

"The truth is I've believed you men were innocent from the start. But as prosecutor, I had no choice but to try and make my case. I'm glad it turned out as it did."

Matthews came over to the defense table as well. "Gentlemen," he said. "Let's get back to Salem. I invite you all to the Easy Pickins Saloon to celebrate."

TWELVE

Having read of the trial in the newspaper and having a particular interest in one of the defendants, Linus Walker had come to San Antonio. As a result, he was one of those in the gallery during the trial, and when the verdict was rendered, he breathed a sigh of relief.

For twenty-six years, Linus had been tasked with being aware of the whereabouts of Lee Edward Holt. It was serendipitous that at the precise moment he needed to track Holt down, his name had appeared in the newspaper. When he heard Andrew Matthews announce that everyone was to convene in Salem at the Easy Picken's Saloon, Linus rode ahead and entered the saloon before the others got there.

When Lee Edward, Hank, and the other members of the Marathon crew arrived, they were laughing and talking.

"Hodge, I want the best bottle of whiskey you have in the house," James McCoy said to the bartender. "No, make those two bottles. The boss man is buying and these boys have a lot of celebrating to do!"

Linus sat alone at a table near the piano nursing a
beer. He watched quietly, not wanting to interrupt the
celebration.

One of the bar girls came to his table. "Hello, handsome," she said. "Would you like some company and
another beer?"

"Sure, get a drink and join me," Linus said.

"My name's Loreen," the pretty young woman said.
"What's yours?"

"Linus." He gave her a dollar. "Go buy yourself a
drink, and keep the change."

"Oh, a generous man," Loreen said, flashing a smile.
"I like generous men."

Loreen returned a moment later, carrying another
beer for Linus and a drink for herself. She joined him at
the table.

"They're celebrating," Linus said with a nod toward
the group of men who were gathered at the bar.

"Yes, they all work for Mr. Matthews at Marathon
Ranch. Two of them were tried for murder today, and
they were both found innocent, so that's why they're
celebrating."

"Yes, I was in the court."

"You were?"

"I was. Do you know Lee Edward Holt?"

"Yes, I know him."

"What kind of man is he?"

"He is one of the most decent men who come in this
place. He's always friendly, always willing to help someone, and like you, he's a generous man."

"I'd like you to ask him to come over to my table to
talk to me."

"Oh, I don't know if he would do that what with
the celebrating and all," Loreen said. "These men are all

his friends, and he's one of the reasons they're cele-brating."

"I'll give you something to say to him that will guar-antee he'll come talk with me."

"What?"

"I know we're drinking to celebrate you two boys being found innocent," James McCoy said. "But I think we should also be celebrating that you killed Dan Willard. Willard was the most no-count son of a bitch I ever knew."

"Yeah, I'll go along with that," one of the others said as they all laughed at McCoy's observation. All but Lee Edward raised a glass.

"Lee Edward?" McCoy said, holding his glass out as if in question as to why Lee Edward wasn't responding to the proposed toast.

Lee Edward shook his head. "I don't think I could celebrate killing someone, even if it was necessary."

"You're a damn good man, Lee Edward," McCoy said as he downed his drink.

A young woman approached the celebrants.

"Loreen, join us for a drink," Hank said. "We're celebratin'."

"I have to speak to Lee Edward first."

"What is it you want to tell me?" Lee Edward asked with a smile.

"Not in front of the others," Loreen said. "Come down to the end of the bar with me."

"Oh, no," McCoy said. "Ain't Holt about the luckiest guy we ever knowed? Now, he goes and gets the prettiest girl all to his own self."

Loreen shook her head. "You guys! You're awful. I just need to pass on a message."

Lee Edward hesitated for a moment wondering what

she could possibly say that the others couldn't hear. At this point, he had no secrets.

"All right," he said as he took his drink and followed her to the far end of the bar. "What's this important message you have for me?"

"Do you see that man sitting at the table by the piano?"

Lee looked over toward the table. "Yes, I see him. What about him?"

"He wants to talk to you."

"What is he, a reporter or something? Tell him no thanks."

Loreen leaned closer to Lee Edward and whispered. "He says he knows who your mother is."

Once, when Lee Edward was a young boy playing on the playground at the orphanage, he fell, and the fall knocked the breath out of him. He lay there for a terrifying moment, wondering if he would ever breathe again.

He felt very much like that now. He had wondered about his parents for his entire life. Could it be possible that this man actually knew who his mother was?

He had to gather himself before he could walk over to the table. When he reached the table, he took in a sharp breath. He knew this man!

"I've seen you before," Lee Edward said. "You used to come to the orphanage and every time you came, you gave money."

"I wondered if you would remember me. My name is Linus Walker."

"Lee Edward Holt," Lee Edward said as he extended his hand.

"Please, have a seat, or if you would prefer, we could have this conversation someplace else."

"This is as good a place as any," Lee Edward said as he

sat across the table from Linus. "Loreen said something that did get my attention."

"What she said is true. I do know who your mother is."

"If that's true, why didn't you tell me or at least Sister Maria, a long time ago when you used to come to the orphanage?"

"It wasn't the right time," Linus said.

"It wasn't the right time?" Lee Edward replied, his voice reflecting his anger at such a response to his question.

"Your mother lives in San Antonio. I can take you to see her."

"Yeah, well, I'm not sure I want to go. If she lives in San Antonio, she had sixteen years to come see me," Lee Edward said with even more emotion. "And she knew where I was."

"I think you should come with me to go see her. Then you'll need to come to Kerrville with me. You'll have to be absent from Marathon for about a week," Linus said.

"Why do I need to go to Kerrville, and why should I be gone for a week?"

"I'm not at liberty to tell you, but believe me, it will be worth it if you come with me."

Lee Edward shook his head. "This all sounds sort of contrived to me. A man who came to the orphanage all those years, and then just happened to be at a trial where I was being tried for murder—yes, I saw you there, and now, out of the blue, you say you know my mother. No, there's something fishy about this." Lee Edward stood. "I'll be joining my family now. Except for Sister Maria and the nuns at Our Lady of Mercy, these people right here are my family."

"I understand how this must be a shock to you,"

Linus said, "but I can say there is a great deal of money riding on you coming with me to Kerrville. If you don't want to meet your mother, then I can't make you do it."

Lee Edward sat down again. "All right, we'll go tomorrow, but if I'm going to be gone for a week, I'll need to get permission from Mr. Matthews before I can go."

"I agree," Linus said. "By Wednesday afternoon, you'll know everything. All I can do is ask you to trust me."

"I suppose I really don't have any other choice, now do I?"

"If you will allow me, I'd like to ride out to Marathon with you. I'd be honored to meet Mr. Matthews."

"All right, I don't suppose I can get in any deeper than I already am, so you're welcome to ride along with me."

* * *

"WELL, HERE HE IS," Ray Dockins said when Lee Edward and Linus rode into the yard at Marathon Ranch. "Am I ever glad to see you're not wearin' black and white stripes."

"That makes two of us," Lee Edward answered.

"Who's this fella you got ridin' with you?" Ray asked as he looked at Linus with obvious curiosity.

"Ray, this is Linus Walker," Lee Edward said. "He's foreman of the Long Trail Ranch."

"Long Trail, is it? I've heard of that ranch. It's a big one, over close to Kerrville, ain't it."

"You've placed it, and yes, it's a good-sized ranch," Linus replied.

"What are you doing with my man here?" Ray asked. "You're not plannin' to hire him away from me, are you?"

"Listen, Ray, I'm going to have to be gone for a while.

Could be as much as a week," Lee Edward said, speaking up before Linus could respond to Ray's question.

"What for? You've already been out of the saddle long enough messin' with this trial."

"I'm going to meet my mother."

"Your mother? I thought you said you didn't have a mother," Ray said, surprised by the announcement.

"I thought I didn't either," Lee Edward said. "But Mr. Walker says that I do, and he knows who she is and where she is."

"Well, all right, by all means, go ahead, if that's what you want to do. I'll clear it with Andy," Ray said. "But Lee Edward, I don't have to tell you this...but I'm gonna say it anyway. Don't get snookered into something, you hear?"

Lee Edward smiled. "Thanks, Ray, you're always looking out for me."

* * *

LEE EDWARD and Linus spent the night in the bunkhouse. When the Marathon men heard Linus was from Long Trail, they began telling tales that may or may not have been true, but nonetheless, it was an entertaining evening. Linus joined the conversation telling stories of trail drives from forty years ago. All in all, Lee Edward felt much better about trusting Linus when they started for San Antonio, early the next morning.

The trip took less than three hours, but to Lee Edward, it seemed a lot longer. When they reached San Antonio, Linus had no hesitation finding the house. It was a small house on Woodlawn, but it appeared to be well kept. Dismounting, and tying off their horses, the two men walked up the steps where Linus knocked on the door. It was answered by a young girl of about twelve.

"Hello, young lady," Linus greeted. "Is your mother home?"

"Yes, sir."

"Would you please tell her that we would like to speak with her?"

Without leaving the door, the girl turned her head and called out.

"Mama! There are two men who want to talk to you."

Lee studied the young girl as they waited for her mother to answer the call. Could it actually be that this girl was his sister? He had never had any family at all, but now, if Linus was to be believed, he had a mother and it seemed, a sister.

The woman who answered the girl's call appeared to be in her late forties. He could see that she had once been very attractive, but years and hard work had robbed her of much of her beauty.

"Linus Walker," the woman said, the expression of her voice and on her face indicating surprise, wonder, and concern. "Lord, it's been a long time since I saw you last."

"Hello, Molly," Linus said. "May we come in?"

"Yes, of course." She turned to her daughter. "Emma, my dear, why don't you run along over to Sally's house? This man and I knew one another a long time ago, and you'd probably get tired listening to all the things we will talk about."

"All right, Mama. Mrs. Margrabe is teaching Sally and me how to cross stitch," her daughter said.

"Well, when it's time to come home, bring me a sample." She leaned down and kissed her daughter on the top of her head.

What an innocent gesture, but to Lee Edward, it was as if a knife had been stuck into his heart. In all the years he was at the orphanage, Sister Maria kissed him only one time, and that was when he was leaving.

"All right, Linus, what is this all about?" Molly asked when she turned her attention back to the two men.

"Could we have a seat somewhere? I have a lot to talk about," Linus said.

"All right, come on into the parlor. It's not like the Big House, but it's comfortable." She managed a nervous titter.

Lee Edward followed Linus and Molly into the parlor. There was a sofa, a table in front and two chairs. Between the chairs, there was a small table barely large enough to hold an oil lamp. Lee Edward noticed that the lamp had a freshly trimmed wick and a sparkling globe. He smiled as he thought of the times he had been assigned the duty of cleaning lamp chimneys. He wondered if that task was assigned to the daughter who was learning cross stitch.

"Would you like some coffee?" Molly offered.

"Yes, that would be good, thank you," Linus replied.

"Just a minute and I'll get us some," Molly said, hurrying out of the room.

Lee Edward wanted to take advantage of Molly's absence to ask Linus some questions, but he held his tongue. He hoped that the answers to his questions would come out soon enough.

Molly returned a moment later carrying a tray with three cups of coffee, a pitcher of cream, and a bowl of sugar. She set the tray on the table in front of the sofa where both Lee Edward and Linus were sitting. They reached for a cup but passed on the cream and sugar preferring their coffee black. Molly, however, took both sugar and cream, her hands shaking so much that she spilled some of the cream on the tray.

She took a sip of the coffee and then set it back on the tray. She folded her hands and held them tightly in her lap. "Now, Mr. Walker, suppose you tell me what this is about?"

"I think you may have guessed by now," Linus said.

Molly studied Lee Edward for a moment, then her eyes filled with tears.

"Oh," she said. "Oh, my. Is this...is this...?"

"Molly Littlefield, this is Lee Edward Holt, late of the Our Lady of Mercy Orphanage. And yes, this is your son."

"Holt? Your name is Holt?"

"Yes, the woman who took me in her arms when you left me gave it to me. Lee Edward Holt was Sister Maria's father's name and I've been proud to carry it for twenty-six years." Lee Edward's voice was challenging.

"I see."

"Ma'am, I have one question—why did you leave me there?" Lee Edward asked

"I...I had no choice. There was no way I could have taken care of you, or even fed you for that matter," Molly said. "I'm glad you had Sister Maria."

"She was my mother," Lee Edward said pointedly. He watched as the woman cringed at his comment. "Or at least, she was the only mother I ever had."

"When you were born, I wasn't married, and there was no way I could have taken care of you. Then, when I did get married, I couldn't tell Earl about you. Please, try to understand."

"I don't have to understand because it doesn't matter. I never knew you, so I never missed you. As I said, when I think of a mother, I think of Sister Maria. She loves me, and she and the other nuns raised me." Lee Edward turned to Linus.

"Mr. Walker, I see no reason to continue this visit. May we leave now?"

"Lee Edward, please," Molly pleaded.

"I'll be waiting for you outside," Lee Edward said to Linus.

"He hates me," Molly said after Lee Edward left.

"I wouldn't go so far as to say that he hates you," Linus said. "But you have to understand that this has come as quite a shock to him. He never had any idea of who his parents were, or even if they were alive."

"How...how did you find him?"

"I watched you deliver him to the orphanage, and I've kept up with him ever since."

"And he never asked you about me?"

"He was never aware of any connection between us."

"Then why were you...?" Molly stopped in mid-sentence. "It was Jake, wasn't it? Jake asked you to keep up with him."

"Yes."

"And so now, you're going to introduce him to Jake?"

"Jake is dead, Molly. He..." Linus paused. He was about to tell her he had been shot, but decided against it. "He died this month."

"I'm...I'm sorry to hear that."

"He never got over you, you know."

"Yes, well, all I can say is he had a funny way of showing it," Molly said. "Never once did he try to contact me."

"Jake regretted that for the rest of his life."

"Do you...do you think my son will ever forgive me?" Molly asked tearfully.

"From what I have seen of him, Lee Edward is as fine a young man as I have ever met," Linus said. "Right now he's in shock, learning, after twenty-six years, that he has a living mother. Once he gets over that shock, he may want to reach out to you."

"Oh, I pray that he will," Molly said. "Linus, I did go see him. I went four or five times whenever the orphanage had some kind of program. I knew which child was mine, even though no one told me. But when he began to favor Jake so much, I stopped going. It was too painful knowing what I had done—and what I had lost. I should have waited for Jake. The boy and I could have managed somehow.

"I have prayed so hard for him over all these years, and yes, I have asked God over and over to forgive me for what I did. I so wanted...Lee Edward...to have a good and rewarding life."

"Well, your prayers were answered, in ways you could never know."

"I'm glad," Molly said without inquiring any further about Linus's rather cryptic response.

Thirteen

Hannah Austin had carried a small stool out to Jake's gravesite. She had gathered stones to outline his grave, and she was in the process of arranging them. Hannah had now lost two husbands. When her first husband, Davy Hunter, had died, she was left with a four-year-old daughter and a two-year-old son.

Davy had owned and operated a profitable livery stable in Kerrville. Alex Gilliland and Jose Castenada had worked at the stable since the beginning, and Hannah had thought that they would continue to work for her after Davy died. But they did not.

After about a year, Alex and Jose opened a competing livery at the other end of the street. Her business continued to dwindle, and it was all Hannah could do to make any money at all. In an attempt to survive, she sold her house and converted the area that Davy had used as a tack room into a place to live. With the money she raised from selling the house, she bought an old Conestoga wagon, and she stored it in the livery. This was where she and her children slept.

She smiled as she thought of that old wagon. Jake had never gotten rid of it. He had built it into a traveling wagon, complete with a wood-burning stove, similar to what a sheepherder would use. It was now moved from place to place when a cowboy had to stay a long way from the home place, and there was no line shack close by.

Just then, Hannah looked up to see Mary Beth approaching.

"I was looking for you, and I thought I'd find you out here," Mary Beth said. "Do you mind if I join you?"

"Of course not," Hannah said. "I wish I had a stool for you, but I only brought one."

"It's all right," Mary Beth said. She kneeled beside Edna's grave and began straightening the stones around her grave. "What do you think causes these rocks to move?"

"I don't know—animals, I guess."

"Do you remember when Papa Jake asked you to marry him?" Mary Beth asked.

Hannah laughed. "Of course I do. I'm surprised that you do."

Then Mary Beth began speaking in a deep voice in an attempt to mimic Papa Jake. "Mrs. Hunter, it has come to my attention that you do not have a husband, and you may know that I don't have a wife. Would you consider marrying me?"

They both laughed until tears came to their eyes.

"And then you said, 'But I have two children.' And then he said, 'You can bring them along,'" Mary Beth continued.

"He was a wonderful man, and I miss him so much already," Hannah said.

"So do I," Mary Beth said. "What do you think is going to happen when we meet with Mr. Fitzgerald?"

"I don't know," Hannah said. "I don't understand why it's taking so long to read Jake's will, and I don't know why Linus has been gone so long. He knows how much I need him right now."

"You mean to rein in Abe?"

"That, among other things. I know what it's like to have people you have depended on to leave you high and dry."

"Like Mr. Gilliland did," Mary Beth said.

"Exactly," Hannah said.

"If Mr. Walker leaves, I don't know what we're going to do. Abe is acting like a fool."

"Where is he now?"

"When I came out here, he had assembled the men in the chow hall. I just can imagine what he's saying."

* * *

In the Long Trail Chow Hall

"I've called this meeting to let you know there are going to be some changes around here. As you all know, I will be the new owner. It is my intention to keep Walker on as my foreman if he wants the job, but he'll be more of an adviser than an actual foreman. As the owner, I'll be assuming most of the duties of the foreman, and that includes hiring and firing. I want it well understood that you will be taking orders from me and not from Linus Walker."

"I don't know about that," one of the hands said. "What does Linus have to say about this? Since this meeting affects him, why ain't he here?"

"Gather your things, Kirby," Hunter said. "You're fired."

"What? All I did was ask a question," Kirby said.

"That's just it. I will not have my orders questioned."

"I've got pay coming," Kirby said as he stood up from the table.

"As soon as Walker gets back, he'll figure out how much you're owed, then he'll get the money to you."

"How 'm I supposed to live until then?"

"That's not my problem," Hunter said. "Tanner, gather up Kirby's gear and escort him off the ranch."

"Come on, Tim," Billy Tanner said.

As they left the chow hall, Hunter was still giving detailed instructions as to the changes he would be putting into effect immediately.

"No more than two of you will be allowed to go into town at any one time."

* * *

"I CAN TELL YOU RIGHT NOW," Tanner said to Kirby as the two of them rode away from the corral, "there'll be others joining you soon, including me. I don't see how anyone's going to be able to work for that son of a bitch."

"I've got no place to go, Billy," Kirby said. "I don't have enough money to buy grub, let alone find a place to live."

"Why don't you go up to the old sheep wagon? Nobody's used it for two or three years, and it'll keep you out of the weather. A few of us can meet up there and move it so it's closer to water."

"Is there any food there?"

"Don't worry about food. One of us will get some food up to you."

"Thanks, Billy. But I can't stay there for too long, I'll

go crazy. I'm going to have to find another job pretty soon."

"You're a good worker, you always hold up your end, and all the men like you. I'm sure I'm not the only one who doesn't want to see you go. Wait until Mr. Walker gets back before you do anything," Tanner said.

"When do you think that'll be?"

"I don't know. All he said when he left was that he had something Mr. Austin had asked him to take care of in San Antonio. And knowing Mr. Walker, he won't be lollygagging around. He'll take care of whatever it is he needs to do, then he'll be back."

* * *

FROM SAN ANTONIO, it was an easy ride to Kerrville, and though Linus had not yet told Lee Edward why they were going, Lee Edward trusted him.

"Have you been to Kerrville before?" Linus asked.

"Never have," Lee Edward said. "Kids at the orphanage didn't do much traveling, and since I've been at Marathon, I've been pretty tied up with work. I did go with Mr. Matthews to Fort Worth one time to get a bull, but that's the longest trip I've ever made," Lee Edward said. "I hope I have a job when I get back. Mr. Matthews would have every right to fire me for being gone this long."

"Trust me, it's very important that you be in Kerrville. I don't want to tell you why just yet, at least not until we see the lawyer."

"Wait a minute! Why do I need a lawyer? The jury found me innocent."

"Lawyers handle a lot of legal business besides murder trials," Linus said.

"But I don't have any legal business."

Linus held up his hand. "Just wait. Just wait until you meet Buford G. Fitzgerald."

* * *

For the ride from San Antonio to Kerrville, their conversation, when they talked at all, was incidental. And because they mostly rode in trail, rather than side by side, there was very little of that.

When they reached Kerrville, Linus led Lee Edward directly to the Schreiner's Bank. Linus had said nothing about visiting a bank, so Lee Edward wondered why they were there. Then he saw the sign, Buford G. Fitzgerald, Attorney at Law, and because Linus had told him they were here to see a lawyer, he knew he was about to find out why he had come on this long trip.

Fitzgerald's law office was in the same building as the Schreiner's Bank. Entry into the office was by a door that was at the east end of the building and marked by a hanging sign.

The two men dismounted in front, then stepped inside.

Fitzgerald was bald-headed, and a rather large man, whose stomach strained at the buttons of his shirt. He wore a gray suit and a red bowtie.

"Here we are," Linus said.

"And you're certain you have the right man?" Fitzgerald asked.

"Lee Edward Holt, yes, I am absolutely certain."

"Very well, be back at two o'clock this afternoon."

"We'll be here," Linus said.

"Mr. Walker, you owe me some sort of explanation," Lee Edward said as they left the lawyer's office. "We rode all the way from San Antonio to see this..." He looked at the sign. "Buford G. Fitzgerald, and now you tell me I have to wait until two this afternoon."

Linus pulled out his pocket watch and looked at it. "It won't be long now. It's eleven already. Trust me on this, Lee Edward. You won't be sorry you came."

"You keep saying that, but I have to tell you, it's damn frustrating."

Linus started to say something, and Lee Edward held up his hand.

"If you tell me to trust you one more time, I just might knock you on your ass."

"What I was going to say is, why don't we get something to eat?" Linus asked.

Lee Edward chuckled. "Well now, that is a pretty good idea. The jerky you gave me last night is long gone," Lee Edward said. "Do you know where to go?"

"Oh, yes, I know this town very well."

"Then lead the way."

"We're going to the Gardens," Linus said.

Lee Edward followed Linus down the main street of Kerrville. The town was small, though it looked to be very prosperous. The name Schreiner came up over and over again—the Schreiner Bank, the Schreiner Mercantile, the Schreiner Freight Company, the Schreiner Wool Market—were some of the establishments Lee Edward saw on the way to the restaurant.

"I would guess Mr. Schreiner must be doing quite well," Lee Edward said.

"I'd say so," Linus said. "See that big two-story house built with limestone—that's his."

Lee Edward laughed. "I was thinking that might be a convent."

"No, it's far from a convent," Linus said. "This is it,

the Gardens, and I have to say, it's not owned by Charles Schreiner."

The building did not look impressive. Lee Edward thought it resembled a livery stable or something similar. It was built with pieces of slab lumber that stood side by side but didn't quite close the gaps. He did notice that the smells coming from the place were tantalizing.

Lee Edward raised his eyebrows. "Name's the Gardens, huh?"

Linus laughed. "Just you wait." He opened a door that hung on leather hinges, and because of that, the door didn't swing but had to be lifted.

"I hope it's worth it," Lee Edward said.

When he stepped inside, there was a rectangle built of stone that rose up to about three feet. On top of this was a metal grate much like those used when the cook for a chuck wagon was cooking over an open flame. And indeed, this was an open flame.

A man was in the process of moving pieces of meat. Some, Lee Edward knew were quarters of beef, but other pieces were much smaller.

"Ah, Señor Walker, it has been too long since you come to the Gardens," the man said as he wiped his hands on a cloth tied around his waist. "I wonder how is the señora? I have not seen her since—"

Linus stopped him before he could continue. "She's fine, Jose. She will be coming into town soon, I think. What has just come off the pit? My friend and I—*nosotros estamos muy hambrientos!*"

"For you, Señor, I have *cabrito*, you want?"

"Yes, sir, and a big bowl of *frijoles* to go with it."

"You go out," Juan said. "I have Carina bring it to you."

Linus went to the back of the building and opened a door, once again on leather hinges.

"You go first," he said.

Lee Edward stepped through the door, and he was amazed by what he saw. There were several gazebos scattered about following a path that went down to a river. A table with benches was under each gazebo, but what had caught Lee Edward's attention were the vines that covered the tops. There were orange finger-like blooms and there were what seemed like hundreds of hummingbirds flitting about.

"So this is the garden," Lee Edward said. "It doesn't make any difference if the food is good or not, just sitting here is worth it. I think what you ordered is goat. Is that right?"

"And beans," Linus said. "You won't be disappointed."

* * *

LINUS WAS RIGHT. When the meal was over, they walked down to a bench that was close to the Guadelupe River. Lee Edward went over to examine one of the gazebos.

"When I get back home, I'm going to try to build one of these. What kind of vine do you think this is?" Lee Edward said as he sat down beside Linus.

"It's a trumpet vine," Linus said. "Do you think you would ever want to leave Marathon?"

"No," Lee Edward said without hesitation. "Those people and Sister Maria and the others are my family. I guess that's not exactly right if you consider that woman in San Antonio, but I don't intend to ever see her again. What did you say her name was?"

"Molly Littleton." Linus pulled out his watch again. "It's time we mosey on back to Fitzegerald's office."

Lee Edward took a deep breath, but he didn't move off the bench. The river was so calm—not a ripple in sight as it moved along. Would this afternoon be like that for him?

* * *

OUT AT THE Long Trail Ranch, Mary Beth Hunter had three dresses lying on her bed trying to decide which one to wear. One was blue chambray, one was yellow gingham, and one was white pongee. She thought about why they were going to town. What would Papa Jake want her to wear? She smiled as she went to her clothes press and pulled out a pair of jeans and a blue checked shirt. Pulling on her boots, she was ready to go, except for her hair. She thought about tying it back, but Papa Jake always liked it when her long hair cascaded down her back, so stroking it with a brush a couple of times, she headed for the stairs.

"Mary Beth, can't you hurry in there," Abe called. "Fitzgerald said two o'clock and I don't want to be late."

"Don't rush her," Hannah said. "We have plenty of time. And even if we are a little late, I'm sure they won't start without us."

"Walker should be here," Abe said. "I hate leaving the ranch with nobody in charge. Where is Walker, anyway? He said he'd be gone a few days, but he didn't say where. I should have demanded to know where he was going and how long he'd be gone." Abe was pacing back and forth.

"The ranch will be here when we get back," Hannah said.

"Yeah," Abe replied with a big grin. "And it'll be mine."

"What about me?" Mary Beth asked as she came

down the stairs. "What makes you think Papa Jake left the ranch to you?"

"Mary Beth!" Hannah said when she saw her daughter. "Out of respect for Jacob Austin, I would have thought you would have dressed a little more ladylike."

"That is exactly why I am dressed like this," Mary Beth said. "Papa Jake would be proud."

"She doesn't have time to change now," Abe said. "Let's go."

Hannah, Abe, and Mary Beth left the house to climb into a red Landau carriage, being driven by Clem Porter, one of the cowboys.

"We're going in this?" Hannah said. "We could have taken a buckboard."

"No way," Abe said. "I intend for us to arrive at this meeting in a style that's befitting me...us," he corrected.

"Mr. Hunter, do you want the top up or down?" Porter asked.

"Leave it down, Porter. When the people in town see this fancy carriage, I want them to see who's riding in it."

* * *

When Lee Edward and Linus returned to the law office, Lee Edward saw that there were five chairs set out in a semi-circle facing Fitzgerald's desk.

"Have a seat, gentlemen. We'll start as soon as the others arrive," Fitzgerald said.

"What others?" Lee Edward asked.

"You'll see," Linus said.

"All I can say is, this is damn odd," Lee Edward said.

Linus raised his finger, but before he could say anything, Lee Edward spoke again.

"I know. You want me to trust you on this," Lee Edward said with a little chuckle.

About ten minutes later, two women and a young man arrived. Lee Edward couldn't help but notice how pretty the younger woman was. He was not accustomed to seeing a woman in jeans, and he smiled as she selected the chair next to his. He stood and pulled the chair back for her, then held it as she sat down.

"Thank you, sir," the young woman said with a pretty smile.

"Walker, what are you doing here?" Abe asked in a voice filled with contempt. "I wondered where you were. You've got no business coming to town unless it's on an errand for me, or else I give you permission. And you certainly have no business being here today."

"Mr. Walker is here at Jacob Austin's request," Fitzgerald said.

"Yeah? Well Jacob Austin isn't here anymore, is he? I'm in charge now, and I say Walker should be out at the ranch where he belongs."

"Abe," Hannah said, putting her hand on her son's arm. "Please, sit down and let it be."

Abe sat down, but the expression of anger remained on his face.

"May we get started?" Fitzgerald asked.

"Yeah, yeah, go ahead," Abe said with a flick of his hand.

"Mrs. Austin, before your husband died, he left this letter with me and asked me to give it to you at the appropriate time. This, I believe, is the appropriate time."

"Thank you," Hannah said, taking the envelope.

"Do you recognize that it is Jacob Austin's hand-writing?"

Hannah looked at the writing on the envelope. "I do."

"You may read it at your convenience," Fitzgerald said.

"Thank you. I'll wait until these proceedings are over."

"Yeah, and after this is over, Walker, you and I are going to have us a serious discussion," Abe said. He looked at Fitzgerald. "All right, let's get on with it. I've got things to do back at the ranch," he added smugly.

"Mr. Hunter, please," Fitzgerald said.

"All right, all right, get on with it," Abe said.

"We are gathered here for the reading of the will and last testament of Jacob Randolph Austin."

Lee Edward looked at Linus with a questioning expression on his face. "Why am I here?" he whispered.

"Just wait," Linus said, speaking so quietly that only Lee Edward could hear him.

Fitzgerald began to read:

"I, Jacob Randolph Austin, a resident of Kerr County, in the state of Texas, on this date, August 12, in the year of our Lord, 1885, hereby make, publish, and declare this to be my last will and testament, thereby revoking any and all previous wills and codicils made by me.

"I attest that I, Jacob Randolph Austin, am of sound mind and body.

"Any and all debts due and payable, including funeral and burial expenses, the expenses of the administration of my estate, shall be..."

"Get on with it, Fitzgerald," Abe interrupted. "Quit reading all that gibberish and get on with the important stuff."

The lawyer looked up at Abe with an irritated stare.

"If I may continue, Mr. Hunter," Fitzgerald said.

"Yeah, yeah, go ahead," Abe said. He smiled. "I guess I can afford to wait."

"I appoint as the executor of my estate, my trusted friend and longtime valued employee, Linus R. Walker."

"Damn, what do we need an executor for? That's just a waste of money," Abe said, once again, interrupting the reading of the will.

"Ahem," Fitzgerald said, clearing his throat before he continued to read.

"To Linus Walker, I leave the sum of two thousand dollars and decree that he will be retained as foreman of Long Trail Ranch for as long as he chooses to do so."

"Don't get too comfortable, Walker," Abe said. "I'll keep you on as long as your work satisfies me, but once I own the ranch, there's not a court in the land that would say I can't fire you, no matter what this piece of paper says."

"Mr. Hunter," Fitzgerald said with more disgust.

Abe let out a long-suffering sigh. "All right."

Fitzgerald continued the reading.

"To Hannah Hunter Austin, my wife of eighteen years, I leave the house in which she currently resides and the sum of five thousand dollars."

Mary Beth patted her mother's arm. "I told you Papa Jake wouldn't make you leave the house."

"To my beloved stepdaughter, Mary Beth Hunter, I leave one-half of the ranch, known by the county of Kerr and the state of Texas as Long Trail, generally accepted to number 85,000 acres, plus or minus. In addition, I bequeath the cattle, horses, and all equipment and structures, with the exception of the aforementioned dwelling."

"What?" Abe shouted. "What the hell is he leaving half the ranch to Mary Beth for? What does she know about ranching?"

"Abe, please, you must quit interrupting the reading," Hannah said.

"All right, you've got half the ranch," Abe said, pointing to his sister. "But I'll damn well be the one who runs it."

"To my son, Lee Edward Holt, raised at Our Lady of Mercy Orphanage, I leave one-half of the ranch, known by the county of Kerr and the state of Texas as Long Trail, generally accepted to number 85,000 acres, plus or minus. In addition, I bequeath the cattle, horses, and all equipment and structures with the exception of the aforementioned dwelling."

"What?" both Lee Edward and Abe shouted at the same time.

"That's right, Lee Edward. Jacob Austin was your father," Linus said.

"What the hell is this? What do you mean that this man, who not one person in this room has ever seen before, is Jake's son?" Abe asked, speaking so loudly that spittle was flying from his mouth.

"I know who he is. I have followed him from his birth," Linus said. "I have signed a sworn affidavit attesting to the fact that Lee Edward Holt is Jacob Austin's son."

"This is unthinkable!" Abe said. He pointed at Lee Edward. "I don't know what's going on here, but you can damn well believe that I'll take this to court. This will not stand."

"And finally, to Hannah's son, Abraham David Hunter, I leave the sum of one thousand dollars."

Fitzgerald looked up from the document. "And that, ladies and gentlemen, concludes the reading of the last will and testament of Jacob Randolph Austin, late of Kerr County, Texas."

Lee Edward and Abe sat there, both of them in total shock over what they had just heard.

"No," Abe said. "This isn't right. The ranch belongs to me."

"Not according to Jake's will," Linus said.

"You!" Abe said, pointing his finger toward Linus. "You had something to do with this, didn't you? You were afraid I'd fire you, so you found someone to pretend to be some long-lost son. Well, you won't get away with it."

"Mr. Hunter," Fitzgerald said. "I was present when Jake made this will. When he said that he wanted to leave half of his ranch to his son, Lee Edward Holt, I questioned him about that, telling him that I had never heard of such a son. He assured me that it was true and shared the circumstances of Mr. Holt's birth. He wasn't proud of this episode from his past and hoped by his will, to make up for his neglect of his only son and heir."

Abe glared at Lee Edward. "What did you do to him? How did you convince him to claim you as his son?"

"I never met the man," Lee Edward said solemnly.

"What? What do you mean you never met him?"

"As the will stated, I was raised in Our Lady of Mercy Orphanage from the time I was one week old."

"Then how would anyone know that you are who you claim to be?"

"I know," Linus said. "I have kept track of Lee Edward from the day he was left at the orphanage. And over the years, Jake has donated a substantial amount of money to the orphanage. I was charged with the delivery of the bank drafts at least twice a year, and sometimes more often. I reported to Jake after every visit."

"All right, you come out to the ranch. But if you've never worked on a ranch, I guarantee you'll walk away from it," Abe said. "I give it a year at the most."

FOURTEEN

"COME ON, LET'S GO HOME!" ABE SHOUTED ANGRILY AS he stormed out of the lawyer's office. He vaulted into the Landau without waiting for his mother or sister.

"All right, you have some explaining to do," Lee Edward said as he turned toward Linus.

"Yes, I'm sure you have questions," Linus answered. "What do you say we go have a drink? I'll try to explain everything."

"I very much have questions," Lee Edward agreed.

"Mr. Fitzgerald, I thank you for taking care of this for Jake," Linus said.

"It was a pleasure and, it was...shall we say, interesting?" he added with a smile. He shook Lee Edward's hand. "Son, if you find you need a lawyer, I'd be happy to represent you."

"Thank you. I know where to find you," Lee Edward said as he rose from the chair.

"Linus," Lee Edward asked after they left the lawyer's office. "Why did Jake Austin leave half the ranch to his stepdaughter but nothing to his stepson?"

"Mary Beth loved him like a father, and he loved her in return. And Abe is an arrogant little jerk, as you saw for yourself today."

"I guess you can't really blame him. I'm sure he expected to inherit half the ranch, just as his sister did," Lee Edward said.

Linus laughed. "No, he expected to inherit the whole ranch, and he's been acting like he owned it ever' since Jake was—died," Linus said. "I'm thinking you're gonna have nothing but trouble from him."

* * *

LEE EDWARD WAS surprised when Linus entered the mercantile. He had assumed they would be going to one of the four or five saloons he had seen.

"Howdy, Emmett," Linus said to the clerk standing at the front counter. "Can you set us up with a couple of cool sarsaparillas?"

"Sure, Linus, go on back and take a seat. I'll run out to the ice house and grab a couple."

Lee Edward followed Linus to the back of the store, where there were three small round tables with two chairs sitting at each one. They were no sooner seated when Emmett returned with two bottles.

"Here you go," he said. "Just got a new supply from San Antone a couple days ago. Mr. Schreiner don't never want to be out of his sarsaparilla."

"Thanks," Linus said as he took a long drink from the bottle. "Do you like sarsaparilla?"

"I don't know," Lee Edward said. "This will be a first."

Linus looked pointedly at Lee Edward. "There's a lot you don't know, isn't there?"

Lee Edward studied the bottle before he took a

drink. "That's what's worrying me. How am I going to own half an 85,000-acre ranch, let alone run it? As you know better than anyone, for sixteen years, I was as cloistered as a nun, and then for the last ten years, I've done what somebody else told me to do. How am I going to start telling somebody else what to do? And like you said, Abe Hunter is going to be one hard person to get along with."

"You heard what was in Jake's will. I'll be there to help you with whatever you need," Linus said. "Don't underestimate yourself. I was at that trial in San Antonio, and I saw so many of the hands from the Marathon there to support you. And then when they followed you to the Easy Pickens—they all treated you with respect. That's not something that comes easy. You have to earn respect from a bunch of knot-headed cowboys and you had it in spades."

Lee Edward took a swallow of the drink. He smiled as he nodded his head.

They sat together in silence while they drank the sarsaparilla, each waiting for the other to start the conversation.

Finally Lee Edward spoke. "The first thing I have to do is go back to Marathon to tell Mr. Matthews and Ray Dockins that I'll be leaving. I have to tell you, that will be hard."

"I'll come with you if you'd like."

"Thanks, Mr. Walker, I appreciate that."

Linus laughed. "I work for you now. You can call me Linus. The question is what will we call you?"

"What do you mean, what will you call me? You know my name."

"I know what name you're using, but your name is Austin."

"No, it isn't. My name is Holt, Lee Edward Holt, and I would never think of changing it."

Linus smiled. "Then Lee Edward Holt it will be."

* * *

"I DON'T BELIEVE THIS," Abe said to his mother and sister as they were going back to the ranch. "Who the hell is this Holt, anyway? Nobody's ever heard of him, and here he comes, out of the blue, and claims to be Jake's son. There's something fishy going on here, and I'm going to find out what it is. It wouldn't surprise me if Walker didn't find somebody who would agree to do this. And even if he really is Jake's son, wouldn't you, his wife, know about it? And another thing—why would Jake leave half the ranch to Mary Beth and not to me?"

"No, sir, this whole thing is a lie."

Hannah and Mary Beth remained quiet for the entire drive back to the ranch.

When the carriage rolled to a stop in front of the house, Hal Crader, one of the cowboys, happened to be standing out front.

Abe climbed down from the carriage. "Crader, what the hell are you doing standing around here? Don't you have something better to do?"

"Uh, yes, sir," Crader said, confused by Abe's bitterness.

"Porter, get this Landau put away now," Abe added.

"Yes, sir," Porter said. Porter had been listening to the conversation on the way back to the ranch. He knew that Abe Hunter owned none of the ranch. Porter had to fight to keep a smile away from his face, and he could hardly wait to tell the others what had happened.

"At least we weren't turned out of our house," Hannah said, hoping in some way to placate her son's anger.

"It's not *our* house. It's *your* house," Abe said in the same tone he had used when talking to Crader and Porter.

Shortly after they entered the house, Abe went to the liquor cabinet, grabbed a bottle of whiskey, and stomped through the kitchen and out the back door.

"He's really upset," Mary Beth said.

"Can you blame him?" Hannah replied. "He was so certain he'd inherit Long Trail, and not just half of it like you were given."

"Mama, did you know anything about this?"

"No, dear, I didn't know that Abe would be excluded from the will."

"No, I mean, did you know that Papa Jake had a son?"

"I had no idea."

"But Mr. Walker knew, didn't he?"

"Apparently, he did."

"I wonder why Papa Jake never mentioned anything about this to us."

"From what I understand from today, Jake abandoned Mr. Holt and his mother. I'm sure that bothered him, and maybe he didn't want to share his guilt with us," Hannah said.

"And yet he left Mr. Holt half of this ranch."

"Yes, he did, and we'll have to live with it."

"I wonder how it'll be?" Mary Beth asked.

"How what will be, dear?"

"How will it be for me to be working with Mr. Holt?"

* * *

As Mary Beth and her mother were discussing the strange turn of events, Abe was sitting out on the back porch. He had already drunk nearly half the bottle of whiskey, but it hadn't made the anger go away.

"How the hell could he have done something like this to me?" Abe mumbled. He took another swallow of whiskey.

"To hell with it. I'm glad the son of a bitch is dead."

* * *

It was a two-day ride back to Marathon, so for the first night, Lee Edward and Linus stopped in a small town called Welfare. With a population of less than three hundred people, it had a large general store, with both a restaurant and rooms to let. The sign read The Joseph and Bessler Store.

"Hello, Carl, Gus," Linus greeted.

"Linus Walker! It's good to see you again," Gus said.

"I suppose you'll be wantin' a room for the night?" Carl asked.

"Yes, give me number six if it's available. I'll need one with two beds."

"It's yours," Carl said. "Fifty cents."

After securing the room, the two men went to the back of the big store to the restaurant. It wasn't a restaurant with a menu—there was no choice in the food you ate. Tonight it was rabbit stew.

"Good to see you again, Linus," the cook said. "I'll put extra pepper on yours, just the way you like it."

"Thanks, Toby. You always know how to take care of me."

"Everyone seems to know you here," Lee Edward said.

"Lord knows they should. I've spent many a night here."

The stew was delivered, and Lee Edward was pleased to see how good it was. They ate in silence for a few minutes, then Lee Edward asked a question.

"What was he like?" Lee Edward asked.

"You mean your father?"

"Yes."

"Jake was a good friend, the best friend I ever had. And he was one of the most principled men I ever knew," Linus said.

"Principled? Hmm, I'd have a hard time calling him that. Any man that has a bastard child is not principled in my book," Lee Edward said. "Was my mother a whore?"

"No. No she wasn't," Linus said in a defiant tone.

"Then why didn't he marry her?"

"Your father wanted to marry her, but there were extenuating circumstances."

"Oh, I'll just bet there were," Lee Edward said in a sardonic tone of voice.

"When Jake learned that you were placed in an orphanage, he had me keep up with you. That's why you saw me there so many times."

"But it was you who came—never Jake. No, I can't call him principled."

"I'm sorry you feel that way," Linus said.

"Why weren't my mother and father married?"

"Your father wanted to marry Mollie, but she refused to wait for him. And she wasn't willing to endure the humiliation of having a child with a married man."

"Oh, I see now. My father was already married," Lee Edward said. "Adultery—another virtue."

"I wouldn't put it like that."

"Well then, how would you put it?"

"He was married, but not to Hannah. His first wife was named Edna."

"Hannah, Edna, it doesn't make any difference. The fact is, my father committed adultery with my mother," Lee Edward said.

"There were issues," Linus continued. "Edna was sick. She had what doctors called dementia. It affects the mind, and even though her body was healthy, over time, she forgot everything, who Jake was, where she was, even who she was. Jake tried to take care of her, but at the end, she was so bad she never left her bed."

"Where did my mother come from?"

"She was the daughter of the traveling minister. Jake hired her to look after Edna. And it was during that time that he and your mother fell in love. He wanted to marry her, but because of Edna's illness, there was no way he would ever abandon Edna. That's what I mean when I say he was a principled man.

"He asked your mother to wait until Edna died, but Molly wanted to marry him right away. She didn't tell Jake she was with child, so she did the only thing she thought she could do—she ran away."

"Where did she go?"

"She wound up in San Antonio," Linus said. "Jake hired a detective to find her, but when he got word where she was and that she would soon deliver a child, he sent me to persuade her to come back. But you had already been born. I was watching when she left you at the orphanage."

"And you didn't try to stop her!"

Linus lowered his head. "No. It was a mistake, and I know that now, but I was about your age when this was happening. My thinking was that you'd be better off at an orphanage. After Molly left, Jake never hired anyone else to care for Edna. He did everything himself. Wouldn't let anybody else touch her. It was a sad time at Long Trail."

Lee Edward was quiet for a long moment. "Thanks for telling me all this," he said. "You have to admit that it's quite a bit to take in all at once."

"I know it is," Linus said, "but don't forget, you now own half of a very large and productive ranch."

"Humph," Lee Edward said. "Apparently, my father bought off his conscience."

* * *

LATE IN THE afternoon of the next day, Hank Everson was working on the gate at the entrance to Marathon Ranch when he saw two riders approaching. He stopped working and stood at the gate waiting for them, smiling as he recognized Lee Edward and Linus Walker.

"Well, Lee Edward, you must have had one hell of a celebration," Hank said. "We've been wondering where you were."

"Am I in trouble with Mr. Matthews and Ray?" Lee Edward asked.

"No, they said you deserved some time to celebrate. They asked me why I wasn't celebratin' with you, but I told them I wasn't invited."

Lee Edward chuckled. "You weren't invited because I wasn't exactly celebrating. A lot has happened since I saw you last."

"Does it have anything to do with Mr. Walker here?"

"As a matter of fact, it does," Lee Edward said. "I'll tell you all about it after I've spoken with Ray and Mr. Matthews. And if everything goes all right, I'll have a proposition for you."

"Now you've got my curiosity up," Hank said. "What's this all about?"

"Have a little patience, Hank. I have to speak with Ray and Mr. Matthews first."

"All right, but you're goin' to have me wonderin' just what's a' goin' on."

Lee Edward smiled at Hank but didn't speak as he and Linus continued on down the lane toward the Big House. They rode around the Big House then dismounted in front of the foreman's cabin. Apparently, Ray had seen them arrive, because he stepped out onto the front porch.

"Lee Edward," he said. "I'm glad Mr. Walker's brought you home. I hope you're gonna spend the night with us again. My boys sure enjoyed hearin' your stories. If I hear one of 'em tell me how you got them cows out of the quicksand up on the Cimarron one more time..."

"I enjoyed the evening," Linus said. "You've got a good bunch of cowboys here, all working together, and I know that kind of spirit only comes about when there's a good foreman."

Lee Edward thought he saw Ray's face flush when Linus paid him such a high compliment, but it was hard to tell with his sun-weathered face.

"Is Mr. Matthews around? We need to speak with him."

"Don't tell me my best hand is in some sort of trouble again."

"Not that I know of," Linus said. "At least he's not in any trouble with the law." He grinned as he looked at Lee Edward.

"Well, the next thing is, are you tryin' to hire Lee Edward away from Marathon, because if you are, I have somethin' to say about that," Ray said.

Lee Edward turned to Linus. "You see why this is going to be difficult."

"Now what does that mean?" Ray asked.

"Come along with us, and let's go find Mr. Matthews," Lee Edward said.

Ray led Lee Edward and Linus up onto the back porch of the Big House, then knocked on the door. The door was opened by Charlotte, the cook and housekeeper.

"Do you know if Mr. Matthews is here?" Ray asked.

"I don't know, but Mrs. Matthews is out in the sunroom. She's fussin' with her ferns."

The three men walked into a little room that was off the dining room. It had windows on all sides, and Dottie Matthews was watering what seemed like a dozen or more ferns. Some were on stands, while others were hanging on chains suspended from the ceiling.

"Lee Edward," Mrs. Matthews said. "Mr. Matthews has been wondering when you would get back. We're all so pleased that everything turned out the way it did at the trial. You know, had it turned out differently, Mr. Matthews would have gotten you the best lawyer in the state of Texas. We can't be losing you anytime soon."

"Thank you, Mrs. Matthews," Lee Edward said.

"Lee Edward and this here fella need to talk to the boss," Ray said. "Is he around?"

"I believe he's in the office," Mrs. Matthews said. "I think he's trying to stare some numbers off the page, but they just won't go away. He'll be happy to take a break."

"We'll find him," Ray said.

The door to Matthews' office was open, and Ray stuck his head in. "Mr. Matthews, Lee Edward's back, and he's brought someone with him. They want to talk to you."

"Sure, come on in."

"I'll leave you three," Ray said.

"Thank you, Ray," Lee Edward said as Ray left, closing the door behind him.

"Lee Edward," Mr. Matthews said as he came around his desk to shake his hand. "And who have you brought to see me?"

"Linus Walker, sir. He's been here before. He's the foreman at Long Trail Ranch."

"Long Trail? Yes, I know that ranch. It's a big spread over in Kerr County, isn't it?" Matthews got a worried expression on his face. "Mr. Walker, you're not here to hire Lee Edward away from me, are you? Because he's a damn good man, and I wouldn't want to lose him."

"That would be very difficult for me to do, Mr. Matthews," Linus replied. Then he smiled. "You see, the truth is, I now work for Mr. Holt."

"What?" Matthews asked, with a puzzled expression on his face. "What do you mean, you work for him?"

"As of two days ago, Mr. Holt became the owner of Long Trail Ranch."

"What?" Matthews asked again, literally spitting out the word.

"Actually, I'm only half-owner," Lee Edward put in.

"Yes, but you'll be the one who manages the ranch," Linus added.

"Would one of you please tell me what this is all about?" Matthews asked as he went back to his chair, and quite literally, fell into it.

"Mr. Matthews, you know my story," Lee Edward began. "How I was left at Our Lady of Mercy when I was still an infant. I never knew who my parents were until now. I had seen Mr. Walker, because he often came to the orphanage. At the time, I didn't know that Mr.

Walker was the connection between me and my parents."

"Let me guess. You just told me that you are half-owner of Long Trail Ranch, so I'm assuming that Jake Austin was your father?"

"So, I have just learned," Lee Edward said.

"Such a shame about Jake. Every rancher in the state is concerned about that," Andrew said. He drummed his fingers on his desk. "I guess this means you'll be leaving Marathon."

"Yes, sir."

Matthews sighed. "Well, I'm happy for you, Lee Edward. You'll be taking on a big responsibility, but I've no doubt that you're up to the task. You'll do fine, just fine. You're as good a hand as I've ever had, so I'll hate to lose you."

"Mr. Matthews, I'd like to take Hank Everson with me. If you adamantly object, I won't ask him to go. But I'm going to be surrounded by strangers when I go to Long Trail, and I'd like to have someone with me that I know and that I can trust. And Hank has become a very good friend."

"I hate having to lose both of you," Matthews said with a sigh. "But I can understand your reason for wanting him. All right, Lee Edward, if Hank is willing to go with you, I won't try to stop him."

"Thank you, Mr. Matthews, I appreciate it very much." Lee Edward smiled. "And I appreciate the education you've given me."

"Education?"

"In the time I've been here, I've watched how you've handled the responsibility of owning and managing a large ranch, and I hope I've learned something from you."

Matthews chuckled self-consciously. "I'm flattered, Lee Edward." He extended his hand. "Does Hank know you're taking him away from me?"

"Not yet. I wanted to talk to you about it first."

"That was very decent of you." Matthews smiled. "It will be a pleasure to know you now as a fellow ranch owner."

It was Lee Edward's time to laugh. "A fellow rancher. That's going to take some getting used to."

FIFTEEN

DOUBLE DIAMOND RANCH

"I THINK WE'VE GOT 'EM RIGHT WHERE WE WANT them," Ruben Pugh said. "Jake Austin was too damn stubborn for his own good. And even if he had agreed to sell, he'd have wanted way too much money. I can deal with that fool Hunter. He's young, and from what I've heard, he isn't much of a worker."

"Yeah, don't nobody over there like 'im," Bull Travers said.

"That helps," Pugh said.

"You want me to bring 'im over to see you?"

"No, not yet. Let's give him a taste of how much work it is to run a ranch. And if it's like you say, if none of his people can get along with him, it won't take long before he'll be ready to walk away. When I make him an offer, all he'll see is the money—more money than he's ever had in his life."

"Yeah, I think so too," Travers said.

"And you know the best part of it?" Pugh asked with a satisfied smirk. "I'll buy Long Trail for less than half of what I once offered Austin."

"Boss, when you get it, I want you to fire Walker first thing. They won't be no need for two foremen. Especially one who thinks he's all high and mighty."

"Worry not. He'll be the first to go. Walker was too close to Austin, and we don't need anyone like him around."

"When will you do it?" Travers asked.

"As soon as I take possession of the ranch."

"No, I mean, when will that be? When will you get the ranch?"

"It's like I said. We'll give Abe Hunter a few weeks to realize he's in over his head—then I'll make the offer."

* * *

MARATHON RANCH

Some ninety miles southeast of the Double Diamond, Hank Everson was waiting outside the Big House. When he saw Lee Edward come outside, he approached him

"I swear, Lee Edward, if you ain't got me so damn curious about what's goin' on, that I'm about to have a conniption fit," Hank said.

"Hank, gather up all the men that are handy and ask them to meet me in the chow hall. I'll want you there as well."

"There's only about six of 'em that's in shoutin' distance. The others are out movin' cattle. The water's gettin' low in the north pasture."

"That's fine. Gather up as many as you can, and they can spread the word to the others."

"All right." Hank had a questioning expression on his face. "You'll be in the chow hall?"

Lee Edward nodded his head. "Oh, and Hank, be sure to tell Ray."

"You can tell 'im yourself, he's comin' over here now."

Hank left just as Ray arrived.

"So, Lee Edward, are you goin' to tell me what's goin' on?" Ray asked.

"I asked Hank to gather up whoever he could, to meet me in the chow hall so I can tell them goodbye."

"Damn it, I knew it," Ray said as he turned to Linus. "You hired Lee Edward right out from under us. Whatever you offered to pay him, I know Mr. Matthews will pay more."

"That's not very likely, as I now work for Mr. Holt," Linus said as a smile formed on his face.

"What?" Ray asked, the expression on his face mirroring his confusion over the strange comment. "What are you a sayin'? Did I hear you say you're a workin' for Lee Edward?"

"That's what I said," Linus said.

"Have you been eatin' loco weed? Lee Edward can't hire nobody. I hand out his pay, and it's barely enough to keep him in a drink now and then and a new pair of boots when he needs 'em."

"He means that I now own Long Trail Ranch," Lee Edward said in a statement that was as void of emotion as he could make it.

Ray pulled off his hat and ran his hand through his thinning hair. "You better not be kiddin' me, because if you're tellin' a tall one, I'll take you over to the horse trough and throw you in it myself."

"What Lee Edward is saying is true," Linus said. "He is the rightful heir of an 85,000-acre ranch."

"Well, I'll be damned."

"It's actually only half the ranch," Lee Edward said. "You know how I've never known who my parents were? Well, it turns out that my father was Jacob Austin. He just died, and he left the ranch to me and to his step-daughter."

* * *

FIFTEEN MINUTES LATER, Lee Edward was standing in front of eight very curious men.

"Guys," he said. "I asked Hank to get you together here, so I could tell you all what has happened to me, and what it means. I never knew my father, and I know most of you are aware of my background. As it turns out, my father was Jacob Austin, owner of the Long Trail Ranch. Mr. Austin died this month, and Mr. Walker, here, took me to hear the reading of his will. You could've knocked me over with a feather when I heard the lawyer say I had inherited half of Long Trail Ranch. It's all pretty over-whelming to me, and it's hard to get my head wrapped around what's going to be happening. I've told Mr. Matthews about this, and he knows I'll be leaving Marathon as soon as I can get my gear together. I wanted you all to hear this from me, and I wanted to say good-bye. You know I lived sixteen years in an orphanage, and I thought I had friends. But those boys don't hold a candle to all of you. I will always think of you as my family."

The room was silent as the men took in what Lee Edward had said.

"Dayum!" someone said after a minute or two.

"Son of a bitch!" another added.

These weren't pejorative words—they were words of awe and wonder.

"I'm goin' to miss you, Lee Edward," Hank said as he avoided making eye contact.

"You don't have to miss me if you don't want to."

"What do you mean?"

"Hank, I'm asking you in front of everybody. Will you come work with me at Long Trail?"

"What? Hell yeah, I'll go with you!" Then Hank stopped. "Uh, what does Mr. Matthews say?"

"He said he'd be damn glad to get rid of you," Lee Edward replied, and the others laughed.

"We're goin' to miss you, Lee Edward," one of the men said. "Oh, I mean, Mr. Holt."

Lee waved his hand. "I'll always be Lee Edward to any of you." He smiled. "But don't tell any of the hands over at Long Trail that. I intend to be one hard-nosed son of a bitch to them."

Again, the men laughed.

"Sure you will be," one of the men said. "You'll have them cowboys sayin' prayers ever' night before you know it."

"Hank will keep me in line," Lee Edward said. "Get your gear, and let's get headed out. I guess we'll be stopping in Welfare on the way back."

He turned to Linus, and Linus shook his head yes.

"Uh, I don't own my horse. It belongs to Marathon," Hank said.

"Damn, mine does too. I didn't even think of that," Lee Edward said.

"Go ahead and take them until you get over there, then you send them back," Ray said. "I'm not gonna be worrying about losing a couple of horses to somebody who owns an 85,000-acre ranch."

Lee Edward laughed. "You keep forgetting it's half a ranch."

* * *

NO MORE THAN AN HOUR LATER, Lee Edward, Linus, and Hank were on their way to Long Trail.

Sixteen

"Since Jake left the house to Hannah, I guess I'm going to have to find a place to stay," Lee Edward said. He used the name Jake, because even though Jake Austin was his father, that wasn't a concept that he felt comfortable saying.

"My suggestion would be to build a house for yourself," Linus said. "In the meantime, you can stay in the foreman's house with me."

"Oh, that won't be necessary, I can stay in the bunkhouse with the hands. Lord knows I've lived in a bunkhouse long enough. And, in a way, I suppose you could say I've lived in a bunkhouse my entire life, 'cause what was the orphanage if not a bunkhouse? I sure didn't have my own private room."

"I'm not sure that would be a good idea," Linus said.

"Why not?"

"Well, think about it. You're going to be their boss. It wouldn't be fair for you to have such meager quarters because you own the ranch. And for that same reason, it wouldn't be fair to the men to have their boss in their midst. They would be intimidated by you."

"Why would that be? I haven't changed just because I own the ranch. I'm moving into the bunkhouse."

"Linus is right, Lee Edward," Hank said. "You know how sometimes we might have said a few things that we wouldn't have wanted Mr. Matthews to hear, don't you? If you stay in the bunkhouse, nobody will ever be able to loosen up."

Lee chuckled. "Yeah, I guess it would be hard to call me a son of a bitch if I lived right in the middle of everyone."

"Thanks, Hank," Linus said. "I'm glad you came along. Someone's going to have to be the one to set the boss straight."

* * *

IT WAS two long days ride from Marathon to Long Trail, so Lee Edward, Hank, and Linus spent the first night in Bandera. The most prominent building was a Catholic Church, around which the town was founded. They decided not to visit a saloon, because they thought they might stay too long, and they really needed to get to bed, knowing they had an equally long ride the next day.

Fortunately, the hotel where they stayed had a dining room, so they had supper.

"Tell me some more about Jake. What was he like?" Lee Edward asked as he picked up a piece of fried chicken.

"Well, obviously anything I have to say about him will be prejudiced, because we were the best of friends."

"How did that work out for you?" Hank asked. "I mean,

you being good friends, but him being your boss. I sort of have a personal reason for asking this, I mean, what with Lee Edward bein' my friend, but now he's goin' to be my boss."

"And don't you forget it," Lee Edward said with a laugh.

"Well, in a way, you could say that Jake always was my boss. We were kids together on the ranch that his father owned, and my father was the foreman."

"This same ranch?" Lee Edward asked.

"No, it was a ranch up in Wyoming. And when Jake's father, your grandfather, died, Jake sold the ranch and bought land down here in Texas."

"What happened to your father and my grandmother when Jake did that?"

"Well, even before Jake sold the ranch, Mrs. Austin had gone back to Chicago, and my father returned to Kansas City, where he bought a hardware store."

"Did your father feel that Jake had abandoned him?"

"No, not at all. Pop had been wanting to do that for a while, anyway."

Lee Edward chuckled. "So you're not going to have anything bad to say about Jake, are you?"

"Not a thing. I just wish I had been with him when he was shot. I might have been able to prevent it."

"Wait a minute. He was shot?" Lee Edward said.

"Yes, while he was riding the fence line."

"I hadn't heard that. Do they know who did it? Did he have any enemies?"

"I don't know that he actually had any enemies, but he and one of his neighbors weren't exactly friends. They disagreed over where the boundary was between their properties. But I'd hardly think that the disagreement was enough to cause Ruben Pugh to have Jake shot.

Besides, where I found him was far away from that disputed piece of property."

"So what you're telling me is that I have a neighbor I'm going to have to watch out for," Lee Edward said.

"Yes."

"I'll give it a little time after I've settled in, then I'll go talk to him and see if we can find some way to take care of the problem."

"That wouldn't be a bad idea, but I don't know how willing Pugh would be to cooperate with you. He's a real pain in the ass."

* * *

THE THREE MEN got an early start the next morning and reached Long Trail by mid-afternoon. When they reached the ranch, the first thing they did was ride up to the corral so all the men who were working close to the bunkhouse could meet Lee Edward and Hank. Dismounting, they tied their horses to the top rail of the fence. There were only five men working nearby as all the other hands were out on the range.

"Linus, you old coot, am I ever glad to see you ridin' up!" one of the men said. "We've been through hell with the new boss. He's some son of a bitch."

Linus smiled. "So you think the new owner's a son of a bitch, do you, Buck?"

"Yeah. Well, hell, Linus, don't you? You been around him more'n anybody."

"I don't know." Linus looked over toward Lee Edward. "Tell me, Mr. Holt. Are you a son of a bitch?"

"I don't know, I try not to be," Lee Edward said, matching Linus's smile.

"Who's this?" Glen Atkins asked.

"Oh, yes, I haven't introduced you yet, have I? Gentlemen, this is Mr. Lee Edward Holt. He's your new son of a bitch."

"What?"

Linus laughed. "I'm sorry, I mean Mr. Holt now owns Long Trail."

All the men looked at Lee Edward in surprise. "Wait a minute, are you saying what Crader told us is true? Abe Hunter don't own Long Trail?" one of the other men asked.

"That's exactly what I'm saying."

"Well, I'll be damn!" Glen said, with a big smile on his face. "Mr. Holt, are we glad to see you."

"What about you, Linus? Will you still be foreman, or will this here feller be?" The man who asked the question pointed to Hank.

"Let me answer that, Linus," Lee Edward said.

"All right."

"Gentlemen, as Linus told you, I'm the new owner of Long Trail. Well, actually I only own half of it."

"What? You mean to tell us that son of a bitch owns the other half?" Buck Adams asked.

"No, the son of a bitch's sister owns the other half," Lee Edward said.

All the men laughed.

"We can handle that," Glen said. "Miss Hunter's one fine lady."

"To answer your question," Lee Edward continued, "yes, Linus will still be your foreman. And this gentleman is Hank Everson. Hank was my closest friend when the two of us rode for the Marathon brand."

"Wait a minute," one of the men said. "Are you telling us you were a cow hand, and now you own Long Trail?"

"Half of it," Lee Edward corrected.

"I'll be damn."

Lee chuckled. "Yeah, I was surprised too."

"Buck, the horses that Mr. Holt and Hank rode in on, belong to Marathon. How about you and Glen taking them back?" Linus asked. "You'll be gone for about four days, two days there, and two days back."

"We'll give you money to stay in a hotel so you won't have to camp out," Lee Edward added.

"All right," Buck answered as a smile formed on his face. "We can sure do that."

"Men," Lee Edward said. "Although I'm well versed on handling cattle from the saddle, this ownership thing is all new to me. So, until I can sort of learn what's going on around here, you and I too, will be depending on Linus to keep things on track."

"Hank," Linus said. "We've got a couple of empty beds in the bunkhouse. Go pick one out."

"All right," Hank said. "I'll bring my things in now."

As Hank was getting settled, Lee Edward followed Linus to a house that was about a hundred yards from the Big House.

"There are two bedrooms," Linus said, "so you'll have your own private room. As you can see, there's also a kitchen, but..." Linus paused for a moment, then continued. "Since Carol died a while back, the kitchen's not been used. I generally take my meals with the hands over in the chow hall, if you don't mind. Moses is our cook, and he's the best we've ever had."

"Why would I mind? I've been eating with a group my whole life."

"I thought you'd be all right with it."

"I take it Carol was your wife. Any children?"

"No, I'm sad to say, we never had children."

"Listen, Linus, if you don't mind, I think I'll go call on

Mrs. Austin. We didn't speak following the reading of the will, and I'm sure she was as shocked as I was at the outcome," Lee Edward said. "If she's going to live here, I'm hoping we can be friends. Oh, and I should probably meet with the young lady who owns the other half of the ranch. It would seem to me like she and I would need to get along if the ranch is to be run smoothly."

"You'll have no trouble getting along with either one of them," Linus said. "They're both fine folks."

"And from what I saw, the young one is pretty, too," Lee Edward said with a little chuckle.

Linus chuckled as well. "She is at that."

Leaving the foreman's house, Lee Edward walked across some empty grassland to the Big House. When he knocked on the door, it was opened by an older Mexican woman.

"*Sí?*" she said.

"I would like to speak with Mrs. Austin."

The woman stepped back from the door, inviting Lee Edward inside.

"Who was at the door, Alenada?" a woman called from another room.

"It is a man, *señora*, who wishes to see you."

"Bring him in, please."

Alenada looked back toward Lee Edward, and with a nod of her head, invited him to follow her.

The room Lee Edward entered was large and well-appointed. One wall had floor-to-ceiling shelves filled with hundreds of books. There were two women in the room, both standing. The older of the two was quite attractive for her age, but the younger one was beautiful. Her blonde hair seemed to catch a beam of sunlight from the windows, her eyes were a bright blue, she had high cheekbones in a perfectly formed face, and though she was slender, there was no doubt that she was a woman.

"Mr. Holt," Hannah greeted.

"Mrs. Austin, Miss Austin," Lee Edward replied.

"I am Mary Beth Hunter," the younger of the two responded.

"Yes, of course, I should have remembered."

"What can we do for you, Mr. Holt?" Hannah asked.

"Nothing in particular. I just thought that as I will be living here on the ranch, it might be good if we got to know each other a little better."

"Living here? You mean living here, in the house with us?" Mary Beth asked, the tone of her voice showing her concern.

"Oh, no, I'm sorry if I gave you that impression. No, I'll be living with Linus."

"Oh, yes, of course. I'm sorry."

"You needn't be; that's a perfectly understandable concern." Lee Edward smiled. "And I'm happy to relieve your mind of that worry."

"I'm Hannah," the older woman said as she extended her hand to Lee Edward. "After Davy, my first husband, died, I tried to run the livery stable he owned in Kerrville, but that wasn't going so well. Edna had died, and I was trying to raise Mary Beth and Abe by myself. That's when your father asked me to marry him. I have to confess, I knew nothing about you being Jake's son."

Lee Edward laughed. "Well, you aren't alone on that," he said. "I knew nothing about Mr. Austin being my father."

"Then, how do you know that Jake was your father?" Hannah asked.

"Because Linus told me. Apparently, he and Mr. Austin were friends of long standing."

"Interesting that you would call your father Mr. Austin," Mary Beth said. "Even I called him Papa, though I knew he wasn't my birth father."

"You have to realize that I'm twenty-six years old, and it has only been in the last week or so that I found out who my mother and father were."

"Is your mother still alive?" Hannah asked.

"Yes," Lee Edward said.

"I wonder why Jake never mentioned her."

Lee Edward shook his head. "I have no idea. I know that Jake was not married to Molly, that's my mother, and that's why she left me in the orphanage when I was a week old."

"You call your parents Jake and Molly?" Mary Beth asked.

"Yes," Lee Edward said. "Since I never knew them, it's hard to start calling them anything but their names."

"Oh, bless your heart. How awful that must have been not to know your parents," Hannah said.

"Not as bad as you might think," Lee Edward replied. "You can't miss something that you've never had."

* * *

WHEN LEE EDWARD returned to the house, Linus was waiting for him.

"Mr. Holt," Linus started, and Lee Edward held up his hand.

"You are the only person who has known who I was for my whole life. Please, call me Lee Edward."

Linus smiled. "All right. Lee Edward, the men wanted me to talk to you about Tim Kirby."

"And who is Tim Kirby?"

"He's a young cowboy who worked here for a couple of years," Linus said. "Abe fired him."

"What did he do? Did he deserve it?"

"Not to my way of thinking. Apparently, he asked Abe a question, and Abe didn't like it. He fired him and had Billy Tanner escort him off the property."

"Was it a personal attack against Abe?"

"I wasn't there, but from what I've been told, all Kirby did was ask if I would be kept on as foreman," Linus said. "I can vouch for him. He's a good man, and you wouldn't be makin' a mistake by rehiring him."

"Where is he now? Does anyone know?"

Linus smiled. "Come with me, I'll show you."

The two men rode across open range for quite some distance, then behind a rise, they saw a small structure that was on wheels.

"A sheep wagon? Is that where Kirby is?"

"Yes, that's where he is, but I wouldn't call that a sheep wagon. That's where Hannah and the two kids were living when Jake married her."

"They lived out on the open prairie like this," Lee Edward said.

"No, Mrs. Austin's husband ran a livery stable, and she tried to keep it going, but a woman running a stable in Kerrville just didn't work," Linus said. "She bought this wagon and pulled it into the stable. It wasn't fixed up like this, but Jake turned it into a movable line shack. It's worked pretty well."

"I'm glad you told me this. I guess Mrs. Austin has been through some rough times."

"And Mary Beth and Abe, too. When Jake brought those two out to the ranch, they were like wild things," Linus said. "But Jake had the patience of Job. It worked for Mary Beth, but Abe—well, I don't want to paint too black a picture about him. Maybe you and he will get along."

"It would be nice."

Just then, a man came into sight carrying a bucket of water. He waved.

"Am I ever glad to see you," Tim Kirby said. "My cupboard's almost bare. Two tins of tomatoes, and that's it. I did snare a rabbit a couple of days ago, but I ain't seen another one close by."

"I'm sorry, Tim, I didn't think to bring you any food," Linus said.

"What? You rode all the way out here and didn't bring food?"

"That's right," Linus said. "I was thinking maybe you'd like to sit down at the table in the chow house. Moses had something that smelled awful good when we left."

"I'd love to take you up on that, but what about Hunter? He's liable to shoot me on sight."

"I don't think so," Lee Edward said. "I'm the man who's going to rehire you, if you would like to come back to work."

Kirby looked at Linus. "Is he taking your place? Damn, don't tell me that son of a bitch fired you."

"Mr. Holt is the new owner of the ranch."

"What? How? I mean, what the hell happened to Hunter?"

"Hunter was left out of Jake's will—well, he got a thousand dollars, but he owns nothing that's part of the ranch. Not a horse, not a saddle, not an acre. The new owners are this man and Mary Beth," Linus said.

"You didn't answer my question, Tim. Would you like to come back to work for me?"

"Hell yeah," Kirby said, slamming his fist into his hand.

"I'll have Billy bring you a horse, and you can go back to your old place in the bunkhouse," Linus said.

"Thank you, mister—I don't think I heard your name."

"Holt, it's Lee Edward Holt."

"Well, Mr. Holt, Thank you a thousand times, no, a million times. There ain't gonna be one man at Long Trail who works harder than I will. Sittin' out here all by my lonesome makes a body think about a whole lot of stuff."

Lee Edward chuckled. "Linus said you're a good hand, so I'll be happy to have you back."

* * *

SAN ANTONIO

Molly Littlefield was looking at her twelve-year-old daughter, as Emma was doing needlework. She had not told Emma the reason the two men had come to visit with her. Ever since Earl had died, Molly had felt the deep responsibility of raising Emma alone.

"Look, Mama," Emma said as, with a smile, she held up the hoop to show Molly the intricate design she was embroidering.

"Oh, you're getting better and better," Molly said. "All your stitches are perfect."

"I'm glad you like it, because when I'm finished with the pillow slip, I'm going to give it to you."

"What a nice present that will be."

Molly looked at Emma for a moment longer, then she took a deep breath to brace herself.

"Emma, do you remember those two men who came

to the house the other day? That was the day you went over to Sally's house."

"Yes, I remember."

"The youngest man was named Lee Edward."

"Uh, huh," Emma said, not taking her attention away from her needlework.

"Emma, Lee Edward is your brother."

"My what?" Emma asked, looking up in surprise.

"His name is Lee Edward, and he's your brother."

"No, that can't be. I'm the only child you and Daddy had."

"That's true. So actually Lee Edward is your half brother, because I am his mother, but Daddy wasn't his father."

"Why didn't he live with us?"

"Because when he was born, I couldn't take care of him, so he went to an orphanage, and that's where he lived until he grew up."

"So, I have a big brother! When will we get to see him again?" Emma asked.

"I'm...not sure," Molly said.

"All right, but when he comes again, will I get to see him?"

"Of course you will, darlin'."

While Emma returned to her needlework, Molly let her mind drift back to a little over twenty-six years ago.

* * *

LONG TRAIL RANCH

"Molly," Jake said. "Edna's bed needs to be changed. Would you take care of it, please?"

"All right," Molly said. "Does she know she messed?"

"I don't think so."

Molly walked into the bedroom. Although it was the middle of the day, the bedroom was in shadow, because all the curtains were drawn.

Edna was sitting in a chair. She was forty years old, which was fifteen years older than Molly. At one time, Edna must have been an attractive woman, but dementia had done more than cripple her mind. Her appearance was that of someone many years older.

"Ma, are you mad at me?" Edna asked. Edna had been calling her ma for some time now, and Molly didn't try to correct her.

"No, dear, I'm not mad at you."

Edna didn't say another word while Molly changed the linens on the bed, then changed Edna's clothes.

Jake came back into the bedroom just as Molly was putting on Edna's gown.

"How are you doing?" Jake asked.

"Who are you?" Edna replied.

"I'm your husband, remember?"

Edna's face was a blank stare.

Jake patted Edna's hand. "Just stay comfortable." He turned and left the room.

When Edna was back in bed, Molly went out to see Jake.

"Jake, we have to talk," Molly said.

"About Edna?"

"No. About us."

"What about us?"

"I'm going to have a baby."

"Oh. I'm sorry to hear that."

"That's all you have to say? That you're sorry to hear that?"

"What do you want me to say?"

"Oh, I don't know. Something like let's get married, perhaps?"

Jake sighed. "Molly, you know that I love you. But you also know that I can't marry you."

"Get a divorce, for heaven's sake. Good Lord, Edna doesn't even know who you are."

"I wouldn't feel right, leaving her under the condition she's in."

"You won't have to leave her. Everything could go on just like it is. I'll live here, and I'll take care of Edna until the day she dies. Nothing needs to change."

Jake shook his head. "No, I can't do that to her. I just can't."

"But you can let me bear your bastard child."

"It's like you said, nothing needs to change. We can just go on as we are until Edna is no longer with us. You and the child can live here."

Tears streamed down Molly's face. "No," she said. "Everything is changing. I'll have my baby without you."

"Please don't say that. Stay, and when Edna dies, we can get married."

"No. This is the end of it, Jake. I will pack my bags and be gone. I never want to see you again."

"But the child—it is my child, too," Jake said.

* * *

MOLLY WAS true to her promise. Not once, in the twenty-six years remaining to Jake Austin, did she see him again.

Molly gave birth to a healthy boy, and she had every intention of keeping him. But within a week, she realized she could not support nor care for a child. Reluctantly but secure in the knowledge that she was doing the right thing, she took the baby to Our Lady of Mercy. It had been her intention to go back for him at some time in the future.

But four years later, Molly married Earl Littleton. Her relationship with Earl was not like what she had felt for Jake. Earl was a man of strong faith, but he was rigid and disciplined. When she told him she was going to have a child, he was most upset. Their child was not a part of his plan for his life. She never once told him she had had a son out of wedlock, and she worked at putting that child out of her mind.

But now, he had come back into her life. Or had he?

SEVENTEEN

LONG TRAIL RANCH

THE NEXT MORNING LEE EDWARD WOKE UP, DRESSED, then walked with Linus over to the chow hall. He was welcomed by the men when he came in, including those men he hadn't met the day before. There were introductions all around and a few more comments as to how happy everyone was that Abe Hunter was not their new boss.

Breakfast was pancakes, fried eggs, and ham.

"Damn, is every breakfast like this?" Lee Edward asked.

"Well, Moses is puttin' on a bit of the dog for you this morning," Billy Tanner said. "But he's a real good cook, and I think we're lucky to have him."

Lee walked back to the kitchen where a Black man was cleaning up the residue of breakfast.

"Moses? I'm Lee Edward Holt, and I wanted to tell you what a fine breakfast that was. I've worked on a ranch for a few years, and I've never had better."

"I 'preciate that, specially comin' from you," Moses said. "'Cause I know you're the boss man now."

"Well, if you know that, I'll be looking for you to slip me an extra pancake, or maybe a larger piece of pie, sometime."

Moses laughed out loud. "I specs I better not do that, Mr. Holt. I got twelve other cowboys I need to keep happy."

Lee laughed as well. "You do indeed. You're a good man, Moses, and I'm glad we're going to be working together."

"Yes, sir, me too."

* * *

AFTER BREAKFAST, Lee Edward threw his saddle on one of the ranch horses and rode out with the men who would be working today. The ranch had seventy-five hundred head of cattle, and the men were checking to see that windmills were working, that tanks were full of water, and that the cows were where they were supposed to be. They were also rounding up yearling calves that had somehow been missed at the round-up.

Lee was moving in and out of the herd, expertly cutting out any unbranded animal.

"I tell you one thing, our new boss handles a horse damn well, don't he?" Clem Porter said.

"He sure as hell does," Hal Crader replied.

"Well, boys, what can I tell you," Hank said. "He's been doin' this since he was sixteen, 'n there wasn't a man on all of Marathon what didn't think he grew to be the best of the bunch."

"So he was what, an ordinary cow hand? What was somebody like him doin', bein' an ordinary cowboy?"

"On account of that's what he was," Hank answered. "He didn't know nothin' 'bout him being Jake Austin's son 'n all this 'til Linus Walker come 'n told him all about it."

"Whoa, one's breakin' away!" one of the men yelled, and Lee Edward started after the running cow, guiding his horse skillfully with his knees and swinging the loop over his head. He closed on the cow, threw the rope, and looped it over the errant cow's head, bringing it to a halt.

Now, with the rope still attached, he brought the cow back to the herd.

"Yeah, I see what you mean 'bout him knowin' his way around a ranch," one of the men said.

* * *

AFTER DINNER, Lee Edward gravitated normally toward the bunkhouse but stopped himself before he joined them. Linus had cautioned him about mingling with the men, pointing out that his presence might intimidate the men. And, recalling his own time in the bunkhouse, he knew how uneasy he and the others would have felt if Andrew Matthews had come into the bunkhouse.

He headed for the foreman's house where Linus was waiting for him.

"You really did cowboy before you came here, didn't you?" Linus said. "You were damn good out there, and I think you made a positive impression on everyone."

"I didn't see Abe anywhere today. Does he ever come out and get his hands dirty?"

"Not often, and when you see him, you'll understand why," Linus said. "More often than not, he's all thumbs. There's no way he could rope a cow like you did out there."

* * *

ABE DIDN'T GO OUT with the others, but he did mount up and leave the home place. He rode around the ranch, making certain that he stayed out of sight. He was upset with Linus for going along with having this interloper as the new owner.

Who the hell is he, anyway? It wasn't right for Jake to just drop Lee Edward Holt on them the way he did.

Of course, Jake didn't leave the whole ranch to Lee Edward, he only left half. And the other half he left to Mary Beth, not to him.

Abe was thinking that Jake always was a son of a bitch. It's just that he had no idea how much of a son of a bitch he really was.

From his distant point of observation, Abe saw that twelve yearlings had been culled from the herd and were being driven into the pen where the calves were brought to be branded. Unlike the larger pastures, this was a relatively small pen.

When Abe saw all the men going in for dinner, he waited until no one was outside, then he rode over, opened the gate, and shooed the cattle out of the pen. When they had all disappeared out of sight, he rode over to the chow hall and went inside. The men were eating, carrying on conversations, and laughing. Lee Edward Holt, Abe noticed, was as deep into the conversation as any of the hands.

"Walker!" Abe shouted. "What the hell is everyone doing in here when you've got cows to bring in?"

"We got them all in this morning," Linus answered. "They're in the branding pen."

"Really? Then would you mind telling me why there isn't a single cow there? Oh, wait, you don't have to tell me, I know. The reason there isn't a cow in sight is because the gate's standing wide open. Seems to me like it wouldn't be that hard for someone to close the gate."

"The gate *was* closed, Mr. Hunter, 'cause I closed it," Crader said.

"Oh, then I guess one of the cows just reared up and unlatched it," Abe said sarcastically.

"It was closed and secured, Abe, because I checked it," Lee Edward said.

"Yeah, well, either you didn't check it all that well, or it come undone. I don't know what happened, all I know is all the cows got away 'n they're probably back with the herd now."

"Gentlemen, maybe we should eat our dinner rather quickly," Lee Edward suggested. "It looks like we've got it all to do over again."

"Boss, I know damn well I closed that gate," Crader said. "And I latched it, too."

"I know you did, Crader, because I checked it myself," Lee Edward said. "But somehow the gate came open, and the cows got out. So, we'll need to bring them back in."

"All right, you heard the man," Linus said. "So let's hurry through dinner so we can get out there again."

"Will you be coming out with us, Abe?" Lee Edward asked,

Abe shook his head no. "I'm not a *vaquero*, Mr. Holt. My interest in this ranch is purely as a supervisor, in this case acting on behalf of my sister. So I'm cautioning you not to make any major decisions without seeing me first."

"I wouldn't think of it," Lee Edward replied.

Lee Edward watched Abe Hunter ride back up to the Big House, no doubt to have his dinner. In the meantime, he, Linus, Hank, and the others, went back out to, once again, round up the maverick cattle.

* * *

"I wasn't sure you would be here for dinner," Hannah said when Abe came back into the house.

"Oh, where did you think I'd be?"

"I thought you might be eating with the cow hands."

"I've never eaten with them before. What makes you think I'd eat with them now?"

"I don't know. I just thought you might use it as a way to get to know Mr. Holt better."

"Speaking of Holt, I know now how I plan to handle him," Abe said.

"What do you mean 'handle' him?" Mary Beth asked, speaking for the first time.

"I mean a way to meet him on an equal basis, as far as managing the ranch is concerned."

"How will you be equal to him? He owns half the ranch," Hannah said.

"Yes, and Mary Beth owns the other half," Abe said. He smiled at Mary Beth. "Meet your new ranch manager."

"What are you talking about?"

"Holt only owns half the ranch, and as half-owner, he can't make any decisions without the approval of the other half-owner," Abe explained. "You are the other half, but I don't expect you're going to want to get into the actual running of the ranch, are you?"

"No, I was thinking that if Mr. Holt is running the ranch, he, with Linus' help, would just take care of things. Right now, I see no need to get involved unless there's a problem."

Abe smiled. "But that's exactly my point. I don't think Jake would leave half this ranch to you if he didn't want you to get involved. He had to know Holt has never run anything before and if he messes up, where does that leave us?" Abe waited for Mary Beth to answer, but she stayed quiet. "And because you aren't going to take an active role in running the ranch, and I have no intention of being completely left out, I'll represent you in dealing with Holt.

"That means I'll have just as much say as he does in the running of Long Trail."

"Does Mr. Holt know about this?" Mary Beth asked.

Abe nodded his head. "I told him I'd be acting in a supervisory position for you, and he understands he can't make any decisions without my approval."

"Abe, try and stay on friendly terms with him," Hannah said. "This ranch has always been a place of peace for me, and I wouldn't like to see any turmoil just because you and Mr. Holt don't get along."

"Mama, you know I can get along with everyone. If there's trouble between us, it will be on Holt."

Hannah let out a long sigh. "All I ask is that you try."

* * *

"LEE EDWARD, you know damn well we closed that gate," Hank said as all the hands turned out to round up the cows again.

"I know we did," Lee Edward replied.

"So then, what the hell happened?"

"I don't want to say what I think happened."

"Why not? I'm thinking it. Hunter opened the gate, didn't he?"

"Like I said, I don't want to say it, but that's exactly what I think happened."

"What I don't know is why he would do something like that."

"You weren't at the reading of the will," Lee Edward said. "Hunter sort of went wild. He expected to inherit the ranch. He didn't know about me."

Hank chuckled. "Hell, you didn't even know about you, did you?"

Lee Edward laughed. "No, I don't suppose I did."

"So, what's going to happen?"

"I think Mr. Hunter and I are going to have to have a conversation."

"Yeah, I think so."

A few of the yearlings that had been rounded up earlier didn't rejoin the herd, so they were easy to start back to the pen. By the time that got the last few into the lot, it was late afternoon.

When the gate was closed, Lee Edward rode over to it, wrapped a piece of chain around the gate post and the end post of the fence. Then he slipped a padlock through the links of the chain and snapped it shut.

"Well, now," Crader said. "One of them cows might have been smart enough to open the gate before, but if that cow ain't got no key to that lock, he ain't goin' to be able to open it again."

"You got that right," Atkins said.

"What are you talkin' about?" Tim Kirby asked. "There ain't no cow that can open a lock whether it's got a key or not."

"Well, then, these cows is goin' to be pretty safe, ain't they?" Atkins asked.

"Unless they start walkin' on two legs," Kirby added.

Lee and Hank, overhearing the conversation, laughed.

* * *

DOUBLE DIAMOND RANCH

"What do you mean, Jake Austin left his ranch to some orphan?" Ruben Pugh asked. "What about Abe Hunter?"

Travers laughed. "Austin left that little son of a bitch hangin' in the wind. No, sir, he left his ranch to some orphan."

"Why the hell would he do that?"

"I don't know."

"I need you to find out all you can about the new guy," Pugh said.

"All right," Travers said. "I'll put Logan on it. He's got a few friends over at Long Trail."

"Yeah, but don't tell Logan I'm the one that wants the information. Make him think you're curious. I don't want the new owner to make any connection with me until it's too late for him to do anything about it," Pugh said. "Then we'll pounce!"

"I got ya."

Travers waited until most of the men had gone in to supper. Logan was at his bunk putting away some gear.

"Hey, Logan, what do you know about this new guy that's takin' up the reins over at Long Trail?"

"You mean Abe Hunter? I know there don't none of the hands like him," Logan replied.

Travers smiled and shook his head. "Huh, uh, Hunter ain't the one."

"Well then who is? I ain't heard nothin'."

"Talk is it's some orphan feller," Travers said.

"I'll be damn. What for would Austin be leavin' that ranch of his'n to some orphan?"

"I don't know. I was hopin' you would."

"No, I ain't heerd nothin' about it."

Travers took two one-dollar bills from his pocket and handed them to Logan. "Tell you what. Why don't you go into town tonight, and if anybody from Long Trail's there, buy him a couple of beers 'n see what you can find out."

"Damn," Logan said with a big smile. "Yeah, I can do that."

* * *

LOGAN GOT to the Saddle and Bit Saloon earlier than just about anyone else. When one of the girls came over to talk to him, he took her upstairs. He didn't ordinarily have enough money to do such a thing in the middle of the month, but Travers had given him two dollars. He was supposed to buy drinks for a Long Trail hand, but Logan knew he could get all the information he needed just by talking. So, he used part of the money to take Abby upstairs. That left him with enough money to buy drinks for himself.

When Logan came back downstairs a little later, he saw Buck Adams and Stump Brewer standing at the bar. Both men were from Long Trail, and having once worked there, he got along well with them. He stepped up to the bar beside them.

"Buck, Stump, what're ya doin' in town?" Logan asked.

"On an errand for Linus," Buck said. "What about you, Curley? I thought Bull wouldn't let Double Diamond men off the range but once a month?"

"Bull Travers is a good man," Logan said. "I'll bet Long Trail's in a hell of a shape with that son of a bitch runnin' things. No, I don't envy you havin' to answer to

Abe Hunter. Too bad it was Jake that was shot and not him."

"We ain't no way workin' for that sumbitch," Stump Brewer said. "We got us a fine boss, now."

"What do you mean? Didn't Austin leave the ranch to Abe?"

"Nope, talk is, Mr. Austin had a bastard kid a long time ago, and the talk around the bunk house is that he wanted to make it up to him, so he left him the ranch," Buck said.

Logan laughed a loud guffaw. "I'll be damned, a bastard! The mighty Jake Austin—just like the rest of us."

"Nobody's told us the whole story, but Mr. Holt is the real thing. Used to be a cowboy just like us," Buck said. "He can ride and rope as good as anybody I ever seen."

"I bet Abe Hunter is fit to be tied," Logan said.

"He's tryin' to horn in on ever'thing. Mr. Austin gave half the ranch to Miss Mary Beth, so now Abe thinks he has to look after her," Buck said. "So far, he ain't caused Mr. Holt to raise his voice—not once, no matter what Abe tries to do. No, sir, Lee Edward Holt is the best thing that ever happened to Long Trail—not that Mr. Austin, rest his soul, was hard to work for. You should have stayed with us, Curley."

* * *

DOUBLE DIAMOND RANCH

"Turns out this Lee Edward Holt fella was Mr. Austin's own son all along," Logan said in his report to Bull Travers.

"You don't say," Travers commented.

Travers carried the report to Pugh.

"His son, huh?" Pugh asked.

"Yeah, I don't know no more'n that about 'im."

"How old is he?" Travers asked.

"I do know that for sure. Curley says he thinks he's about twenty-five or so."

"Good to know," Pugh said, a broad smile crossing his face. "Probably doesn't know a damn thing about ranchin' or about business."

Eighteen

AFTER THE EVENING MEAL WAS OVER, LEE EDWARD stopped at the Big House and knocked on the door. It was answered by Alenada.

"Hello, Alenada. I wonder if I could come in and visit for a while?"

"*Si, señor*," Alenada said, stepping back from the door by way of invitation.

"I'll wait here until you tell Mrs. Austin I've come to talk."

Alenada nodded, then hurried back into the house to notify the others of his arrival.

A moment later, Mary Beth came out to greet him. She had a welcoming smile, and Lee Edward was struck again by how attractive she was.

"Mr. Holt, Alenada said you'd come to visit. Welcome to our home."

"Thank you."

"Come on into the parlor. Mama will join us in a bit."

"All right."

Lee followed her into the parlor. There, she held out

her hand toward a comfortable leather chair, inviting him to have a seat. The chair was near a wide fireplace. There was no fire, but there was the faint aroma of lingering burnt wood.

"I must say that Linus thinks you can do no wrong," Mary Beth said as she lifted the chimney and lit a lamp.

"Linus is a good man."

"It's strange that he kept up with you all these years."

"Under the circumstances, I would say that is true," Lee Edward said. "After all, he was coming to an orphanage. I suppose at any time, one of us could have been adopted—even if it would have been by my own father."

"You have to have some resentment toward Papa Jake."

"Not really. You can't feel resentment for something you never knew. You have to understand, I never felt alone," Lee Edward said. "Despite what people think an orphanage is, I had Sister Maria, and I always felt she loved me."

Mary Beth looked down at her hands. "I hate it that you didn't know Papa Jake. He was so good to Mama and me, and I suppose to Abe, too, although Abe wouldn't always let him be nice to him." Mary Beth smiled as she looked directly at Lee Edward. "He is my brother, but he can be—a lady doesn't say what I'm thinking, so I'll leave it at that."

Lee Edward chuckled but didn't comment.

"Did I miss something?" Hannah asked as she came into the room.

"No, Mama, Mr. Holt and I were just talking."

"I must say you fill Jake's chair very well," Hannah said. "That leather chair was always his favorite. When the fire was blazing, he would sit there 'resting his eyes,' as he called it, but when he began to snore, he would awaken with a start." Hannah looked at Lee Edward. "You do resemble your father."

There was an awkward pause, and Hannah continued.

"Would you like some coffee? And I believe Alenada has some Scotch scones left over from yesterday," Hannah said. "They have currants in them, and I suspect they will be as good today as they were yesterday."

"I would like that very much, Mrs. Austin."

"Oh, heavens, you're part of us now," Hannah said. "Please, use our first names." She laughed. "I am your stepmother after all, but you don't have to call me Mom."

"I guess that's right, isn't it?" Lee Edward said.

"Alenada, would you bring us some coffee and your scones, please?" Hannah called.

"Yes, ma'am."

Hannah was carrying a large envelope with her, and she reached down into it. "I had never seen these photographs before, but I was looking through some of Jake's things, and I found them."

She handed two pictures to Lee Edward. One was of a baby sitting on a high stool, wearing a long christening dress. Lee Edward recognized Linus' handwriting on the bottom of the photograph. It said Molly's baby boy. The other was a group picture of all the children at the orphanage. His face was encircled, and an arrow pointed toward it. Again, in Linus's handwriting, it said Lee Edward Holt, twelve years old.

Lee Edward handed the pictures back to Hannah. "I don't know what to say."

"I would say that your father cared for you, and you were often in his thoughts," Hannah said.

"Yeah," Lee Edward said. The one-word response was dismissive.

Abe Hunter came into the room then, and seeing Lee Edward, stopped.

"What are you doing here, Holt? What do you want?" Abe asked. The tone of his voice was cold.

"I thought that, since we'll be working together, it might be a good idea to speak every now and then."

Abe didn't answer, and there was a pregnant pause, which Hannah filled with an observation

"I don't know why Jake never told us about you. I know that I certainly would have welcomed you to our home."

"If you ask me, there's something fishy about all this," Abe said. "I mean, here you come along after Jake is dead, and you try to convince us you belong here. And not only that, you make the claim that you own half this ranch."

"I made no such claim," Lee Edward said. "When the will was read, and I was told I had inherited half this ranch, it was as big a shock to me as it was to you."

"Oh, yeah, I'm sure it was," Abe said in a challenging tone.

"Abe," Hannah said. "This is my house, and Lee Edward is welcome here."

"I don't know how you can welcome him when it's so obvious he and Walker connived to put this sham together."

"Do you remember the letter Mr. Fitzgerald gave me at the reading of the will?" Hannah asked.

"Yeah, I remember it. What about it?"

"I think I should read it now. It will clear up a lot of questions."

Hannah walked over to the fireplace where the envelope lay on the mantel. She removed the letter and began to read aloud:

"My beloved Hannah

*"If you are reading this, then it means that I have
already slipped the bonds of this life, and have gone on to
the next, where I shall wait until we are again, rejoined.*

*"I have a secret that I have kept from you all these
years. Although my love for you knows no bounds, you were
not my first, nor even my second love. My first wife, Edna,
remained childless throughout our marriage."*

"See there!" Abe shouted. He pointed to Lee Edward.
"I told you he was a fraud!"

Hannah looked up from her reading. "Abe, please do
not interrupt."

"All right," Abe said. "Go on, go on, I'm going to
enjoy this." He smiled at Lee Edward though his smile
was obviously without humor or warmth.

Hannah cleared her throat and continued reading.

*"When Edna became infirm, and without awareness of
who I was, or even who she was, I hired Molly Clinton to
look after her. As time went by, and Molly became more and
more a fixture of this household, we fell in love. As a result
of that love, Molly learned that she was with child. She
begged me to marry her, but because I felt bound by honor to
remain married to a woman who no longer even knew my
name, I rejected Molly's pleas. I asked her to wait,
promising her my love and my support for our child until
such time as we could be married.*

*"Molly refused my offer, and upon the birth of her son,
she placed him at Our Lady of Mercy Orphanage. Over the
years, as you are aware, I have supported that orphanage.
And now, you can understand why I have been so generous.*

"I made the decision not to let anyone at the orphanage,

*including the child himself, know that I was his father. As
he grew, I followed him through the visits of Linus Walker.*

*"And now, you know the name of my son. I am sorry he
does not bear my name, but the name given him by Our
Lady of Mercy is Lee Edward Holt. From what Linus has
told me, Lee Edward is a fine, upstanding young man. I will
be leaving half the ranch to him. I'll be leaving the other
half to Mary Beth. By establishing a shared ownership, I
feel that this will create a bonding which will make Lee
Edward a part of a family.*

*"I hope you understand this, and accept Lee Edward
with open arms.*

*Your Loving Husband
Jake"*

Hannah folded the letter, put it back into the envelope, then smiled at Lee Edward.

"Welcome to the family, Lee Edward."

"I've...I've never had a family, Hannah. Thank you for
reading Jake's letter."

"Yeah, I guess you do thank us," Abe said, his tone
still bitter. "It means that old fool has given you half of
the largest ranch in Kerr County." Abe started to walk
away.

"Abe, please, don't leave," Hannah called after him.

"Don't worry about it. You've got another son now!"
Abe shouted, slamming the door as he stormed out of the
room.

"I'm so sorry," Hannah said.

"I'm the one who should be sorry. None of this would
have happened to you if Jake would have left well enough
alone. I had a life at Marathon Ranch, and I was satisfied

with it. If you think it would be easier, I can go back where I came from."

"No," Hannah said. "I welcome you. Jake quite literally lifted me out of squalor. When I met him, I was mucking out stables. He told me that was not a life for a lady. I grew to love him with all my heart, and now, seeing you here, sitting in his chair, he has given me a piece of him to grow to love as well. No, Lee Edward, please stay. Just give Abe some time. He'll come around; I know he will."

Lee nodded, then stood. "It's been an enlightening evening." He walked over to the door then looked back at Hannah and Mary Beth. "Thank you so much for accepting me."

"You're welcome to come here any time, Lee Edward," Hannah said. She came to him and embraced him. Lee Edward was not expecting that and he pulled away.

"Yes," Mary Beth added. "Any time."

* * *

WHEN LEE EDWARD started toward the foreman's house, he saw the glow of a cigarette in the darkness. As he grew closer, he saw that it was Abe.

"Abe, do you think it might be possible for us to be friends?"

"I doubt it."

"Well, it doesn't make a lot of sense for us to be enemies, does it? Whether you like it or not, fate has thrown us together."

"Just remember one thing," Abe said. "You only own half of this ranch. I own the other half."

"Really?" Lee Edward said. "I thought Mary Beth owned the other half."

"That's the same thing as me ownin' it. 'N you won't be able to do a damn thing unless I approve of it."

"I really hope we can work together. I know that I intend to do all I can to make this arrangement work."

"Yeah, well, we'll just see what you can do," Abe replied.

When Ruben Pugh rode over to Long Trail, he dismounted in front of the Big House. Having seen him ride in, Linus Walker walked over to meet him.

"Something I can do for you, Mr. Pugh?" Linus asked.

"Yes, I'd like to speak with Mr. Holt."

"Mr. Holt is out on the range with the men right now."

"Wait a minute, I've heard he's the owner," Pugh said, "and now you're telling me he's out on the range with the cow hands who work for him?"

"Yes, sir, that's what I'm telling you. If you'd like, I can take you out to meet him."

"I'd like that."

"All right, let me saddle up. It's a bit of ways out there," Linus said.

* * *

PUGH FOLLOWED Linus out onto the range to see Lee Edward. He couldn't understand why Holt would be working with the men he employed.

Pugh was of the belief that if you lowered yourself to the level of your working cowboys, they would lose all respect for you and start questioning any of your orders. He smiled at the thought. Mr. Lee Edward Holt would be an easy man to deal with.

"There he is," Linus said.

The man Linus pointed to was on a horse at full gallop. He was controlling the horse with his knees as he was whirling a loop overhead. Pugh watched as Lee Edward threw a perfect heel catch on a wayward steer. When the steer lifted his legs, he was released, but as he was between Lee Edward and the herd, and seeing the herd in front of him, the animal immediately headed back to rejoin the others.

* * *

WITH THE STEER now back with the herd, Lee Edward saw that Linus and a man whom he did not recognize had come out to the pasture.

"Hank?" Lee Edward called out.

"Yeah, boss?"

"Keep an eye on things here. I need to go see what Linus needs."

"All right."

Lee Edward rode up to the two men. "Linus, I didn't expect to see you out here."

"Lee Edward, this is Ruben Pugh. He owns the Double Diamond Ranch. His ranch shares a boundary with Long Trail."

Lee Edward nodded. "Glad to meet you, Mr. Pugh. I had intended to go meet my neighbors, but I've been pretty busy."

"I can see that, Mr. Holt. I'll just get right to the point. Jake and I were negotiating the sale of Long Trail to me just before his untimely death. Now, I'd like to tender another offer for the ranch."

Lee Edward looked at Linus for confirmation that this had indeed been happening. Without saying a word,

Lee Edward could tell by the expression on Linus's face that this was not something he had ever heard.

"Ah, I see," Lee Edward said. "If we're going to discuss something as important as that, this isn't the place to do it. Come up to the house with me. Miss Hunter will have to be a part of this conversation."

"Yes, I heard that she was a part owner here, but surely her opinion wouldn't be considered."

"Oh, but her opinion will very much be considered."

"Why would you need her need opinion as to whether or not you would sell the ranch?"

"Let's just say it is as you said—she owns half the ranch."

When they reached the Big House, they tied their horses off out front, then walked up to the front door. Lee Edward knocked.

"Why are you knocking on the door of your own house?"

"Because it isn't my house," Lee Edward answered.

"How the hell is it not your house if you own Long Trail?"

"Because Jake left the house to Mrs. Austin. I live in the foreman's house," Lee Edward said. "You seem to know so much about our business. I'm surprised you didn't know that, too."

Alenada answered the door.

"Come in, *Señor* Holt. I will tell the *señora* you are here."

"Thanks, Alenada, but it's Mary Beth that we need to talk to."

Mary Beth came into the room a moment later, smiling broadly. "Hello, Lee Edward, what...?" The smile left her face when she saw Rueben Pugh.

"What are you doing here, Rueben Pugh?" The tone

of her voice as she asked the question could only be described as negative.

"I've come to make a business offer. I was prepared to make an offer to Mr. Holt, but he informed me that anything that has to do with the ranch must include you."

"And what would that business offer be?"

"I'm prepared to make quite a generous offer to buy Long Trail."

"No."

"You haven't heard what I'm willing to pay."

"I don't care what the offer is. Papa Jake wouldn't sell to you, and neither will I."

Pugh turned to Lee Edward. "Mr. Holt, don't you have any input at all into this discussion? Can't you talk some sense into her?"

"If you ask me, her answer made good sense. You see, I don't want to sell the ranch either."

Pugh looked at the two of them, then shook his head.

"I think you both are going to come to regret this someday."

Lee Edward called out to the maid, who had left the room. "Alenada, would you please show this...gentleman out?"

"*Si, señor*," Alenada said, hurrying into the room. "This way, *Señor* Pugh."

Pugh looked at Lee Edward as if he were about to say something else, but he said nothing. He just shook his head, then followed the maid out of the room.

Lee Edward and Mary Beth waited until they heard the front door close, then they both laughed out loud.

"How would you like a glass of sweet tea?" Mary Beth asked.

"I'd love it."

Mary Beth poured both of them a glass of tea, then headed to the back porch to drink it.

Abe came walking up to the back porch then, and when he saw Lee Edward, he stopped and frowned.

"Shouldn't you be out on the range? Isn't there work to be done?" Abe asked. "Why are you here with my sister?"

"It's rather obvious, isn't it? I'm drinking tea," Lee Edward replied, holding out his glass.

"Yeah? Well find someone else to drink it with."

"Abe, I'll drink tea wherever and with whomever I please," Mary Beth said.

Abe didn't reply. He just glared at both of them as he walked by them into the house.

"Do you get the idea that Abe doesn't like me very much?" Lee Edward asked with a little chuckle.

"He'll come around," Mary Beth said.

"Well, Abe is right about one thing," Lee Edward said as he put the glass down and stood up. "I do have work to do."

"What will you be doing?" Mary Beth asked.

"It was doctor for screwworms or replace salt at the salt grounds. Now which do you think I chose?"

"I'd say the salt," Mary Beth said. "Since this operation is half mine, do you care if I go with you?"

"I'd love to have your company."

"Give me a minute to change clothes."

* * *

MARY BETH WAS WEARING butternut pants and the shirt she had worn at the reading of the will. Her pants were tucked into her well-worn boots, and her once-white hat was now a shade of tan. It was quite evident she had been on a horse for more than just pleasure jaunts.

"I think I'm going to ride Dobbin," Mary Beth said. "He hasn't been ridden since—well, it's been a long time."

She put her fingers to her lips and whistled. Within a few minutes, a big red bay came trotting up to her. Reaching into her pocket, she pulled out what looked to be a cookie, and the horse began to nose her hand.

"Hold on, there, Dobbin," Mary Beth said. "You'll get another one."

"If you have more than one, how about sharing with Scout?" Lee Edward asked.

"Nope, I make these only for Dobbin," she said as she gave him a second one. "I bake them myself—apple, oats, molasses, flour, and a little lard. You could do it, too, if you wanted to." She patted the horse on the neck and led him to the tack shed to get her saddle.

Lee Edward knew it would be a mistake to offer to saddle her horse, and he was correct. She chose her bridle and put it on, making sure the bit was the correct size. She grabbed a saddle blanket, put it in place, then slung the saddle up and positioned it so it fit just right. She continued checking all the straps and the cinch before she got into the saddle.

Lee Edward was actually glad she was going with him because he wasn't sure where the salt grounds were. He knew that the ranch had more than one, but Tim Kirby had reported that the one at the northwest corner was the one in need of replenishment. He would have ridden the fence line until he got there, and he was sure Mary Beth knew exactly where they were going.

"Are we ready?" Lee Edward asked.

"I don't think so," Mary Beth said, a mischievous smile crossing her face.

Lee Edward frowned, not knowing what they could need.

"I guess we need a canteen," he said dismounting. "We may need water."

"I thought we were going to the salt grounds. Don't you think we should take some salt?"

Now it was Lee Edward's turn to smile. "I was going to get the packsack when I got the canteen. I was just testing you."

"Sure you were, Holt," Mary Beth said as she started Dobbin out in a walk.

* * *

WITH THE PACKSACKS filled with salt and a canteen filled with water, Lee Edward soon caught up with Mary Beth. He fell in behind the slender young woman as she headed out across the range in a northwesterly direction. He couldn't help but admire her horsemanship. She was sitting deep in the saddle in front of the cantle. Her posture was straight and her legs were secure in the stirrups, as the reins were held loosely in her left hand. She controlled Dobbin by gently laying the rein against his neck to indicate which direction she wanted him to go.

Lee Edward was envious of Mary Beth's childhood. He could imagine Jake or some other cowboy working endlessly with her—teaching her how to jog or lope or gallop a horse—the subtle movement of her body controlling the horse's every move.

He smiled when he thought of his own introduction to a horse. It was after he arrived at Marathon when he realized that he didn't know the first thing about horses. When he was choosing a job, he hadn't thought about that. Ray Dockins had assigned Hank Everson to teach him how to ride, and that had been the beginning of his friendship with Hank.

"Not too much farther," Mary Beth called back to him as she headed Dobbin down a gently sloping ravine. "There's a seep down here and the salt box is about two hundred yards away. Papa Jake had intended to put up a windmill around here, but he never got it done."

"If that is something he wanted, then I'll have to put it on my 'to do' list," Lee Edward said.

"You know you don't have to do everything yourself. We do pay men to work for us."

"I know. It's just that I hate to tell the cowboys to do something out of their regular routine," Lee Edward said. "They work hard."

They rode for another mile or so until they came to the wooden salt box. They both dismounted and Lee Edward emptied the salt while Mary Beth led Dobbin down to the seep where there was enough water to let him drink.

When Lee Edward was finished, he stared at Mary Beth. She was standing there with her blond hair tumbling down her back. He was not accustomed to seeing women in pants, and he noticed the curves in her body.

It occurred to him that, except for the nuns and bar girls, he had never been around many women. His education had been at the orphanage school that had only boys, and when he attended church, the boys made up the choir even if one couldn't sing, so there were no opportunities to talk to girls.

Being around Mary Beth, and Hannah, too, was a new experience. He hadn't realized it at the time, but when Hannah had embraced him, he had instinctively pulled away.

"Your horse needs water," Mary Beth called, "and I could use a drink from your canteen."

"I was on my way down there."

Lee Edward made his way down the ravine. He looked around not knowing what to talk about.

"Is this spring here all the time?" he asked as he handed her the canteen.

Mary Beth nodded. "It is." She took a long drink and handed the canteen back to Lee Edward.

"Then we should dam it up and make a tank out here."

Mary Beth smiled. "You're already thinking like a ranch owner. Always seeing what could be done to improve Long Trail."

"Well, it does belong to us. Might as well make it the best ranch in the county," Lee Edward said as he climbed back in the saddle.

"According to Papa Jake, it already is."

NINETEEN

As Lee Edward lay in bed that night, he thought back over the day. It had been one of the most pleasant days he had ever had. What a strange turn his life had taken.

When he was fourteen years old, Sister Maria had told him the truth about how he had come to live at the orphanage. She had no idea why the woman had chosen to abandon him, but she assumed it was because he had been born out of wedlock.

And now he learned that though he had been born out of wedlock, his father had given him the opportunity to become a part of a real family. Hannah had issued the invitation, and he could see having her as his stepmother. But it was her children that gave him pause.

It was obvious that Abe was resentful and was going to be a problem for him. It was a wholly different thing with Mary Beth. She seemed to be genuine in her acceptance of him, and he was strongly attracted to her, but she was his stepsister. He wondered about the propriety of exploring such a relationship.

Because of all these thoughts tumbling through his mind, sleep was a long time coming.

Mary Beth was also having thoughts that prevented her from sleeping. She thought Lee Edward was a handsome man, but it was more than his looks that occupied her thoughts. There was something about him—something that she found attractive that went beyond his looks. He was friendly with her and with her mother, but what was more important was how he reacted to Abe's hostility toward him. It was met with an equanimity that she found very appealing.

She couldn't help but wonder if he had any thoughts for her. When she was with him, she believed she could feel something. What she did not know was if he felt something for her.

* * *

OVER THE NEXT SEVERAL DAYS, Lee Edward looked for opportunities to be around Mary Beth, and he was pleased to see that she seemed to enjoy those opportunities as much as he did. Then, when Mary Beth made a suggestion to him that he would have said no to anyone else, he listened to her.

"She's your mother, Lee Edward," Mary Beth said. "You can't just shut her out forever."

"Why not? She shut me out."

"She was a young, unmarried woman who had just had her heart broken. How was she going to take care of a new baby? She did what she thought was best for you. I think we should go see her."

"We?" Lee Edward asked. "You mean you'd go with me?"

Mary Beth smiled at him. "Yes, I'd be glad to go with you."

"And what if she turns me away?"

"Well, from what I've heard, you weren't that open to her when Linus took you to meet her," Mary Beth said. "But I'm willing to bet that if you went to see her...and maybe even apologized for how you acted, she would accept you with open arms. You're her son, Lee Edward. And even though she went all those years without seeing you, you know darned well, she thought about you over the years."

"All right," Lee Edward said. "Maybe you're right, and I'll consider an apology, but we'll wait and see what happens."

* * *

SAN ANTONIO WAS TOO FAR for them to go in one day, so when they got to Welfare, they stayed at the same place where Linus had always stayed.

When they walked in, neither Carl nor Gus recognized Lee Edward, but Toby, the cook, remembered him.

When they sat down at the table in the back of Joseph and Bessler's store, Toby greeted them with a wide smile.

"Mr. Holt, what a surprise, you comin' here with your missus. We heard you inherited Long Trail."

"Well Toby, I did inherit Long Trail," Lee Edward said, "but so did Miss Mary Beth Hunter. We're on our way to San Antonio."

"So you'll be wantin' two rooms," Gus Bessler said, having overheard the conversation.

"Yes, sir," Lee Edward said.

"If that's the case, I think Toby can rustle you up a free meal."

"Sounds good," Lee Edward said. "What do you have?"

"I had some good fresh antelope steak today, but that's all gone. I can put some potato soup together for you folks," Toby said. "I know that ain't much, but I can throw in a hot loaf of sourdough bread and a piece of rhubarb custard pie."

"Oh, that sounds good," Mary Beth said. "I was expecting to have Lee Edward throw some salt pork in a pan and whip out day-old biscuits."

"You give me too much credit," Lee Edward said. "I thought you would have done the cooking."

They were both laughing as Toby and Gus left them alone. Then there was an awkward silence.

Finally Mary Beth reached her hand across the table to take his. "Were you embarrassed when they thought you and I were married?"

"No." Lee Edward felt a little catch in his throat. "I sort of liked thinking about the idea."

"Me, too."

"But just thinking about that brings up another question. Really, two questions. How would your mother feel if I started courting you, and more importantly, what about Abe?"

Mary Beth's face flushed as she tried to suppress a smile. "Believe it or not, my mother and I have discussed it. To be honest, she suggested that it would be nice if you and I were to marry. Now, Abe is another story."

Lee Edward sighed. "I rather thought he'd be against any idea of us getting together."

"He'll either come around to the idea or not. But

whatever he says, it's none of Abe's business. If I want you for my beau, then I'll have you for my beau."

"Oh, so I'm your beau now?"

Mary Beth laughed out loud.

"You're my beau if you want to be."

"Yeah," Lee Edward said with a broad smile. "Yeah, I think I do want to be your beau. I'd like that."

When they went upstairs after supper, Lee Edward walked Mary Beth to her room. He unlocked the door and handed the key to her, but she did not step inside. Instead, she looked up at Lee Edward with expectant eyes.

Lee Edward was hesitant. He knew he wanted to kiss her, but having a desire was a new experience for him.

Finally, Mary Beth moved toward him and her lips met his. The kiss was long and deep, and neither wanted it to end. Again, it was Mary Beth who stepped back.

"Good night, Lee Edward Holt. I want you to think about me all night." She gave him another light kiss, then turned and entered her room.

TWENTY

THEY REACHED SAN ANTONIO JUST AFTER NOON THE
next day, and Lee Edward turned down a road that he
knew well. After a few blocks, they came to a limestone
building with a tall bell tower. A wall surrounded the
grounds of the building, and to one side, Lee Edward
heard the familiar sounds of young boys at play.

The two walked up the cobbled path, and Lee
Edward rang the bell. When the door was opened, he was
met by the same young nun who had answered the door
the last time he had come to visit Our Lady of Mercy.
This time when she saw him, he was met with a smile of
immediate recognition.

"Mr. Holt, how pleased we are to see you," the nun
said.

"Sister Margaret, I believe it is," Lee Edward said.

"Yes." Her smile disappeared. "I am so glad you got
Mother Superior's message."

Lee Edward shook his head. "I didn't get a message,
but why should I have gotten one?"

"Poor dear soul," Sister Margaret said. "It's Sister

Maria. She was caring for a very sick indigent who came to us. We did not want to expose the boys to whatever it was he had, so we enlisted the help of our neighbor, Mr. Perez. He allowed the man to stay in his garden hut, and Sister Maria cared for him until his passing."

"And what of Sister Maria?" Lee Edward asked.

"She is in the infirmary."

"Then we will go to see her."

Sister Margaret shook her head. "Mr. Holt, it is not wise. She has typhoid."

"I will go to see her," Lee Edward said. "Will you please show my friend, Miss Hunter, to the plaza?"

"Yes, sir, come with me, ma'am. I know you can make your way to the infirmary."

* * *

LEE EDWARD MADE his way to the church. When he stepped inside, the frescos in their fading colors were so familiar. He moved to the sacristy where the carved wooden cabinet stood. Had it been under different circumstances, he would have opened the door to see his old vestments when he served as an altar boy were there but now was not the time.

He ascended the steps, taking two at a time, until he entered the infirmary. In one corner, he saw a lone bed surrounded with white gauze. Moving toward it, slowly now, he was suddenly filled with fear. What if Sister Maria was dead?

He slid the veil aside and pulled a chair up beside his beloved mother. Taking her hand in both of his, tears began to stream down his face.

Sister Maria opened her eyes, and a small smile crossed her face.

"My dear son, do not grieve for me. I will soon be with our savior."

Lee Edward put his head down on her hand, and she began to pat his hair.

"Be strong and be faithful," she said. "How have you been since last I saw you?"

He proceeded to tell her about the events that had transpired in his life—about Long Trail, about Mary Beth, and even about Molly Littlefield.

"I think your young lady is wise to insist that you reconnect with your mother. You should accept her with love and forgiveness. My son, it will make my passing easier, knowing that you will have another mother to love you as I have always done." Sister Maria closed her eyes.

Lee Edward checked her pulse, and her heart was beating steadily. He sat with her for about an hour, but she never awakened. Finally, he knew he must leave. He leaned down to kiss her hand.

"Goodbye, my mother. I will always love you."

A smile crossed her face, and he knew she had heard him.

* * *

LEE EDWARD JOINED Mary Beth in the plaza. She had been watching the boys play ball. They were kicking around a vulcanized brown leather ball that Lee Edward could have sworn was the same ball that was there when he left. He remembered that for many years when the "mysterious man" came to visit, he had brought a new ball. Had he thought about it, he would have asked Linus where he got them. He decided that from now on, he would arrange for Our Lady of Mercy to receive a supply of new balls.

"There you are," Mary Beth said when she saw Lee Edward coming toward him. "How is Sister Maria?"

"She's not well, but she is at peace," Lee Edward said. "And she brought a sense of peace to me. I know that one of the problems I have had in acknowledging Molly as my mother is that I thought I would be betraying Sister Maria. But in a blessing that only she could give, Sister Maria gave me permission to forgive Molly." He extended his hand to Mary Beth. "Shall we go?"

* * *

LEE EDWARD HAD no difficulty finding the house again. It was strange thinking of this as his mother's house. He and Mary Beth walked up onto the porch, and Lee Edward knocked on the door. A few seconds after he knocked, the door opened, and the expression of curiosity on Molly's face turned to one of anxiety.

"Lee Edward," she said in a hesitant voice, her hand moving toward her mouth.

"I've come to tell you I'm sorry for the way I acted when Linus and I were here before," Lee Edward said.

"You didn't do anything," Molly said.

"Oh yes, I did. That was no way to treat my mom."

Molly stared at Lee Edward for a long moment, then tears came to her eyes. "You...you called me mom," she said in a quiet, awed voice.

"Yes, I did, because you are my mother. May we come in?"

Molly stepped back from the door. "Yes, of course, please come in. I've told Emma about you, and she'll be excited to meet you."

"I'd like to get to know her as well."

"Emma, please come meet your brother," Molly called

as she led Lee Edward and Mary Beth into the parlor. "And his friend," she added.

Emma came into the room then, with a surprised expression on her face. "My new brother is here?"

"Come sit beside me, and you can be a part of our conversation." She pointed to the sofa, which had the effect of inviting Lee Edward and Mary Beth to sit together.

"Did you really grow up in an orphanage?" Emma asked.

"I did."

"Mama, why did Lee Edward live in an orphanage and not with us? I could have had a big brother all this time."

"Emma, she had no choice," Lee Edward said. He thought about going into the reasons behind her choice, but he decided that was better left unsaid.

"Was the orphanage a bad place?" Emma asked.

"No," Lee Edward answered, thinking about his emotional visit. "The Sisters were kind to all of us."

"You mean you have more sisters?"

Lee Edward chuckled, then Molly explained.

"He's talking about the ladies who ran the orphanage, dear. They are nuns of the church, and they are called Sisters. When you talk to them, that's how you address them, such as Sister Maria."

"You remembered Sister Maria," Lee Edward said. "I'm pleased."

"Oh, honey, I knew of Sister Maria long before you mentioned her. When I left you at the orphanage, I put you in her arms."

Lee Edward looked away. "I saw Sister Maria today. She is quite ill."

"I'm so sorry to hear that. I hope she will recover, because she is a young woman."

Lee Edward was silent.

"Forgive me," Molly said, turning to Mary Beth. "Where are my manners. Are you Lee Edward's special lady friend?"

"She is a lady, and she is my friend, so I would say yes," Lee Edward said.

Mary Beth looked at Lee Edward and smiled, before she answered. "My name is Mary Beth Hunter," she said. "And there is nothing to forgive. I'm just very glad that the two of you have come together now."

"Hunter," Molly said. "Of course, Hannah is your mother."

"You know my mother?" Mary Beth asked, the tone of her voice showing her surprise.

"Not exactly," Molly said. "For a while, I subscribed to the Mountain Sun. When I read that Edna had died, I wrote Jake a letter of condolence, but I never heard from him. Then I saw that he and Hannah Hunter had married, and then...well, I stopped taking the paper. Not long after that, Earl Littlefield asked me to marry him, and I did." She hugged her daughter to her. "And I got my baby here."

"Mama, I'm not a baby," Emma said.

"Of course, you're not," Lee Edward said. "How old are you?"

"I'm twelve," Emma said. "Are you and Miss Hunter going to get married?"

"Emma, you don't ask those kinds of questions," Molly said quickly.

Mary Beth was the one to step in. "Lee Edward and I are business partners. We own his father's ranch together, but who knows what will happen?"

"If you marry Lee Edward, then I would have a sister too, wouldn't I?"

"I think we should change the subject," Lee Edward said. "I'd like to hear about you and our mother."

The rest of the afternoon was spent with all four of them sharing stories. Mary Beth talked about Jake in a way that Lee Edward had never heard before. He told about growing up in the orphanage, Emma talked about her friends and school, and Molly told about working as a seamstress and being married to Earl.

"Mom," Lee Edward finally said. "I think it's time for Mary Beth and me to go."

"Oh, no," Molly said. "It's so late in the day. Why don't you spend the night with us? We have a room off the kitchen that has a bed for you, and Mary Beth can have my bed. I'll go in with Emma."

"I'd hate to put you out," Mary Beth said.

"Then you can come in with me," Emma said.

Mary Beth laughed. "I could at that."

* * *

MOLLY, Mary Beth, and Emma prepared supper while Lee Edward sat in the parlor listening to them talk. His thoughts wandered to Sister Maria, and he thought about how she had told him to be strong and faithful.

This trip to San Antonio had been filled with emotions. He had not thought about Long Trail, or Abe Hunter, or Rueben Pugh or any other potential problems he may be facing. When Mary Beth called him to the table, he could envision her as his wife.

Strong and faithful. He would try to live by those words no matter what lie ahead.

* * *

LEE EDWARD and Mary Beth were up before the sun rose.

"Don't you think you should eat breakfast?" Molly asked. "At least let me make some coffee."

"I wish we could," Lee Edward said, "but we need to get back to the ranch. We'll be passing through several towns, and we'll get a bite to eat on the way. The horses will need the rest anyway."

Molly walked to him and hugged him tightly. "I'm so glad we've found one another again. You'll come back, won't you?"

"Of course we will," Lee Edward said, hugging her back. "Who knows? Maybe you'll want to come to Long Trail."

Molly smiled, comprehending what Lee Edward was hinting. "I wouldn't miss it for the world." Then she embraced Mary Beth. "You take care of my son, you hear?"

"I'll do my best," Mary Beth said as she got onto her horse. "Tell Emma we said goodbye."

Molly nodded but didn't speak. She watched as the two rode away into the new dawn.

TWENTY-ONE

DOUBLE DIAMOND RANCH

"You know, Boss, even if you did get Holt to sell to you, you'd only get half the ranch. Mary Beth Hunter owns the other half," Bull Travers said.

"It doesn't matter," Reuben Pugh said. "When I take over the ranch, I won't do it by halves; I'll take the whole damn thing."

"How are you going to do that?" Travers asked.

"You just leave that to me," Pugh said.

* * *

After Lee Edward and Mary Beth returned from San Antonio, there was a perceptive difference in the way they acted around one another. They spent as much time together as they could, Mary Beth often finding reasons to be with him, or to ride around the ranch with him. On one such ride, she showed Lee her favorite place. It was on a little rise that was flanked by a couple of live oak trees that lent their shade to the little ridge. The ridge itself overlooked a swiftly flowing brook.

"I can see why you like this place," Lee Edward said. "It's peaceful."

"That's not the only reason I like it."

"Hmm, do I sense a story coming on?"

"I was six when Mama married Papa Jake. My dad had died a year earlier, and I didn't think Mama should have gotten married, but heaven knows, we were so much better off. Living in a wagon and trying to eke out a living running a stable was no fun for Mama or for Abe and me. As kids, we worked hard—putting out the clean straw or carrying water buckets or getting corn or oats when we could afford them. But I thought Papa Jake was trying to become part of our family.

"One day, Mama sat me down and told me that Papa Jake wasn't going anywhere, and I should just try to like him." She laughed. "As if that was going to be easy. I would sneak away and come to this spot and try to remember what it was like when my father was alive. I refused to call Papa Jake anything but Mr. Austin.

"One day, I was sitting here with my back against that tree. I didn't hear him come up, but he called my name. I about jumped out of my skin because he scared me so. He asked me if he could sit beside me. He sat there with his back against the tree, too, and before you know it, he pulled out some cookies and began munching on one. Then he asked me if I wanted one.

"We sat there until the cookies were gone, but we didn't talk. Then he started to get up, and I climbed into his arms and hugged him. From that time on, I was his girl, and I could do no wrong. And he became my Papa Jake."

"Hearing the stories that you tell, and those that my

mom told as well, I wish I had known him," Lee Edward said.

"You would have loved him as much as I did."

"I have no doubt that I would have," Jake replied. "But what about Abe? Did he and Jake get along?"

"Oh, I suppose they got along well enough," Mary Beth said. "But there was never any real love between them. Abe didn't cross Papa Jake."

"I wonder if that's how it will be between Abe and me, just sort of stay out of one another's way."

Mary Beth smiled at him. "As long as you don't try to stay out of my way..."

"I couldn't do that." Lee Edward kissed her. It started as a small, inconsequential kiss, but gradually grew into something much deeper before they separated. The kiss left both breathing hard.

"Yes, yes," she said breathlessly, kissing him again.

After the kiss, she smiled at him. "You're so concerned about Abe, but let me ask you. Which one of us do you want to take to the Fireman's Ball?"

"The Fireman's Ball?" Lee Edward replied.

"Yes, thank you. I would love to go with you," Mary Beth said.

Lee Edward chuckled. "Well, I'm glad you could accept my invitation."

* * *

THAT NIGHT AFTER SUPPER, Lee Edward went to the bunkhouse. He motioned for Hank Everson to meet him outside.

"What's up," Hank asked.

"I've got a problem," Lee Edward said. "Mary Beth asked me to go to the Fireman's Ball."

"Well, don't you want to go?"

"Of course I do, but I don't know how to dance."

Hank laughed. "The boys and I can help ya out. Come on in, and we'll clear a little space."

After they had moved the card table out of the way and moved a bunk or two, Hank told them what Lee Edward needed. Six men moved into position with Lee Edward and Hank making up a square.

"There ain't much to it," Buck Adams said. "Ya just gotta know what the caller wants you to do. The main thing is to listen to him and try to follow what the others do. Tim, get your fiddle, and let's teach the boss a thing or two."

Tim Kirby pulled out a fiddle that was old and dusty. "I ain't played this for a coon's age," Tim said. "Ain't sure I can do it anymore."

"Of course you can," Hank said. "All we need to do is tell him what the words mean and what he's supposed to do."

Well into the night, the bunkhouse was alive with music as Lee Edward learned what allemande left, do-si-do, promenade, ladies chain, and a host of other calls were.

"Men, I think I can do this," Lee Edward said as he wiped the sweat off his forehead. "I had no idea dancing was this much work."

"Just like ropin' calves," Tim said as he put his fiddle back in the case. "Once you know what you're a doin', it comes easy."

"Well, I appreciate what you've done to help me. I'm going to leave word with Moses to hold off breakfast in the morning so everybody can sleep an extra hour," Lee Edward said as he helped move the furniture back in place.

"Hey, we ain't had an extra hour of sleep since Christmas," Buck Adams said.

Lee Edward smiled. "Well, don't get used to it."

* * *

THE VOLUNTEER FIREMAN'S Ball was held in the wagon yard next to the sawmill. Planed wood planks had been laid out to form a good-sized dance floor. A stage had been built at one end, and along one side, several pieces of canvas had been placed over a frame. Benches were made out of rounds of wood with attached planks.

Lee Edward and Mary Beth had come into town in the Landau while most of the hands who were coming to the dance rode along behind them. The wagons were all being parked at the other end of the street next to the livery stable.

"Miss Hunter, could I have a dance with you?" Buck Adams asked.

"Sure," Mary Beth said.

"Me too," Tim Kirby added.

"All right."

"Don't forget me," Hank Everson asked.

"I'll add your name to my dance card," Mary Beth said.

"If you're going to dance with every one of the men, you're going to be one tired lady when we start home," Lee Edward said.

"I won't mind," Mary Beth said. "I'll just lean up against you and fall asleep."

"And I'll have to carry you into the house just like Sleeping Beauty."

When the Landau was parked, Lee Edward and Mary

Beth fell in behind others who were headed to the dance floor.

"I have to ask all of you'uns if you're a carryin'," the deputy city marshal said. "Iffin you are, Marshal Wallace says I have to take your guns down to the jail. We don't want no trouble at this here dance."

"We don't have a gun, Benny," Mary Beth said.

"I'm sorry, Miss Mary Beth. It's the fella I want to hear from," Benny Carr said.

"Miss Hunter is correct—no gun," Lee Edward said.

"Then you move right on through that gate," Benny said. "And in case you didn't know, they's a molasses can a settin' there. Iffin you want to drop in a coin or somethin', the firemen will be much obliged."

"We'll do that," Mary Beth replied with a broad smile.

"Then all I can say is enjoy the dancin'," Benny said.

* * *

WHEN LEE EDWARD and Mary Beth arrived, there were dancers moving around on the floor. Lee Edward stopped to watch what they were doing, and he listened carefully to what the caller was saying. He smiled as he saw that they were indeed doing the same things Hank and the boys had taught him in the bunkhouse.

"Oh, isn't it wonderful?" Mary Beth asked. "I love coming to dances. Someday, Kerrville will have a grand hotel with a ballroom, and we won't have to dance outside in the heat. Oh look, another square is forming. If we hurry, we can join them."

* * *

LEE EDWARD and Mary Beth danced several dances before they took a break, and with a glass of punch and a couple pieces of penuche candy, they found a seat away from everyone else.

"You surprised me, Lee Edward. I was wondering if you knew how to dance, because I don't expect you had many dances at the orphanage?"

Lee Edward chuckled. "You're right about that."

"Then where did you learn to dance so well?"

"I was told all you have to do is listen to what the caller says. It's like roping a calf. When you know all the moves, it's easy."

Clem Porter, one of the Long Trail hands, came over to them then and in a shy and hesitant way, cleared his throat, then he stood there, silent for a long moment.

"What is it, Clem?" Mary Beth asked.

"Miss Hunter, I was just wonderin', I mean, iffin you wouldn' mind 'n Mr. Holt, why iffin he don't mind neither, uh..." Porter came to a complete halt, then stood there in embarrassed silence.

Mary Beth smiled at him. "Clem, would you like to dance with me?"

A big smile spread across Clem's face. "Oh, yes, ma'am, more'n anything."

"Well then, it looks like the band is about ready to start the next song, so why don't we go find us a square?"

Porter held his arm out, and Mary Beth took it. She followed him out onto the dance floor.

Lee Edward walked over to the punch bowl to refill his cup. He stood under the canvas canopy, listening and watching. He thought about Sister Maria, and how if she could be here, she would be patting her foot under her habit. But then he thought of the last time he had seen her. Typhoid was a deadly disease, and even all the prayers that would be said for her may not have returned her to health. The next time he came to town, he would have to remember to send a note to the Mother Superior inquiring about her health.

"What are you a' doin' here?" someone asked in a belligerent tone.

"Haven't you heard?" Lee Edward replied. "They're having a big party here tonight, so I brought a young lady to the dance."

"Yeah, but it ain't for you. This here dance is for the ons who work, not some high-falutin son of a bitch who don't never get his hands dirty."

"Travers, Mr. Holt does more work in an hour than you do in a whole day," Billy Tanner said. "So why don't you get over there with the other trash from the Double Diamond?"

Bull Travers was a good-sized man, thus the nickname Bull. But he had seen Billy Tanner in a prize fight held at the stock auction last year. Tanner was in four matches, and he won every one.

"It just don't seem right to me, is all," Travers said. "You Long Trail cowboys is different. Why you think ya hafta sidle up to yer boss? At the Double Diamond, Mr. Pugh lets us be. We don't kowtow to nobody."

The music ended, and Mary Beth joined Lee Edward and Billy near the punch bowl. "I saw Bull Travers talking to you. Was there any trouble?"

"No trouble, ma'am," Billy said.

"He's not a good man," Mary Beth said as she got another cup of punch. "But then, anyone who'd be foreman for the Double Diamond brand wouldn't be worth much. Not a one of them who works for Reuben Pugh is worth a plug nickel."

Lee Edward chuckled. "Somehow I get the idea you don't care much for the Double Diamond."

"Wow, you're quick on the uptake, aren't you?" Mary Beth teased.

* * *

THE DANCE ENDED JUST after midnight, and as Lee Edward drove the Landau back home, with Mary Beth resting against his shoulder, Hank Everson, Tim Kirby, Billy Tanner, Clem Porter, Buck Adams, Hal Crader, and Stump Brewer rode alongside.

Lee Edward was just wishing he could be alone with Mary Beth when someone fired a shot from the side of the road.

"Uhhn," Stump Brewer grunted, and he fell from his horse.

Everyone but Brewer and Porter started toward the place where the shot had come from. Porter dismounted to see about Brewer.

"Mary Beth, get down!" Lee Edward said. "Get in the ditch on the side of the road."

"But my dress," Mary Beth complained.

"I can buy a new dress, I can't buy a new you."

"All right," Mary Beth agreed, climbing down from the Landau.

"How does it look?" Lee Edward asked, joining Clem alongside Stump."

"It's just inside his shoulder," Clem said.

Hank returned to the Landau. "Looks like it was just one shooter, and he got away. How's Stump?"

"We're going to have to take him back to town to see a doctor," Lee Edward said.

"Doc's not goin' to like being woke up in the middle of the night," Clem said.

"When someone decides to become a doctor, they expect to be awakened in the middle of the night," Lee Edward said.

"Dr. Telfer won't mind anyway. He's good about that," Mary Beth said. "I'll be coming with you."

"Stump, we're going to put you in the back of the carriage," Lee Edward said.

"I'll ride back there with him," Mary Beth said. "Do any of you have a knife?"

"Lord ma'am, you ain't a' gonna try 'n cut the bullet out your ownself, are you?" Porter asked.

"No, I'm going to cut off some of my petticoat to stuff into the wound so I can stop the bleeding."

"Oh, well then, yeah, I got a pocket knife," Porter said.

Mary Beth cut a strip from her petticoat, then pushed it down into the bullet hole.

"Are we ready?" Lee Edward asked.

"Yes, let's go. And be quick about it," Mary Beth said.

"We'll all go with you to help you get him into the doctor's office," Hank said. "Then we'll come back with you. I don't think you should come back alone, not after this."

"We'll be all right," Lee Edward said.

Hank smiled. "Yeah, I know you'll be all right, because we'll all be with you."

Hank turned to Buck. "Take Stump's horse with you."

Lee Edward turned the carriage around.

"Hang on, back there," Lee Edward called out as he whipped the team into a gallop.

They were back in town in less than fifteen minutes.

Mary Beth directed him to the doctor's office, and as soon as they got there, Mary Beth stepped up onto the porch and began banging on the door as hard as she could.

"Dr. Telfer! Dr. Telfer! Please come! It's Mary Beth Hunter."

The house was dark inside, but after a few more knocks and calls, they saw a light inside.

The man who opened the door was rather short, white-headed, and with glasses. He was wearing a nightshirt and carrying a lantern.

"Mary Beth, what is it?" he asked.

"Stump Brewer's been shot, Dr. Telfer," Mary Beth said. "We got him here as fast as we could."

"Bring him in."

With Lee Edward on one side, and Hank on the other, they helped Stump walk into the house, then follow Dr. Telfer back to his operating room.

"Put him there on the table," Dr. Telfer said. "Let me get some more light so I can see."

Dr. Telfer brought another, larger lantern that was backed by a concaved, mirrored disk. The result was a brighter light that illuminated the wound.

"Who put this in here?" Dr. Telfer asked as he pulled out the petticoat wad that Mary Beth had stuffed down into the wound.

"Uh, I did," Mary Beth replied, not sure now that she should have done it.

Dr. Telfer nodded. "Good job. You stopped the bleeding and might have saved his life. We'll see where this bullet lodged."

The doctor cut off Stump's shirt and undershirt, then examined the wound more closely.

"I don't think the bullet hit anything vital, but it's still in there, and it's going to have to come out."

Dr. Telfer got a piece of gauze and put it across Stump's nose and throat. Then he poured about a teaspoon of chloroform onto the gauze.

"Mary Beth, hold the gauze there until I tell you to lift it."

Mary Beth held the gauze in place, and Dr. Telfer watched Stump until he was sure that the young cowboy was under.

"All right, lift the gauze, but be ready to put it back down if I tell you to."

Mary Beth lifted the gauze, and Dr. Telfer started digging for the bullet. After a moment or two, Stump groaned and moved.

"Put it back," Dr. Telfer ordered.

Mary Beth put the gauze in place and held it there until she was told to lift it again.

It was only a few minutes before Dr. Telfer held up the bullet. "I got it," he said with a grin.

Within ten more minutes, he had sewn up the bullet hole.

"All right, you folks can go home now. Let me keep Stump here with me for the rest of the night and more than likely tomorrow, too, and the next day after that, you can come get him."

"Is he goin' to be all right, Doc?" Hank asked.

"I think he'll be good as new," Dr. Telfer said. "Or at least as good as he was before he was hit."

Mary Beth yawned, and Lee Edward put his arm around her. "Come on, let's get you home and put to bed."

* * *

BOTH HANNAH and Abe were waiting up for them when they got back to the ranch.

"Mary Beth, where have you been?" Hannah demanded. Abe was scowling at both of them.

"We've been at the doctor's office," Mary Beth said.

The expression of anger on Hannah's face was replaced with one of concern. "Good Lord, what happened? Are you all right?"

"Yes, I'm fine, it wasn't me. It was Stump Brewer. He was shot as we were coming home."

"Shot?" Abe asked. "How, where?"

"We weren't far from town when someone took a shot at us from the side of the road," Lee Edward said. "Hank and the boys went after the shooter, but they didn't see who it was. When we saw Stump was hit, we took him back in to see the doc."

* * *

"DID YOU KILL 'IM?" Alan Simpson asked.

"I don't know, I think I did. I know I saw someone fall off his horse."

"Fall off his horse?"

"Yeah, after I shot him though, the others started comin' for me, and I had to get out of there."

"That wasn't Holt, you dumbass. Holt was driving the carriage."

Twenty-Two

RUBEN PUGH WAS SITTING IN AN OUTER OFFICE, reading a newspaper as he waited for his appointment. The clerk came out then.

"Mr. Pugh, he'll see you now."

"Thank you."

Pugh folded over the newspaper, then put it on the table beside the chair where he was sitting. He followed the clerk to the back office.

"It's Mr. Pugh, sir," the clerk said, sticking his head in through the door.

"Yes, come in, Ruben, come in."

Pugh went into the office. "Thank you for seeing me."

"I've gone over your proposal. Are you sure you want to do this?"

"I'm absolutely sure."

"But I thought you and Austin were having some difficulty over property lines?"

"That was with Austin, not with the new owner."

"I certainly hope he appreciates what you're doing for

him." The man shoved some papers across the desk. "These are for you. Everything is in order, I believe."

"Thanks," Pugh said. "I'd just as soon keep this between the two of us."

"I understand."

"Lee Edward, before the next payday, you might want to go to the bank and get your name added to the ranch's account," Linus said.

"Shouldn't Mary Beth be in on that? And what about Hannah and Abe?"

"Jake had Mary Beth's name on the account already." Linus chuckled. "Heck, right now, she's the only one who *can* write a check."

"Do you think the bank will just let me do that—put my name on the account without her being there?" Lee Edward asked.

Linus smiled. "You won't have any problem. Mary Beth wrote out a letter telling the banker that you're half owner, and that she wants you on the account. Burt will recognize her handwriting, and if we have to, we can have Fitzgerald come in and swear you're half-owner."

The ride into town was uneventful, but when they passed where they had been fired on after the dance, Lee Edward left the road to examine the spot.

"Did you find anything?" Linus asked when he returned.

"Not really. It looks like there was only one set of tracks, but I can't be sure of that. I should have come out here the next morning," Lee Edward said. "Do you have any idea who could have done this?"

"It's hard to say. I don't think Stump Brewer was the target," Linus said. "There's no cowboy in the whole county who's better liked."

"Maybe it was just some cowpoke who had too much

to drink, and he was just firing his gun at nobody in particular."

"Or maybe he didn't know who was driving the carriage." Linus looked directly at Lee Edward.

"What do you mean? I was driving," Lee Edward said. "Nobody knows me or anything about me."

"There might be somebody who would stand to gain something if you weren't around."

"Now wait a minute—you aren't accusing Abe of taking a shot at us, because if you are, I don't believe it."

Linus chuckled. "No, I don't think even Abe would stoop that low. He's got his hen feathers ruffled, but he'll get over it. We both know he's kind of sore because he didn't inherit the ranch."

"I hope so," Lee Edward said. "I don't know if you're aware of it, but I'm sort of keen on Mary Beth."

"Oh, I have to say that's some secret," Linus said. "Only me and every other cowboy on the ranch kind of know what you two think about one another."

Lee Edward's face flushed, even through his sun-bronzed skin.

"Mr. Holt, we all think you're moving fast."

"Too fast, do you think?"

"Not as long as Mary Beth doesn't think you're moving too fast and all of us think she's just as starry-eyed as you are. Now don't say I told you, but we've all got bets down on how long it takes you to marry her."

"I guess it was best for me not to have moved into the bunkhouse when I got here."

"I'd say it wouldn't have been a good idea."

* * *

THE RANCH WAS FAIRLY close to Kerrville, so it was an easy ride into town. They rode side by side so they could continue their conversation.

When they arrived in town, Linus stopped in front of the Saddle and Bit Saloon. He dismounted and tied his horse to the hitching rail.

"I thought we were going to the bank," Lee Edward said.

"That can wait," Linus said. "Have you been in here yet?"

"I can't say that I have."

The bar was empty except for the bartender and four men who were sitting at a table near the back. They were engaged in a game of cards, and they didn't look up when Linus and Lee Edward came in.

"Well, if it ain't old Linus Walker makin' his way to town," the bartender said.

"It's been a while," Linus said. "Mr. Holt, this is Sam Gentry, and he's a good man to know."

"Mr. Holt," Sam said as he looked Lee Edward over. Then he began nodding his head. "I guess the gossip's true. You kinda favor your old man."

Lee Edward had a look of surprise on his face.

Linus laughed. "Here I was gonna tell you all about the changes at Long Trail, but you already know about Mr. Holt."

"A lot of talk goes on in a place like this," Sam said. "I know one thing—your cow hands think you're an all right boss, and that's good enough for me." He extended his hand. "Happy to meet you, Mr. Holt."

It felt awkward for Lee Edward to be called Mr. Holt all the time, but as that was how Linus usually addressed him, he accepted it. "And I'm pleased to meet you, too.

But right now, I think my foreman and I could use a mug of beer."

* * *

WHEN THEY LEFT the Saddle and Bit, Linus took him to the Schreiner's Bank, where Linus introduced Lee Edward to Burt Rowe, the bank vice president.

"Is Mr. Schreiner around?" Linus asked. "I want to introduce him to Long Trail's new owner."

"Charles isn't here," Rowe said. "You know he turned Live Oak into a sheep ranch, and he has to spend a lot of time up there."

"I suppose we don't need him. We have to get it fixed so Mr. Holt can start paying some bills," Linus said.

"Good, good," Rowe said. "I was wondering how this was going to be handled now that Jake is gone."

"As I'm sure Mr. Fitzgerald told you, Miss Hunter and I are now co-owners. She sent a letter requesting that my name be added to the account," Lee Edward said.

"That's easy to take care of," Rowe said. He withdrew a paper from a drawer in his desk. "All we need is your signature on this card. You can see Miss Hunter's name is already there."

Lee Edward signed the paper and slid it across the desk. "I'm glad that's taken care of."

"Oh, as a reminder, your first payment will be due by the end of this month."

"First payment?" Linus asked, his voice reflecting his confusion. "What payment would that be?"

"Oh, you didn't know? Just a minute, and I'll show you," Rowe said. He put the signature card back in place and then pulled out another paper.

"Two years ago, when so many cows died during the

big blizzard, Jake borrowed money to replace them," Burt said, "and then last year, when the range dried up and the cattle were so thin, he didn't make enough to pay off the loan. Mr. Schreiner didn't think it was good business to continue to base the loan on the stock, so Jake put the ranch up as collateral."

"You mean the ranch is mortgaged?" Lee Edward asked in a rising tone of voice.

"Oh, indeed it is. To the tune of eight thousand dollars."

"And you say the first payment is due the end of the month?" Lee Edward asked.

"Yes, one-half of it, plus interest," Rowe said. "That would be four thousand three hundred dollars, and it's due by June thirtieth."

"That's only ten more days. Do we have that much in the bank?"

"I believe so," Rowe said. "Why don't we check?"

Rowe riffled through a wooden box until he found the Long Trail account. "All right," he said. "Let's just take a look here."

Rowe examined the record, and as he did so, the easy smile left his face.

"Oh, my," he said. "Oh my, oh my, oh my."

"What is it, Burt?" Linus asked.

"There's only eleven hundred dollars remaining in the account. It would appear that a rather sizable withdrawal was recently made. Nine thousand dollars, to be exact. It was transferred to another account that Mr. Fitzgerald controls."

"Fitzgerald? Can't we get it back?" Linus asked, surprised by the announcement.

"I'm afraid not. The money will be disbursed after the probate closes."

"Will this debt be paid before the money is given to those who will inherit?" Lee Edward asked.

"If it is, I know you can have the two thousand that's coming to me, and I'll bet Hannah will give up her money to keep the ranch," Linus said.

"I'm sorry, it doesn't work that way. The money is in the hands of the court now," Rowe said. "It could be tied up for months, and you don't have that kind of time."

"Is there any way we can get an extension on the loan?" Lee Edward asked.

"Oh, I'm sure we can. Mr. Adams is our loan director. Let's go see him."

"All right."

Lee Edward and Linus followed Rowe from his office to a much smaller one, where they saw a very thin man with a closely cropped mustache. He had papers laid out on a table, and he looked up as they went in.

"Richard, this is Lee Edward Holt. He's the new owner of Long Trail."

"Nice to meet you, Mr. Holt," Adams said.

"Mr. Adams," Lee Edward said.

"We're going to need to give Mr. Holt an extension on the loan Jacob Austin took out with us," Rowe said.

"We can't do that, Burt. The Long Trail note was one of the ones we sold to The Cattleman's Association."

"Oh, that's right, isn't it? They bought four of five loans from us," Rowe said. He turned to Lee Edward. "If you'll go see Mr. Patterson, I'm sure you won't have any trouble getting the extension you need."

"Did you know about this, Linus?" Lee Edward asked after they left the bank.

"No, I didn't know anything about it," Linus said.

"Wouldn't he have checked with you first?"

"Don't forget, Lee Edward, Jake owned the ranch.

There was no need for him to check with me about anything. Though, I must admit I'm a little surprised that he didn't at least mention a loan to me. He was always pretty open about his business, and he liked to keep me up on what was going on, just to have someone to talk it out with."

Their next stop was the Kerr County Cattlemen's Association where Lee Edward was introduced to Marcus Patterson, the association president.

"Mr. Holt is the new owner of Long Trail," Linus said.

"Good, good," Patterson said. "It'll be a good thing to get Long Trail active in the association again."

"Yes, I intend to do that, but apparently you and I have some business to attend to," Lee Edward said.

"Oh, you don't have to do anything. Long Trail is already a member of the association. When I said get you active, I just meant to have you attend our meetings," Patterson said.

"It's not that," Lee Edward said. "The Cattlemen's Association holds a loan on Long Trail. I didn't make the loan, though of course I'm responsible for it. I'd like to have the loan extended."

Patterson shook his head. "Things have changed— your loan now belongs to Ruben Pugh over at the Double Diamond."

"Ruben Pugh?" Linus sputtered.

"Yes, he came in just a few days ago," Patterson said.

"Now, would you mind telling me just why in the hell you sold the loan to that man?" Linus asked.

"Well, he's a member of the Cattlemen's Association, and he's in good standing, I might add," Patterson said. "I'm surprised you didn't know about it because he said he was doing it as a favor to you. Just being a good neighbor."

"A favor, my ass," Linus said. "Let's get out of here."

* * *

"WHAT DO YOU THINK THIS MEANS?" Lee Edward asked when they left the Cattlemen's Association building.

"You've had a couple of run-ins with Pugh," Linus said. "And what was he after every time?"

"Long Trail."

"I'll just say it right out, Pugh is a low-life son of a bitch. He's only been in the county a couple of years, and he's been a pain in the ass for the whole time. He's been buying up small ranches and farms right and left, until I'd say the Double Diamond is almost as big as Long Trail," Linus said. "I'd bet my last dollar that buying this loan is some scheme to take over the ranch. He probably thought the payment date would come around and you'd miss it and then the land would be his."

"What I'm hearing is, he's not going to give us an extension," Lee Edward said.

"Not a chance. Since the original loan was from the bank, Pugh will, no doubt, call in the four thousand dollars that's due."

"Plus interest," Lee Edward added.

"I'm afraid so."

"Well, we won't know if we don't talk to him."

"All right, we'll go over there, but I don't think it'll do any good."

* * *

THE TWO MEN had been riding for about an hour when they saw the sign for the Double Diamond Ranch. There were two joined diamonds under the name of the ranch.

"Not hard to figure out what the brand is," Lee Edward said. "Smart."

"Yeah, well, I like the Long Trail brand better," Linus said. "The bottom of the L forms the top of the T so that the two letters are joined."

"Yeah, I have to agree, that's a good one too. I suppose Jake came up with that."

"No, the brand has been with the land since the very beginning. I don't know who the original owner was. Maybe it was part of a Spanish land grant."

As they started toward the ranch headquarters, they saw a rider coming toward them.

"That's Jim Grayson," Linus said.

"Hello, Walker. What can I do for you, fellas?"

"We need to see Pugh," Linus said.

"What about?"

"Well, whatever it is, it would be between Pugh and us, wouldn't it?" Lee Edward replied.

"Who are you?" Grayson asked.

"This is Mr. Holt," Linus said. "He owns Long Trail now."

"I'll take you to him."

Pugh stood to meet Lee Edward and Linus when Grayson took them to him. He was smiling, but there was more smugness than friendship in the smile.

"Well, well, well, so, we meet again, Mr. Holt," Pugh said. "And I think I might have an idea why."

"I'm sure you do," Lee Edward replied.

"Well, what can I do for you, sir?"

"Let's not beat around the bush here, Pugh. You hold a note due on Long Trail."

"That's true."

"What made you decide to act as a bank?"

"Let's just say I was doing a favor for a neighbor," Pugh said.

"But that wasn't necessary, was it?" Lee Edward asked. "As I understand it, the loan was first made at Schreiner's Bank, and then they sold it to the Cattlemen's Association. There was no need for you to buy the note."

"I guess you could say that," Pugh said. "By the way, you might need to know that in buying the loan, I was able to change the due date. Your loan is due the twenty-eighth of June."

"Wait a minute, that's only a week away," Linus said. "That doesn't leave Mr. Holt much time to raise four thousand dollars. It's going to be pretty damn hard to do."

"Yes, I'm afraid it will be, especially since it isn't four thousand. I'm afraid that in a week, I'm calling the note. You'll owe me the full amount, eight thousand dollars plus six hundred for interest," Pugh said, his smug smile growing even larger.

TWENTY-THREE

"PUGH HOLDS THE NOTE?" ABE HUNTER SAID.

"I'm afraid so," Lee Edward said.

Abe shook his head. "Of all the people in Texas, Ruben Pugh is, without doubt, the worst person to be involved with us."

"Yeah, I have to agree with you," Lee Edward said.

"And there's nothing we can do to stop him," Abe said. "He'll get Long Trail."

"That's not necessarily so," Lee Edward said.

"Oh. Do you have eight-thousand-six-hundred dollars?" Abe asked.

"No, but we do have a sizable herd of cattle, and we've got a week to raise the money. Linus, do you think we can get the cattle to San Antonio in no more than three days and then be back in two if we push it?"

"If nothing goes wrong, we can do it," Linus said. "That will give us two days leeway to beat the date the loan's due."

"This isn't the season," Abe said. "If we take these

cows to market now, we'll get a whole lot less than what we'd get this fall."

"I know that," Lee Edward said. "When I was at Marathon, we had to take cattle to market a couple of times out of season, and we never got less than twenty-five dollars a head. I know Peter Hamilton, one of the buyers there. If we took four hundred head, we'd get ten thousand dollars. That would pay off the note and give us operating expenses until we're ready to make another drive in the fall," Lee Edward said.

"Yeah," Abe said. "Yeah, you're right. I don't think we have any other choice. We have to take them to market."

"I'll let the men know what we have ahead of us," Linus said. "It'll take some preparation, but we're up for it. Especially if it will keep Ruben Pugh from taking over Long Trail."

"Good. Abe and I will be counting on you for that. Won't we, Abe?"

"Uh, yeah," Abe said, surprised that Lee Edward had included him in the comment.

"Linus, how long do you think it'll take us to get ready?" Lee Edward asked.

"Moses will have to get the chuck wagon ready, but knowin' him, he'll work all night," Linus said. "We can start rounding up the cows as soon as I tell the boys, and we should be ready to leave before daybreak tomorrow. It won't be the prettiest trail drive, but we'll get these beeves to San Antonio in three days."

"All right," Lee Edward said. "That's what I want to hear."

Linus nodded, then he and Abe started toward the barn. Lee Edward was going to go as well, but decided he needed to tell Mary Beth what was going on.

* * *

"Did you have any trouble getting your name on the account?" Mary Beth asked.

"No, that part went through easy enough."

"What do you mean *that part*?"

"It turns out we have a loan due by the end of this month."

"That shouldn't be a problem. I know that loan is from when we had to buy more stock after the freeze-out. Papa Jake got an extension more than once, and I know Mr. Schreiner will do it again."

"We don't have a loan with the bank."

"Oh? I thought you said we had a loan due by the end of the month."

"Yes, but it's not with the bank. The loan is with Ruben Pugh."

"What?" The word literally exploded from Mary Beth. "How can that be? Papa Jake would never have taken out a loan from Pugh."

"He didn't. The loan was at the bank, then it was sold to The Cattleman's Association, then re-sold to Pugh."

"I didn't know you could do that."

"I didn't either," Lee Edward admitted.

"What are we going to do?"

"We're going to sell some cows," Lee Edward said.

* * *

The next morning, the cowboys who were going were up before dawn. They called out and shouted excitedly and laughed and whistled at horses and each other. They banged around the barn and corral, loading wagons and preparing equipment for the drive. Moses was getting ready as well, having moved his operation from the kitchen to the chow wagon. He was cooking breakfast in the chow wagon so that the aroma of bacon and coffee permeated the preparation area.

Mary Beth hadn't asked Lee Edward or Abe if she could go on the drive, because she was afraid they would say no. But the more she thought about it, the more she realized she didn't have to ask anyone. Half of the cows they would be selling belonged to her. But just to avoid an argument, she decided to wait until they had already pulled out. Then her plan was to catch up with the herd and join with the others.

She didn't want her mother to wonder where she was, though, so she told her what she was going to do.

"Oh, honey, are you sure you want to do that?" Hannah asked. "It's not going to be a pleasant ride. It takes two days to get there by stagecoach and you know it's going to be longer than that to take a herd. Abe said they will be pushing the cows hard."

"You know I'm a good rider, Mama. Every bit as good as Abe, and I don't see a problem."

"Well, what about this? You'll be the only woman among nine or ten men."

"First of all, most of those men have worked here for at least three or four years or longer, and I trust them. Also, Abe, Linus, and Lee Edward will be part of the drive, and you know they're going to look out for me."

"If there's nothing I can say to stop you, just be careful. That's all that I ask. And know that Lee Edward isn't going to have time to look after you."

"I will, Mama," Mary Beth said, giving her mother a hug.

Within an hour after leaving, Mary Beth caught up with the herd. She could see the dark shapes of cattle moving under a billowing cloud of dust. She could see individual plumes of dust behind running horsemen as cowboys dashed hither and yon to keep the animals from turning back.

Lee Edward had just pushed an errant steer back into the herd when he saw a rider approaching. The person was too far away to be identified when the rider first came into view, and for an instant, he thought it may be someone from the Double Diamond coming to say the cows stayed with the ranch. But as the distance was closed, he was surprised to see that it was Mary Beth. Turning his horse, he rode back to meet her.

"What are you doing out here?" he asked in a sharper tone of voice than he would have wanted to use when he spoke to Mary Beth.

Mary Beth chuckled. "Yes, I'm glad to see you too."

"You know what I mean. This is no place for a woman."

"Perhaps not, but it's a place for someone who owns half of these cows you're taking to market."

Lee Edward took off his hat and wiped the dirt off his face. "All right, but we're going to push these cows as hard as possible. Since you're here and I've seen you ride, I'll expect you to ride herd." He stopped, and a smile crossed his face. "Since you own half the herd, I won't make you ride drag."

"That's decent of you," Mary Beth said. Then, she suddenly darted away from him, and he saw her going after a cow that had strayed away from the herd. She caught up with the cow and then skillfully pushed it back to join the others.

Lee Edward chuckled. He knew that one of the drovers would have handled the errant bovine, but he also knew that Mary Beth had done it, to show that her presence wouldn't be a drag on the drive.

Lee Edward and Mary Beth rode close to one another when they could, but their visiting was curtailed due to the frequent need to attend to one task or another.

It was summer, and throughout the long, hot day, the sun beat down relentlessly on the drovers and the animals. Mercifully, the yellow glare of the midday summer sky mellowed into a somewhat less oppressive blue of early evening. By the time they reached the bedding ground, the sun was a great, red disc that paused for a brief time just above the horizon, having lost much of its oppressive glare and heat. A low layer of clouds was underlit by the sun, and they glowed orange in the darkening sky.

Moses had prepared a quick supper, and as soon as the meal was over, everyone, including Mary Beth, opened their bedrolls and took advantage of the cool respite of the late evening. The herd was spread out before them, a large shuffling shadow within shadows. For the moment, the herd stood still, content with resting for the night.

Hank Everson and Hal Crader were riding nighthawk, and for the moment, Hank was just sitting in the saddle, his horse still, as he looked out over the herd. Hank heard something and jerked his head around, looking toward the source of the sound of creaking leather. Crader came riding out of the darkness.

"I've circled the herd," Crader said. "They all look quiet."

"Good, that's the way we like it," Hank said. "Hope the next two days pass with no trouble."

The two men rode on slowly. The cattle lowed softly, and the whippoorwills called noisily.

After a few minutes of riding, Crader broke the silence with a question.

"How long have you known Mr. Holt?"

"I've known him at least ten years, ever since he came from the orphanage to Marathon," Hank replied.

"Is it true he was just a cowboy?"

"Well, he was a cowboy, yes, but I wouldn't say he was *just* a cowboy. I mean he took on really quick right after he got there, and pretty soon, he was probably the best hand Marathon had. I know Ray thought so."

"Who was Ray?" Crader asked.

"Ray Dockins. He was our foreman."

"Well I'm a heap of glad that he's the boss now and not Abe Hunter."

"What was Mr. Austin like?" Hank asked.

"Oh, he was top-notch. Ever' one that rode for the LT brand liked him. It was really sad when he was kilt, 'n I'm tellin' you right now, I'd like to know who the son of a bitch is that shot 'im, 'cause if I had him in my gunsight, I'd drop him in a cowboy minute."

They rode in silence for a few more minutes until Crader spoke again.

"The ranch is in trouble, ain't it?"

"Why do you say that?" Hank asked.

"The reason I ask is 'cause I know this ain't the normal time we take our cows to market. 'N I figured if it was in trouble, you 'n the boss, bein' old friends like you are, that he might have told you."

"He didn't tell me not to tell anybody else, so I reckon I can tell you," Hank replied. "The truth is, the ranch is in some debt, and if the debt's not paid off by the end of the week, Lee Edward and Mary Beth can lose the ranch."

"Damn, you mean the bank won't give him a little longer to pay it off, seeing as how he just got here?"

"That's just it. The loan isn't with the bank. It's Ruben Pugh that holds the note."

"Wait a minute, they's somethin' fishy here. Mr. Austin and Pugh hated each other. I don't believe for one moment that he would borrow money from Pugh, 'n I don't believe that bastard would make him a loan, even if Mr. Austin did try."

"Pugh bought the loan papers, so now the money is owed to him."

"Damn, I didn't even know a body could do that," Crader said.

"Me neither, but that's what he done."

* * *

AFTER THE COWBOYS had bedded down close to the chuck wagon and the rhythmic sound of soft snores were heard, Lee Edward led Mary Beth away from the encampment. He found a large rock, and they were sitting side by side, looking out over the quiet herd.

"A hard day," Lee Edward said, "and I'm glad you decided to tag along."

"I'm surprised Abe came along," Mary Beth said.

"I am too, but I'm pleased that he came."

"You know he wants to save the ranch as much as you do," Mary Beth said.

"Yeah, well they say it's an ill wind that blows nobody good. Maybe the ill wind of this possible loan default will take away some of the hostility between Abe and me," Lee Edward said.

"Who knows, maybe he'll realize that fate has put us together, and he won't stand in the way of our courtship."

Lee Edward chuckled. "Fate, is it?"

"Yes, fate. I mean, look at us. Both of us use two names. You're Lee Edward, and I'm Mary Beth. Don't you think that is unusual?"

Lee Edward stuck out his hand for a handshake. "It's nice to meet a young lady who, like me, has two names."

"Oh, we can do better than a handshake," Mary Beth said. Reaching up to put the palm of her hand on his cheek, she turned his face toward her, then moved in for a kiss.

After a long and deep kiss, they separated.

"Wow," Lee Edward said quietly. "That fate that you're talking about is a wonderful thing."

They sat together, enjoying their surroundings and talking quietly. Finally Lee Edward tipped her face toward his. He kissed her gently and then called time.

"We'd better get back to our bedrolls," Lee Edward said. "We've got two hard days ahead of us."

* * *

MOSES HAD breakfast ready for them by sun up. Breakfast took no more than half an hour, then the cowboys got the herd moving again. This day was even harder than the day before had been. The day was longer, and Lee Edward could swear that it was hotter.

There had been very little water today, and as the cows became more restless, the cowboys had to work to keep them moving.

Then, at mid-afternoon, there was the unmistakable sound of a pistol shot. The cattle nearest the sound of the shot jumped and started to run. That spread quickly through the rest of the herd so that in a matter of seconds, the herd was running out of control.

"Stampede!"

It was more a cry of determination than fear, because every man on this drive had been through stampedes before, and they knew exactly what to do to stop it.

Lee Edward was riding on the left side of the herd when the stampede started. Mary Beth was riding with him, and to Lee Edward's horror, the herd was swinging toward the left, thundering hoofbeats, bellowing calls, four hundred animals moving together in the blistering heat.

The stampeded cattle raised a huge cloud of dust so thick that Lee Edward could no longer see the herd. He could barely see Mary Beth, and her safety was more important to him than stopping the stampede.

To Lee Edward's surprise, Mary Beth, instead of running away, galloped to the head of the herd to join the other cowboys in turning the stampeding cattle. Lee Edward no longer had time to worry about her. They needed to stop this stampede, and the only way to do it was to force the cattle into milling. By doing that, the cattle would continue to run until they were tired out, then gradually, they would quit running in a circle and return to the long, slow walk they had been on since leaving Long Trail.

Twenty-Four

Learning that Lee Edward Holt was taking a herd of cows to the market, Ruben Pugh, who could move much faster than a herd of cattle on the march, hurried on ahead of them. He had chosen to stay in a barrio close to San Antonio and he had taken a room at the Compadre Cantina. Now, he was enjoying a drink with Josefina, one of the bar girls, who had joined him at his table.

They had just concluded a business arrangement where Josefina had agreed to come visit him in his room after eleven o'clock.

He looked up as Bull Travers came into the cantina, stood just inside the door, looked around, spotted Pugh, then with a grin, crossed through the room.

"Have a seat, Bull," Pugh invited, pushing a chair out with his foot.

"Oh, you should have been there," Travers said. "One

little shot, 'n them cows started runnin' like they had a torch tied to their tail."

"Did they get them under control?"

"I stayed on for about half an hour, 'n they hadn't got 'em stopped yet. It's goin' to, for sure, cost 'em an extra day."

Pugh smiled. "One extra day is all I'll need. How many head do you think he's bringing?"

"I didn't get a good count, but I'd say it's close to five hundred," Bull said.

"That's good enough."

* * *

WITH THE HERD

"We're not goin' to get there tomorrow," Linus said.

Linus, Lee Edward, Mary Beth, and Abe were sitting around a low-burning campfire, drinking coffee. Supper had been served a couple of hours earlier, and most of the others were doing the same thing in at least two more little groups. Crader and Porter were riding night hawk.

"You really don't think we'll get there tomorrow?" Abe asked. "By my calculation, we've only got about thirty-five more miles to go."

"The cattle pretty much wore themselves out in the stampede," Linus said. "We'll get there tomorrow, but it'll be too late for us to get anything done. We'll have to wait over until the next day before we can get the cattle penned up and sold," Linus said.

"It'll be close, but we can do it," Lee Edward insisted. "I'll not come this close and have us lose Long Trail."

"Son, I hate to be the one to tell you this, but no matter how much you want to save Long Trail, you have to realize it might not be possible. We all want what you want, but..." Linus shrugged. "What we need now is sleep, but Lee Edward, if you have any favors you could call in with the Good Lord. Now's the time to do it."

Lee Edward smiled. "I've had some practice here lately. I'll do my best."

Pugh was already in San Antonio. He had arrived late in the afternoon and taken a room at the Horseshoe, a hotel near the stockyard. He was spending the night with Lily Simmons, a lady of the evening. It was over quickly, and now Pugh was lying beside her in the bed.

She was snoring.

Pugh woke her up.

"Oh, honey, you want to do it again?" Lily asked.

"No, I want you to get dressed and get out of here."

"But it's the middle of the night," Lily said.

"I don't give a damn what time it is; I want you out of here. I paid for this room, you didn't."

"But I'll have to walk six blocks to get back to my room. And I'm scared to walk that far when it's dark."

"That's your problem, not mine."

Pugh lay in bed as Lily was getting dressed. He wouldn't let her light a lamp, so she was dressing in the darkness. When she was dressed, she left his room without another word.

Pugh thought about how he would prevent Holt from getting enough money to pay off the loan. He had two plans. Travers and half a dozen Double Diamond riders were about twenty miles northwest of San Antonio, waiting for the Long Trail herd. The herd would reach that point on the third day.

If successful, Holt would be denied the opportunity to get his herd to market in time to get the money and pay off the loan. If Travers failed, Pugh had another plan ready.

"We slowed 'em down," Travers said. "But they've already got the herd moving again. They'll more 'n likely get here today."

"Will they be here in time to get their cattle sold?" Pugh asked.

Travers shook his head. "I don't see how. They're more'n thirty miles away. But they'll be here in time to sell them first thing in the morning."

Pugh smiled. "That doesn't matter. I have a plan that will stop Holt."

"How?"

"I'll sell Hamilton a thousand cows today. That'll put my cows in front of his at the San Antonio Cattle Market. And with it being off-season, they won't have the hands or the railcars to handle both mine and his. By the time Holt gets here, the pens will be full, and he'll have to wait until the cattle on hand are processed."

"Well yeah," Travers said. "But all Holt will have to do is hold his herd until the cattle you sold are shipped out."

"By then, it'll be too late for him to pay off the note I hold." Pugh laughed. "By this time next week, there won't be a Long Trail Ranch. It'll be nothing but 85,000 new acres added to the Double Diamond. And I'll get it all for eight-thousand-six hundred dollars. Now what do you think about that, Bull Travers?"

"It's a damn good idea, boss, but where are you gonna get a thousand cows in time to do that?"

"It'll be easy," Pugh said. "There are small ranches all around San Antonio that would be glad to sell off some cows. I'll buy them above market price, then resell them here in San Antonio."

"You're a smart man," Travers said with a broad grin. "I like workin' for a smart man."

As Pugh was sharing his plan with Travers, Lee Edward was in the office of Peter Hamilton, the chief processing officer for the San Antonio Cattle Market.

"Lee Edward Holt," Hamilton said with a wide smile. "Is it true what I heard from Ray Dockins? A Marathon cowboy now the owner of Long Trail Ranch?"

"That's true."

Hamilton extended his hand for a handshake. "Well good for you. I guess we'll be doing business together then, won't we?"

"Yes, sir," Lee Edward answered. "As a matter of fact, that's why I'm here. I have four hundred head ready to ship, well, actually three hundred ninety-eight. We lost two during the drive. What are you paying now?"

"Thirty dollars for utility animals."

Lee Edward smiled and nodded. "That'll do nicely. They'll be here today, but too late for you to take them. But they'll be ready first thing in the morning."

"All right," Hamilton said.

"I'd like to lock in the price," Lee Edward said. "You won't be out any money until the cattle are delivered, but I'd like for you to give me a written commitment to take them."

"Ohhhh, I don't know if I can do that," Hamilton said. "Thirty dollars is for utility animals, and without seeing what you have—why I don't think I can do that."

"What are you paying for canners?" Lee Edward asked. "I can guarantee my cows are better than that."

Peter Hamilton walked over to a ticker machine in the corner of his office. He put on a pair of glasses and began examining a long piece of paper that was falling to the floor.

"It looks like canners are going for twenty-four dollars. I don't know what the market will be in the morning, and if you say your cows are a better grade than canners, I'll agree to twenty-three dollars, sight unseen," Hamilton said. "How many do you say you have?"

"Three hundred ninety-eight. A mix of steers, bullocks, and heifers."

"Sounds like you're selling off some choice stock."

"I am," Lee Edward said. "A little matter has come up, and I have to raise money in a manner of days."

"I've worked with you before, and I trust you. I'll give you today's market price for canners, but I can't go higher."

Hamilton did some figuring on a separate sheet of paper, then looked up. "That'll be nine thousand five hundred-fifty-two dollars. Cash on the barrelhead."

"Sounds good to me." Lee Edward jumped up and shook hands with Hamilton. "You won't be sorry. I'm bringing you prime beef."

With the booking commitment in hand, Lee Edward galloped out to join the approaching herd, which was now nine miles from San Antonio.

* * *

WHEN MARY BETH and Abe saw him coming, they rode out to meet him.

"Did you get it?" Mary Beth asked.

Lee Edward held the booking paper up. "Nine thousand five hundred fifty-two dollars' worth," he said.

"Which is more than enough to pay off the note," Abe said. "You did it!"

When the three of them rode back to join the herd, Linus came out to meet them.

"Well," Linus said with a smile on his face. "I don't have to ask. I can see by the expressions on your faces that you got the herd sold."

"Same as," Lee Edward said. "We've got the cattle booked. Will we still get to San Antonio before dark?"

"Oh, yeah," Linus said. "We'll be there by six, and it won't get dark for at least a couple more hours."

* * *

RUBEN PUGH DISMOUNTED in front of the headquarters of the Alamo Ranch. He knew the ranch owner, Ike Bailey, and though they weren't particularly friends, Pugh had done business with him before. It was Pugh's plan to buy a thousand head of cattle. He knew that Holt was bringing a lot less than that, but he needed to fill up as many holding pens as possible so that they wouldn't be able to accept another herd until the cows he sold them were shipped out.

"Ruben, what can I do for you?" Bailey asked by way of greeting.

"I need to buy a thousand head of cattle and get them to market today."

"That's kind of a rush, don't you think?" Bailey asked. "My hands couldn't even cut out the ones you want in that length of time."

"They don't have to," Pugh said. "I've got twenty men from the Double Diamond who will take care of them."

"Do you want steers?"

"I don't care," Pugh said. "I want the number—I want a thousand head of cattle."

"That's a strange request, but if that's what you want to do, I'll sell them to you," Bailey said. "But it'll cost you."

"How much do you want for them?" Pugh asked.

"Thirty-five dollars a head," Bailey said.

"What! Commercial grade cattle aren't bringing that much."

"Probably not, but the way I see it, for some reason, you want a thousand head today. Now, you can pay my price or go on down the road and see if you can find somebody else who'll sell 'em to you for less," Bailey said. "I wasn't plannin' to sell today, so you can take 'em or leave 'em." Bailey turned around and started walking away from Pugh.

"Wait, hold up a minute," Pugh said. "I'll have to go to the bank, but I want to have my men working the cows by noon. I'll be back with a draft before they drive them to the stockyard."

Ike nodded his head. "I have a feelin' I don't want to know what you're a doin', but I'll be proud to take your $35,000."

"I don't see this as the way one friend treats another, but you're right, I do need the cattle."

"In cash," Bailey said.

"If that's the case, you need to come to the bank with me," Pugh said. "And my men start rounding them up now"

* * *

TWO HOURS and thirty-five thousand dollars later, Pugh rode up to the San Antonio Cattle Market with a bill of sale for a thousand head.

"Mr. Pugh," Peter Hamilton said. "I don't normally see you until around October. What brings you to town?"

"I have a thousand head of cattle I want to move," Pugh said.

Patterson looked at a blackboard that was behind his desk. "A thousand head, you say? You can bring them in after Wednesday of next week, and I can take them off your hands."

"No," Pugh said. "You don't understand. I need to sell them now."

"Where are they?"

"They're more than likely on the trail. I just bought them from Ike Bailey out at the Alamo Ranch."

Hamilton stroked his chin. "Hmm, you just bought them from Bailey, and now you want to sell them? Ruben, that doesn't make any sense."

"It makes perfect sense to me. I need to get the cattle in here this afternoon."

"I wish you'd have come a little earlier. My pens are full. I just took on four hundred head this morning, and I'm going to have to crowd 'em up to find room for them. I don't know what's going on, but Swift and Armour are backed up, too. I got my orders how many car loads I can send through Ft Worth, but they're not takin' a lot right now," Patterson said. "If you weren't in such a hurry, I could see if I can send your cows to Kansas City, but it'll cost you money."

"But Holt's cows aren't here yet. I know that his herd's at least eight or nine miles out of town. If you found room for his four hundred head, then I'll only send four hundred, too. My cattle will be here by mid-afternoon, and he'll be the one who has to wait."

"How did you know it was Holt's cows I bought?" Hamilton waved his hand. "It doesn't matter. I'm sorry, Ruben, but I signed a contract with Lee Edward. I'll buy your cows, but you'll have to wait your turn."

* * *

"That son of a bitch pulled one over me," Pugh told Travers. "Holt has his cattle under contract, and Hamilton won't move off the commitment he's made."

"What are we going to do with the thousand head you bought from Bailey?"

"It's either sell them back to him or drive 'em to the Double Diamond," Pugh said.

"Let me get this straight," Bailey said. "This morning, you had to have the cows. Now you don't need them, so you want to sell them back?"

"Yes, it shouldn't be any problem for you. They haven't been moved off your ranch."

Bailey studied Pugh for a moment, then he nodded. "All right," he said. "I'll buy them back from you."

"Good."

"For twenty dollars a head."

"Twenty dollars?" The words exploded from Pugh's mouth. "I paid you thirty-five dollars a head!"

"Yes, you did, but you seemed desperate to have them, so you were willing to pay a premium price for them. I don't want 'em back, but now it seems you need to get rid of 'em just as much as you wanted 'em this morning. And as I say, it's going to cost you."

Pugh gritted his teeth. "All right, damn you, all right," he said, his words dripping with anger.

Twenty-Five

After they returned to Long Trail, Mary Beth went into town with Lee Edward to deposit the draft they had received from the sale of the cattle.

"We'd like to make a deposit in the amount of nine thousand five hundred dollars," Lee Edward said. "And we'll want fifty-two dollars in cash."

"Yes, sir," the teller said as he went about the business of entering the figures in the Long Trail account.

As soon as Lee Edward got the fifty-two dollars, he counted out twenty-six dollars and gave it to Mary Beth. "Here's your half," he said.

"Thank you. It's a pleasure doing business with you, sir," Mary Beth said with a happy smile.

"Now, what would you say is the most elegant restaurant in town?" Lee Edward asked.

"Oh, that would be the Hill Country Inn, without question," Mary Beth replied.

Lee Edward smiled. "Good. I'll let you take me to lunch there."

"Wait, are you saying you want me to take you to

lunch?" Mary Beth asked, emphasizing the words 'me' and 'you.' "Doesn't the gentlemen usually take the lady to lunch?"

"Well, I suppose so, but in this case, you got just as much money from this deal as I did."

"But you are the gentlemen of this duo."

"I suppose that's right," Lee Edward said. "So, you talked me into it. I'll take you to lunch." His smile broadened.

The Hill Country Inn was constructed of irregular pieces of limestone but perfectly joined. They were greeted by the proprietor as soon as they stepped through the door.

"Hello, Mary Beth, it's been quite a while since you've stopped by."

"Hello, Conrad," Mary Beth said. "It has been a while, but we've been busy out at Long Trail."

"I'm sure you have been," Conrad said. "What a tragedy. The whole town is still upset by what happened to Mr. Austin."

"Thank you, Conrad," Mary Beth said. "You haven't met Lee Edward, Papa Jake's son."

Lee Edward extended his hand, not wanting to get into an extensive conversation. "A nice place you have here, Conrad. Mary Beth said it was the best in town."

Conrad smiled. "We like to think so. Why don't you sit over here by the window? You can look at the river."

Mary Beth and Lee Edward followed Conrad. There was a white cloth on the table and a single candle inside a chimney. Conrad lit the candle and proceeded to tell them what was available. Both Mary Beth and Lee Edward chose the quail.

"I was very pleased to see how Abe acted during the cattle drive," Mary Beth said.

"I was too," Lee Edward said. "I think he cares for Long Trail as much as we do."

"I hope so. I think he realized how awful it would be if we lost the ranch," Mary Beth said. "But it's going to be a little easier now that the ranch is saved. I wonder what Pugh is going to say when he finds out we have enough money to pay off his note?"

"He already knows."

"He already knows? How? How do you know that?"

"When we delivered the cattle, Peter Hamilton told me that Pugh tried to sell a thousand cows. Peter told him that he had already contracted for our cattle, and it would be a few days before he could take delivery. That's when Pugh called off his sale."

"Oh, my, he was trying to block us out, wasn't he?" Mary Beth asked.

"There's no doubt in my mind, but that's what he was intending to do."

"It really is a good thing you went to see Mr. Hamilton before we actually got our cattle there."

"I had an idea Pugh would try something, and do you remember the gunshot that started the stampede?" Lee Edward asked. "I wouldn't doubt but that somehow, he was responsible for that, too."

"I'd sure like to see his face when you pay off his note," Mary Beth said.

"Why don't you go with me tomorrow?"

"Oh, yes, I'd love to go," Mary Beth replied enthusiastically. "What about Abe? Will he go, too?"

"He could if he wanted to, I guess," Lee Edward said. "I want him to know he'll always have a place to live."

"Will you want to move into the Big House someday?" Mary Beth asked.

"No, Jake left that to your mother, and I suspect she will leave that to Abe," Lee Edward said.

"Then where will I go?"

"I've been looking at your favorite spot—the place where you and Jake made up," Lee Edward said. "I'm thinking that is a perfect spot to raise a family."

"Whose family?"

Lee Edward didn't answer, but a grin overtook his face.

"Lee Edward Holt, are you trying to tell me something?"

Just then Conrad came with their meals.

"Yes, I'm telling you I'm hungry."

* * *

WHEN THEY RETURNED to Long Trail, Lee Edward took the horses out to the barn while Mary Beth went into the house.

"Hello, dear. Did everything go all right at the bank?" Hannah asked.

"Yes, it went well."

"I was beginning to worry—you were gone longer than I expected."

"Well, we had lunch at the Hill Country Inn," Mary Beth said.

"The Hill Country Inn, huh?"

"Yes, we had quail, and it was delicious."

"Would you say that Lee Edward is courting you?"

Mary Beth was surprised by her mother's question. "Would you be all right with that idea?"

"I certainly would. I think Lee Edward is a fine gentleman, and after what he's done for us, I want you to ask him to come for supper tonight. Abe told me how close we came to losing Long Trail."

* * *

MARY BETH PRESENTED Hannah's invitation to supper, and Lee Edward graciously accepted.

During the meal, talk turned to the money that was due.

"Before we left town, Mary Beth and I went back to the bank." Lee Edward lifted the satchel he had sitting beside his chair. "I have eight-thousand-six-hundred dollars in cash."

"Oh, my!" Hannah's hand went to her mouth. "Wouldn't it have been easier for you to carry a draft?"

"Yes, it would be, and if anyone other than Ruben Pugh held the note, that's what I would have done. But I wouldn't put anything past that man," Lee Edward said. "If he asks to be paid in cash, then that's what he's going to get."

"I think that was a smart move on your part, Lee Edward," Abe said. "Why don't you stay here in the house tonight? I'll go bunk with Linus."

Lee Edward smiled at Abe's endorsement.

"Why, thanks, Abe. I think I'll do that."

* * *

THE NEXT MORNING, which was the last day to pay the note, Lee Edward and Mary Beth left Long Trail for their ride to Double Diamond.

"I'm glad that you and Abe seem to have settled your differences," Mary Beth said.

"Yes, I am too. It will make things much easier."

"I knew he'd come around," Mary Beth said.

"We'll have some money left over after we pay off this note. And I have a few ideas about how I'd like to use it," Lee Edward said. He looked at Mary Beth. "Maybe start a house."

"That's a good idea. I'll be interested in seeing..." Mary Beth started to say, then she interrupted her comment. "Lee Edward, look ahead of us. Those two men—they're just sitting there. Do you think they know we have all this money?"

"We'll be ready for them," Lee Edward said. He pulled his pistol and then lay his gun hand across the saddle in front of him so that it wasn't easily seen.

As they approached the two men, both men raised their pistols and pointed them at Lee Edward and Mary Beth.

"You're carryin' a lot of money, and you're either going to give it to us, or you're goin' to die," one of the men said. "Now, which is it going to be?"

"Neither," Lee Edward said, lifting the pistol from his saddle.

The sudden and unexpected appearance of a gun in Lee Edward's hand startled the two would-be robbers, and that moment of shock was all Lee Edward needed. He pulled the trigger twice, and the two men who had stopped them fell from their horses.

"Oh!" Mary Beth said, shocked by what she had just seen. She put her hand over her mouth as she looked at the two men, now lying still on the ground. "Did you... did you kill them?"

"Yes, I didn't have time not to."

"How did they know we were carrying a lot of money?" Mary Beth asked.

"One of two ways," Lee Edward said. "It was a large

withdrawal, and it's hard to keep that a secret. I wouldn't be surprised if everyone in Kerrville knew about it."

"I guess I can see that," Mary Beth said. "But you said there were two ways. What's the other way?"

"We'll be meeting him in about half an hour."

"Pugh? You think he would do something like this? But why would he? He's about to get the money anyway."

"Mary Beth, Pugh doesn't want the money," Lee Edward said.

"What? What do you mean he doesn't want...?" Mary Beth halted in mid-sentence, suddenly understanding what Lee Edward was talking about.

"He wants the ranch," she said.

"Yes, any way he can get it."

"But surely he wouldn't kill for it."

"He already has."

Again, a flash of clarity crossed Mary Beth's mind. "You mean Papa Jake, don't you?"

"Who else would it be? He was killed on the ranch, a long way from the public road. That means that his killer, or killers, knew the terrain, and they made him a specific target."

"Now, I'm frightened," Mary Beth said.

"Come on, I'm going to take you back home until I've gotten the note back."

"No, I think it's important that I go with you."

"All right. It's only about another fifteen minutes to the Double Diamond gate."

They resumed their ride, speaking very little, each thinking about what was to come.

"I wonder if we'll run into any other men like those two." Mary Beth said.

"If we do, we'll deal with them." Lee Edward checked his gun and replaced the two expended bullets.

When they reached the turnoff road leading up to the Double Diamond main house, there was someone waiting for them. It was Bull Travers, and he looked surprised to see them.

"I see you got here," Travers said. "Any trouble along the way?"

"Why do you ask? Should there have been trouble?" Lee Edward asked.

"Uh, no. I'm glad you made it all right. Mr. Pugh said that if you showed up, I should take you up to see him."

"Well, we've showed up—both of the owners of Long Trail, so why don't we go see Pugh and get this over with?"

Travers turned his horse around and started up the drive toward the home place. Lee Edward and Mary Beth followed.

"Wait here," Travers said when they reached the house.

Travers went in, and Lee Edward and Mary Beth remained mounted until he came back outside.

"Mr. Pugh will see you now."

Lee Edward and Mary Beth both dismounted. When he did so, Lee Edward took a pannier down from his horse.

"Uh, Mr. Pugh said he would only see you," Travers said to Lee Edward.

"He'll see both of us, or he won't see either of us." Lee Edward put his hand on Mary Beth's elbow and led her into the house with him.

Pugh was sitting behind a desk in his office. He looked up at both of them, showing obvious displeasure that Mary Beth was with Lee Edward.

"I told Travers I'd only see you. There's no need to get Miss Hunter in the middle of this."

"Miss Hunter owns half the ranch, so anything that involves the ranch also involves her."

"You have the money to pay off the note?"

"You know damn well I do, Pugh. You tried to stop me by trying to sell Peter Hamilton a shipment of cattle before we could get there."

"It was a legitimate transaction, the cows I tried to sell, I owned. Anyway, I'm afraid you're too late."

"How can we be too late? This is the date you gave us."

Pugh stared at Lee Edward, his eyes narrowing. "Because there's no time to get the draft to the bank."

"We have cash," Lee Edward said, reaching down into the satchel he had brought in with him. He began taking out the money and laying it on Pugh's desk.

"Eight-thousand-six hundred dollars, as agreed upon. Count it if you want to, but I'll thank you for the note."

With a sigh of disgust, Pugh jerked open the middle drawer of his desk, took out an envelope, then slid it across the top. "Here," he said.

"I want a receipt for the eight-thousand-six-hundred dollars."

"Why do you need that? You have the note."

"Let's just say I don't trust you any farther than I can spit."

Pugh wrote out a receipt and handed it to Lee Edward.

"Thank you." Lee Edward looked at the receipt and then folded it and put it in his vest pocket. "By the way, I left your greeting party on the side of the road between Long Trail and the turnoff to Double Diamond."

"What makes you think I had anything to do with those two men?" Pugh asked.

Lee Edward smiled. "I don't know, Pugh. Why do you think I might have a thought like that?"

* * *

WHEN LEE EDWARD and Mary Beth rode back toward Long Trail, the bodies of the two men that Lee Edward had shot were gone.

"Where are they?" Mary Beth asked.

"I don't know, but I think we should go see the marshal."

Twenty-Six

It was nearly noon when they arrived in Kerrville.

"What do you say we have a bite to eat before we see Marshal Wallace?" Lee Edward asked.

Mary Beth smiled. "I think that's a wonderful idea," she said.

The smell of roasting meat was coming from the Gardens where Linus and Lee Edward had eaten before.

"I can't pass that up," Lee Edward said as he came to a stop in front of the building. "Shall we?"

"Sure," Mary Beth said as she dismounted and tied off her horse. "This is like coming home, and I mean that quite literally. Did you know this was where we were living when Papa Jake married Mama?"

"No, Linus told me this was an old livery barn, but he didn't tell me it was the one your mother was trying to run."

"It was," Mary Beth said as they swung the door open and entered.

"Ah, Miss Mary Beth, you come to visit." The man

was standing over the pit applying a sauce over the pieces of meat that were spread on the grill.

"No, Juan, we are not here to visit." Mary Beth laughed. "We've come to eat."

Juan moved to a side table. "Right now, I take *pecho de vacuno* off the pit. You taste." He handed Lee Edward a small piece of meat.

"That's what we want," Lee Edward said. "Whatever it is, it tastes fantastic."

"Gringos call it brisket. You sit by river and I bring it out myself. Carina—she not work today," Juan said.

Mary Beth and Lee Edward went out into the garden and found a table under a gazebo. Once again, the hummingbirds were everywhere.

"Who would have thought such little birds could be so mean to one another," Mary Beth said as they watched one and then another try to drive the competing birds away from the orange flowers of the trumpet vine.

"Not unlike people," Lee Edward said. "You know Pugh did send those men after us, don't you?"

"Well, I wouldn't be surprised," Mary Beth replied.

"No surprise to it. Remember what he said? He said, what makes us think he had anything to do with those *two* men."

"Yes," Mary Beth said. "We didn't say anything about there being two men."

"Exactly."

"And yet he acted as if he thought we were going to give him a bank draft."

"He knew we had cash. He was just trying to convince us he wasn't involved."

"Lee Edward, do you think Marshal Wallace will do anything?"

"I don't know Wallace well enough to say, but if I was

guessing, I'd say he probably won't. In my mind, Angus Pugh has his fingerprints all over the killing of Jake Austin, and yet the marshal hasn't done anything about it," Lee Edward said.

Just then Juan brought out a pile of sliced meat and a round of cornbread. "You eat. You will like and then you will come again."

"You can bet on that," Lee Edward said as he began tearing off a piece of the hot bread.

* * *

AFTER EATING, Lee Edward and Mary Beth led their horses down to the marshal's office to make their report. They were met by Deputy Carr.

"What can I do for you two?" Carr asked.

"Is Marshal Wallace around?" Lee Edward asked. "We're here to see him."

Carr shook his head. "No, seems like there was a murder out on Dee's Road. Two men were found dead."

"That's what I want to talk to him about," Lee Edward said. "I shot those two men, but it wasn't murder, it was self-defense."

"Wait a minute, there were two of them and one of you, but you claim it was self-defense?"

"Yes."

"That doesn't seem right," Carr said. "If two men were about to kill you, how'd you get the drop on 'em?"

"They were cautious, I was careful."

"Do you have any way of proving what you say?" Carr asked.

"He has me," Mary Beth said. "I was there. I saw what happened. Lee Edward is telling the truth. There were two men who tried to rob us. They had their guns out, and I was afraid they were going to shoot us, but Lee Edward shot them before they could shoot us."

Marshal Wallace came into the office then and saw Lee Edward and Mary Beth standing there.

"Holt, Miss Hunter," the marshal greeted as he took off his hat and put it on a peg. "What can I do for you?"

"The two men that were found dead on Dee's Road? I killed them."

Marshal Wallace spun around quickly. "Are you confessing to the murder of those two men?"

"I said killed, not murdered," Lee Edward said. "We were carrying a lot of cash on our way to the Double Diamond. I believe these two were sent by Ruben Pugh to steal the money before I could pay off the note he held on Long Trail."

"Well, it turns out both men had paper out on them, so I can believe they wanted to rob you. But, hell, any man in town could have wanted to do that. You know, it was damn stupid of you two to ride out of here with that much cash. Did you not notice Jolly Dirk Catron standing at the door when you left the bank?"

"We weren't paying attention," Mary Beth said.

"Well, Jolly Dirk was listenin' to your whole conversation. He hightailed it down to the Saddle and Bit and told ever'body in sight what you two was a doin'." Marshal Wallace clucked his tongue. "Stupid. Damn stupid. And now you think Ruben Pugh had something to do with this?"

"When I paid off the note, I told him about being stopped on the road by someone who wanted to steal the money before I could pay it. He told me that he didn't have anything to do with sending those two men after me."

"Well, then, there you have it—it's your word against his," Wallace said.

"Except that he said he didn't have anything to do with sending those *two men* after me. Neither one of us said anything about it being two men."

Wallace nodded his head. "I tend to believe your story. The two men were a couple of brothers from up around Waco who go by the names of Jed and Pete Billings. As a matter of fact, there's a reward out on each of 'em to the tune of five hundred dollars. Since you said you killed 'em, that money's yours."

"But what about Ruben Pugh? I think he hired them?" Lee Edward said.

"Could be," Wallace said. "But I can't prove it. Not after what Jolly Dirk was a tellin'."

"What about when he told us he didn't have anything to do with the two men who stopped us?"

Wallace shrugged his shoulders. "No witnesses. Wouldn't hold up in court."

"What do you mean, no witnesses?" Mary Beth asked. "I was there, I heard Pugh say those words."

"Your testimony couldn't be used as a witness comment, because everybody knows you own half of Long Trail. That gives you what's called a vested interest in the case."

"So nothing happens to Ruben Pugh?" Lee Edward asked.

"Nope."

Lee Edward glanced over at Mary Beth, then let out a long sigh. "All right, Marshal, thanks for nothing. Come on, Mary Beth, we're wasting our time here."

"Holt!" Wallace called out as Lee Edward and Mary Beth started to leave.

Lee Edward turned to look back at the marshal.

"I don't want you to be taking any of this into your own hands. If anything happens to Ruben Pugh, you're going to be my first suspect."

Lee Edward nodded his head. "I can understand that, because you already went through this once before."

"What are you saying, Holt? Are you accusing me of somethin'."

"Not at all, Marshal. I know you have plenty of suspects for the murder of Jake Austin. You're going to make an arrest any day now." Lee Edward took Mary Beth's arm, and they walked out of the building without giving the marshal a chance to reply.

* * *

LEE EDWARD and Mary Beth were riding down the main street when they heard church bells ringing.

"I wonder why church bells are ringing today. It's not Sunday. It's not even Wednesday night prayer meeting," Mary Beth said.

"Listen," Lee Edward said. "That's not ordinary ringing. They are tolling."

Even though Lee Edward and Mary Beth were at the other end of the street, they waited until the bell had struck twenty-eight times, and then was silent.

"God rest her soul," Lee Edward said and then he made the sign of the cross.

"How do you know it was a woman?" Mary Beth asked.

"At the beginning the bell rang three times, twice, and then the toll started for each year of the person's life. If it had been a man, the death knell would have rung nine times," Lee Edward said.

"In all the years I've heard bells toll, I never knew that."

"I have to give Sister Maria credit for all I know about religion," Lee Edward said. "She wouldn't be happy with me if she knew I took two lives."

"She would forgive you. You had no choice."

"Before we go home, let me go by the post office. I've been meaning to write a note to Sister Superior to see how Sister Maria is. God may have performed a miracle, and she recovered from typhoid," Lee Edward said.

The post office was at the back of Schreiner's Mercantile and when the two walked in, the clerk addressed them.

"Mr. Holt, I believe."

"Yes, I'm Lee Edward Holt."

"I've published the list of unclaimed letters in the last two issues of the *Mountain Sun*. Did you not see your name?"

"I'm sorry I did not."

"Well it must be important. It has a black seal on the back with some kind of writing in it." The clerk headed to the back of the store to retrieve the letter.

"Hope it's not something bad." He handed the letter to Lee Edward.

"I know what it is," Lee Edward said. He didn't look at it but put it in the pocket of his vest.

Lee Edward and Mary Beth rode back to the ranch. Only the plodding of the horses broke the silence.

When they arrived, they dismounted in front of the barn.

"You two have been gone all day," Linus said as he took the reins to their horses. "We thought old Ruben may have gotten the best of you."

"It's not because he didn't try," Mary Beth said. She

took Lee Edward's hand and looked up at him. "Are you all right?"

"Yes, but I think I'm going out by my father's gravesite for a while."

"Do you want company?" Mary Beth asked.

"I don't think so."

Lee Edward started toward the Alamo tree that stood guard over the graves of Jacob and Edna Austin. When he got there, he found a small stool and sitting down, he took out the envelope. He rubbed his finger over the wax seal that said Our Lady of Mercy. On other correspondence, the seal was white. The black could mean only one thing. Breaking the seal, he withdrew the note and held it to his nose. The scent of incense immediately took him back to his days at the orphanage.

My dear Lee Edward,

It is with great sorrow that I take pen in hand to tell you that our beloved Sister Maria Claire passed life's earthly bounds fifteenth instant, in the year of our Lord, 1886. I know how important you were to her life, and how impactful she was to yours.

There is something you should know. Before that fateful day when you were left at the doorstep of Our Lady of Mercy, Sister Maria had not yet taken her perpetual vows. She was questioning her commitment to a life of charity and was preparing to vacate her calling. When I placed you in her care, her life of prayer and devotion took on new meaning. You, Lee Edward Holt, are responsible for allowing Sister Maria to fully commit to a life of spiritual service in the community of sinners. She truly loved the Lord our God, but she held a special place in her heart for the love she had for you. And I believe, by observing your deeds, that you shared that love for Sister Maria. I ask that you take comfort in your time of sorrow, knowing that our dear Sister Maria is now in communion with our Lord and Savior, Jesus Christ, and the Blessed Mother, Mary, and all the saints who surround His table. She is in the arms of God.

And now I want to speak directly to you. The church teaches about forgiveness. Please look into your heart and examine those seeds of darkness that you harbor. Forgiveness is a blessing that allows clouds to be lifted. For your physical and spiritual growth, I beg of you in the name of Jesus and knowing the love of your dear Sister Maria, please consider forgiving those who have wronged you. Remember, you are a child of God and He loves you.

Sister Maria's dying wish was that you have her cross. Please keep it in remembrance of her. Know that she will continue to look down upon you from her place in heaven.

With prayers of love and grace, you will continue to receive the blessings from all those of us at Our Lady of Mercy who live and work in the path of service to our Lord.

In the name of our Blessed Savior, I remain.
Reverend Mother Mary Elizabeth O.L.M.

Lee Edward read the letter through again before putting it aside. He withdrew the simple silver cross on its black leather cord. Seeing it, he envisioned Sister Maria. From his very first memories of her, she had always worn this cross around her neck. The letters INRI were engraved in small letters at the bottom of the cross. She had told him they stood for the Latin words the Romans had put on the cross when Jesus was cruci-fied. Jesus of Nazareth, King of the Jews.

Lee Edward squeezed the cross in his hand as tears rolled down his face. How much of his character had been formed by growing up in an orphanage and with the guidance of Sister Maria.

He had killed men, and he felt remorse over that, but Mary Beth was right. He had killed because he had to. He hoped Sister Maria would understand that.

Looking down, he saw the rocks outlining both his father's and Edna's graves. And then he thought about the Reverend Mother's words about forgiveness. She said clouds would be lifted.

He had said that inheriting the ranch was a way for his father to assuage his guilty conscience, but if that was true, Lee Edward was the benefactor. And it was more than the land—Lee Edward had inherited a family. He thought that Jake had been especially perceptive in leaving half the ranch to Mary Beth. It was as if he knew Lee Edward would marry her.

"Yes!" Lee Edward said. "I will marry Mary Beth, and Dad, I have you to thank for bringing us together. I may not fully understand everything that had to be done in the past, but whatever it was, I forgive you. I wish I would have known you, but Mary Beth did know you and she loved you and in my book, that's good enough for me."

He stood up, and putting the letter in his pocket and the cross around his neck, he walked back to the house.

* * *

FOR THE NEXT two or three days, chores around the ranch consumed all the hands. Linus had announced it was time to break a few of the green horses that had grown up on the ranch. The boys rounded up the first ten and brought them up to the corral. Linus and Lee Edward were standing at the fence, watching.

"Pick out the one you like best, and we'll put him in the picket," Linus said.

Lee Edward pointed to a red bay colt. "Let's start with him."

Linus smiled. "Your dad would be proud. That's Dobbin's get. Would you like to try your hand working with him?"

"It's been a while, but I'll do my best," Lee Edward said. He stepped into the circle of pickets and began twirling his lariat. On the first throw, he caught the horse's forefoot.

Several of the men laughed. "I'd say it's been a while," Clem Porter said. "You missed that horse by a mile."

"I don't think so," Hank Everson said as he jumped down off the top rail. "In a minute, you're going to see the Marathon way of training a horse."

Hank joined Lee Edward, and they brought the horse down and tied the horse's legs much as one would tie a calf at branding time. While they had the horse down, they were able to put a bridle on him. As soon as he was up, Hank got an empty feed sack and handed it to Lee Edward. Lee Edward allowed the horse to smell the sack and then began to rub the sack over the horse's neck and ears. He was talking to him in a soft voice and the horse began to immediately calm down.

"I'll be damned," Porter said. "I never seen anything like that. How long will it take before the boss tries to ride that bronc?"

Hank smiled. "It'll be weeks. Our boss has the patience of Job, but there won't be a better horse on the ranch when he finally does climb up on him."

"If it takes that long, all I can say is, I'm glad we ain't got but twenty horses to break."

"Would you rather be up there bustin' your ribs when the horse starts buckin'?"

"There's somethin' to be said by doin' it the old way, but I'm game to try somethin' else."

The training continued, and true to Hank's word, it was a slow process. Even Mary Beth and Abe came out to watch how Lee Edward trained Dobbin's colt. When at last, Lee Edward was ready to put the saddle on, the three-year-old was as gentle as a puppy dog.

"Do you know you haven't been to town for a while?" Mary Beth asked as she approached Lee Edward just after breakfast.

"I guess not," Lee Edward said, "but I don't have to." He gave Mary Beth a peck on the forehead. "My partner buys all the supplies and pays all the bills while I get to play around the ranch."

"I wouldn't call breaking horses playing, but it's been fun to watch the cowboys start training them your way."

"It works. If you handle a horse with respect, he'll do whatever you want him to do," Lee Edward said.

"And I suppose you would use that same technique with a wife?"

"Well, if it works for a horse..."

Mary Beth hit him on the arm. "Stop it. I'm going to hitch up the wagon because Mama's going to town with me. She wants to enter her preserves in the county fair."

"What about her pickles? She should enter a jar of those, too," Lee Edward said.

Mary Beth laughed. "She wants to win and as long as Lulu Ford enters her pickles, nobody else can win."

"Are they that good?"

"They're good, but Hudson Ford is one of the judges."

"Enough said. Let me get my town duds on, and I'll join you."

* * *

WHEN LEE EDWARD, Mary Beth, and Hannah got to town, there were wagons everywhere. On the outskirts, they saw a big red and white striped tent had been erected.

"That's where we're going," Hannah said, pointing to the tent. "Get as close as you can so I don't have to carry my crate any farther than I have to."

"If you wait, I can carry it for you," Lee Edward said.

"No, no," Hannah said. "If you're late, you have to put your jars in the back and I don't think they even sample them. You two just wander around. Look at some of the animals the kids have brought in, or go taste some of the food that's for sale. If Cadianne Hebert is selling meat pies, pick up a dozen or so. You know how much Abe loves those."

"We'll do our best," Mary Beth said.

Just then, they heard a gushing sound and immediately they saw a balloon lift off in the open field behind the tent.

"Oh, Lee Edward, isn't that one of the most beautiful sights you've ever seen?"

"Let's go see if they're taking people up." After they found a place to park the wagon, Lee Edward took Mary Beth's hand. They began running down the street toward the site where they expected the balloon to be.

As they ran, several people who recognized them were cheering and yelling catcalls. "Holt, don't let her get away! Mary Beth, run faster!"

When they got to the spot, there was a tan-colored

ball that seemed to be suspended over the park. As they drew closer, however, they saw that it wasn't suspended, but rather it was attached to a long rope.

There was a professionally painted sign near the spot where the balloon was descending.

PROFESSOR GIDEON KOCH
AERONAUT TRAINED BY THADDEUS LOWE
ASCENSIONS PROVIDED
$2.00 PER PASSENGER

When the balloon was lowered, an elderly gentleman and a child of about ten stepped out of the basket.

"That was fun, Grandpa," the boy said. "Did you really go up in a balloon during the War between the States?"

"That man"—and he pointed to the name Thaddeus Lowe—"built eight of 'em. President Lincoln recognized that it was a great way to watch where the Rebels were, and yes, I went up more than once."

After overhearing the conversation, Lee Edward turned to Mary Beth.

"Are you ready?"

"I have to say, I'm a little scared," she said.

"You heard the man. Abraham Lincoln put these things in the air."

* * *

PROFESSOR GIDEON KOCH stepped out of the basket and headed toward them. He was wearing striped trousers, a cut-a-way jacket, and a red silk scarf.

"Is this thing safe?" Lee Edward asked.

"My dear boy, I have personally had over a thousand ascensions. It is, indeed, safe."

"How high will this thing go?" Lee Edward asked.

"If the balloon is free, the altitude is practically unlimited. But as you can see, this balloon will be tethered. Our altitude will be limited to five hundred feet."

"That's high," Mary Beth said. "Are we sure we want to do this?"

"Don't forget, you'll have me with you," Lee Edward said. "If we fall out, I'll grab you and turn over on my back so I can cushion your fall when we hit the ground."

Mary Beth laughed. "You are insane. All right, Professor Koch, you've got yourself two passengers."

Professor Koch opened the gate to the basket, and Lee Edward and Mary Beth stepped inside. Koch adjusted a valve, and the balloon began to rise.

"Oh! Oh, oh!" Mary Beth said, grabbing hold of Lee Edward.

"Is this where I'm supposed to give you a hug?" Lee Edward asked.

"Yes, yes!"

Lee Edward took her in his arms, but as the balloon continued its ascension, Mary Beth became intrigued with what she was able to see.

"Oh, look, there's our ranch. And the Double Diamond. Oh, and there's Twin Sisters Mountains, and Haddenbrook Hill, and Bachelor Mountain." Mary Beth turned to look the other way. "Oh, my, I can see all the way to Gobbler's Knob. This is marvelous!"

"Look at Long Trail," Lee Edward said. "I can see that Linus has them working today."

"I wish we had a looking glass, then we could..."

"Be my guest, ma'am," Professor Koch said, handing Mary Beth a pair of binoculars.

"Thank you," Mary Beth said with a big smile as she accepted the offer. She held the binoculars to her eyes. "Lee Edward, look! I can see Dobbins out in the horse pasture!"

Lee Edward took them, located the horse, then identified a couple of the cowboys he could see riding out.

"There's Crader and Porter," Lee Edward said.

They remained aloft about half an hour, and during that time, they studied not only the surrounding terrain, but they could also look down on Kerrville. It was with some reluctance that they returned to the ground, giving up their cocoon of silence.

Mary Beth was filled with ebullience when they walked away from the balloon. "I am so glad we did that. It was as if a cloud was lifted."

Lee Edward stopped dead still. "What did you say?"

"I said I was glad we did that," Mary Beth said, not understanding why Lee Edward was acting the way he was.

"No, you said it was as if a cloud was lifted." Lee Edward remembered a similar sentence from the Reverend Mother's letter. This was the happiness forgiveness had given him.

He took Mary Beth's hands in his. "Mary Beth Hunter, will you marry me?"

"Oh, Lee Edward, you've made me the happiest woman alive. Yes, I will marry you, but I've always dreamed of a wedding at Christmas. Can we wait that long?"

"As long as you've said yes, I can wait as long as you like."

"Let's not tell anyone yet," Mary Beth said. "Let it be our secret."

* * *

ON THE RIDE back to the ranch, Mary Beth rested her head on Lee Edward's shoulder while Hannah sat on a seat in the back of the wagon. Hannah prattled on about how she didn't win the blue ribbon for her peach preserve, and how Claude Watson had raised the biggest watermelon she had ever seen, and of course, how Lulu Ford had won a blue ribbon for her mustard pickles.

Lee Edward and Mary Beth didn't hear a word she said.

* * *

OVER THE NEXT FEW DAYS, the atmosphere at Long Trail was one of harmony. There was no danger of anyone fore-closing on the ranch. A strong camaraderie had been built among the cowboys and with Lee Edward and Linus. Even Abe Hunter, who at one time had been bitterly disliked by the men, by his most recent actions, had earned the respect and friendship of Long Trail hands. The men were proud to be riding for the LT brand, and they shared that pride with anyone who would listen.

Twenty-Seven

"Morning, Miss Mary Beth," the cook said when she wandered over to the chicken coop.

"Hi, Moses," Mary Beth said. "I came to see if any more hens are on the setting boxes."

"Yes, ma'am," Moses said. "I told you if we got some Rhode Island Reds, we get more nesters." He went over to one of the boxes and put his hand under the chicken. She ruffled her feathers and began to cluck. "Hold on there, Henrietta, I ain't gonna rob your nest. I'm just a countin'."

"How many eggs does she have?" Mary Beth asked.

"Yesterday, she had seven, but today I think I count nine," Moses said. "If all these old clucks do as much as Henrietta, here, we're gonna be needin' us a bigger chicken pen."

"I think we need a bigger one anyway," Mary Beth said. "The more chickens we raise, the more chicken and dumplin's you can make for us."

"I shore 'nuff can do that. Mr. Linus—now that man can eat a heap of dumplin's."

"We all can," Mary Beth said. "I need to get some oats for Mr. Holt today. I'll stop by the hardware store and pick up what we need."

"Make sure you get that tall wire," Moses said. "We don't want no coyotes raiding our chicken house."

"I'll see what they have at the hardware store."

* * *

MARY BETH GOT to town right at ten o'clock. Her first stop was the bank where she drew out enough money to buy the oats and what she thought would be enough to buy the fencing. Her next stop was the feed store where she bought fewer bags of oats than she usually did because she didn't want the wagon to be too heavy for the horses to pull easily. And her last stop was Sikes Hardware.

"Miss Hunter, what can I get for you today?"

"Moses wants to build a bigger chicken yard. I'll need the tallest wire you have and some posts and staples," Mary Beth said. "Oh, and Alfred, I want some of those new leather gloves I've seen some of the cowboys wear."

"Let me see what I can get for you." Mr. Sikes went around back and then came back in. "I've got some wire for you, but I'm out of posts. You stay here while I run down to the sawmill. I'll have Newt bring up a supply."

"You don't have to do that. I can go down there myself. I only need about five posts."

"No, I'll do it for you," Sikes said. "You just wait right here."

Mary Beth was in the back of the store, taking staples out of a keg that was sitting on the floor. Without any warning, she felt someone reach around from behind her. She tried to fight, but the person was much bigger than she was. Then a sweet-smelling cloth was slapped over her nose. She felt dizzy, then weak, then nothing.

It wasn't unusual for Mary Beth to go into town and stay until late in the afternoon. But it had grown dark, and Mary Beth still hadn't returned. That was unusual, so unusual that Hannah shared with Abe and Lee Edward, that she was very afraid that something had happened to her.

When Mary Beth came to, she was lying under a canvas cover that was nearly suffocating her. Her hands and feet were tied, and she had a gag over her mouth. From the sound and the movement, she realized she was in a wagon, but she had no way of knowing where she was or where she was going. She had never been so frightened in her life.

The wagon continued to roll for a time that was so long that Mary Beth had no idea how long she had been in this wagon. She wanted to call out, to demand where she was, but the gag was secure enough that, try as she might, she was unable to make a sound.

Finally the wagon stopped, and the canvas was pulled back. Her eyes could not make out anything around her as it was now dark. In her mind, she calculated that she had arrived in town around eleven, she spent almost an hour at lunch, then her errands had probably taken about two hours before she got to the hardware store and she'd been there for about half an hour before she was taken. She had no idea how long she had been in the wagon before she regained consciousness, but she had been in this wagon at least since she had awakened. Could Lee Edward find her? But how could he? She had no idea where she was or even in what direction from Kerrville she had been driven.

She closed her eyes. *Please God, let him find me.*

"How ya doin' in there, little lady?" a man said.

"Uhmm, uhmm?" Mary Beth said, trying to speak.

"Hard to talk with a gag, ain't it?" someone said.

Mary Beth tried to position herself so that she could see the speaker, but even if she were to manage, she could not be sure if this was the person who had abducted her.

"Well, there ain't no need to keep that thing on any longer. You're far enough away now that you can scream as loud as you want to, 'n there ain't nobody but the coyotes and the bobcats a' goin' to hear you," her captor said as he pulled the gag out of her mouth. He laughed. "Ain't nobody a' goin' to see you, neither."

"Who are you, and why have you done this?" Mary Beth asked.

"Oh, you'll know soon enough."

* * *

WHEN IT WAS late in the evening and Mary Beth hadn't returned, they began to worry. Lee Edward told Hannah that he and Abe would go look for her. Lee Edward and Abe went into town, riding side by side.

"What do you think happened?" Abe asked.

"Let's not panic yet," Lee Edward said. "She was going to be pulling such a load, something could have happened to the wagon—a wheel or an axel—it could be anything."

"Or someone could have kidnapped her," Abe said.

Lee Edward had thought that all along, but he didn't want to voice his thinking. Things had been going too smoothly at the ranch. Never once did Lee Edward forget that Ruben Pugh wanted Long Trail, and he knew, too, that Pugh would stop at nothing to get what he wanted.

When they rode into town, the several saloons were doing a good business and the sounds drifted out on the street. Lee Edward and Abe did not stop nor look at any of those businesses. They went directly to Sikes Hardware.

"Look," Abe said. "That's our wagon, but the horses aren't there."

"I hope Alfred Sikes has a good explanation for this. Let's round him up and see what he knows."

Abe knew where his house was, and they were there in a minute.

"Sikes! Alfred Sikes!" Lee Edward yelled as Abe banged on the door.

A moment later, a rather small man with a gray beard and wearing a nightshirt and cap answered the call.

"What is it?" Sikes asked anxiously. "Is something wrong?"

"Alfred, did you see my sister in your store today?"

"Yes, she stopped by this morning. Wanted wire and posts for the chicken yard."

"Do you know why she left the wagon in front of your store?" Lee Edward asked. "And do you know what happened to our horses?"

"Yes, I do know about the horses. I closed up early today, and when I saw the horses standing there, I took them out of their traces and took them to the livery. I left her a note. Did she not find it?"

"I don't believe she did," Lee Edward said. "Now, get dressed."

"What?"

"Get dressed. I want to search your store."

"Search my store for what?" Sikes asked, still confused by the whole thing.

"For Mary Beth Hunter," Lee Edward said. "She was there today, wasn't she?"

"Yes," Sikes replied. "Yes, yes, she was."

"Did you see her leave?" Abe asked.

"No. I went down to the sawmill to get some posts and when Newt and I brought them back, she was gone," Sikes said. "Like I said, her rig was there, so I thought she was off visitin' someplace. When she hadn't come back when I closed up, like I said, I unhitched her horses."

"Right now, let's see if we can find something. Will you come with us and open your store?" Lee Edward asked.

"Yes, of course, as soon as I can get dressed," Sikes replied.

Half an hour later, Lee Edward, Abe, and Alfred Sikes were looking through his store.

"Lee Edward, look," Abe said. He pointed to a wicker basket that was sitting on the floor. In the basket were staples, a pair of wire pliers, and a pair of leather work gloves. "She was here, all right. But what happened to her?"

"I think this might give us a hint," Lee Edward said. A moment earlier, he had picked up a cloth, and now he held it out toward Abe.

"What is that?"

"Smell it," Lee Edward said.

Abe took a sniff of the cloth, then jerked it away from his nose.

"Chloroform," Lee Edward said, even before Abe asked about it.

"Damn, that's how they got her," Abe said.

"Yes, but how did they get her outside, past everyone?"

"I think I might be able to answer that," Sikes said. He pointed to a door. "That leads into my store room."

"Is there a back door?" Lee Edward asked.

"No, but there's a window. I normally keep it locked though."

The three men went into the storeroom, and Alfred pointed to the window. The lock was broken, and the window was raised. "That's how they got her out," he said.

* * *

MARY BETH'S feet were untied, and she was yanked out of the wagon and forced to walk into a dilapidated cabin. Once inside, a lantern was lit, and she saw four men, one of whom she recognized.

"Bull Travers," she said. "I might have known that Pugh had something to do with this."

"So, now you know," Travers said.

"What do you want? What's going to happen to me?" Mary Beth asked.

"That all depends on Mr. Lee Edward Holt."

"He will never turn Long Trail over to Rueben Pugh," Mary Beth insisted.

"Mr. Pugh's not asking for the ranch. He's asking for money," Travers said.

"Money?"

"Yeah, it's called ransom. Holt gives us the money and we give him you," Travers said.

"Where are we?" Mary Beth asked.

"It don't matter to you. If the ransom's paid, we'll take you out of here. If it ain't, we'll bury you here." Travers' cackle could have come from the depths of hell.

* * *

AFTER FINDING the cloth with the chloroform, Lee Edward and Abe headed for the marshal's office. When they went in, Deputy Carr was asleep in one of the cells of the jail.

Abe went back and began shaking him.

"Benny, Benny, wake up!"

Benny sat up quickly, grabbing a pistol from under his pillow. "You're under arrest!"

"Benny, you were sleeping. It's me, Abe Hunter, and we need the marshal."

Benny scratched his head. "The marshal ain't here."

"We know that," Lee Edward said. "We think Mary Beth has been kidnapped and we need help."

"It's the middle of the night. How's the marshal gonna help you?"

"Well, could you at least tell him what we think has happened?"

"I can in the mornin'," Carr said. "His rheumatiz is botherin' him and he took a whole bottle of elixir. I don't expect I could wake him up lessen I throwed a bucket of water on him, and iffin I did, he'd be howling like a polecat."

Lee Edward took a deep breath. "All right, we're going back to the ranch to let Hannah know what's happened, but we'll be back first thing in the morning."

"I'll do some lookin' tonight," Benny said as he rose from the bunk. "I'll check the bars and see if she's showed up in one of them. With the fair still goin' on we got lots of foreigners in town, and maybe she run off with one of them."

"There is no way my sister is going to run off with a stranger or show up in a bar."

"Ya never know," Carr said. "People do some crazy things sometimes."

* * *

THE NEXT MORNING, after a sleepless night, Lee Edward and Abe rode back to town. They headed for the marshal's office.

Marshal Wallace was sitting on a bench in front of the jail. When he saw Lee Edward and Abe coming, he stood up.

"I've got something for you," Marshal Wallace said. "It'll shed some light on what you're a facin'."

Lee Edward and Abe followed the marshal into his office.

"This was layin' on the floor this morning." He picked up a rock. "And this was tied around it." He handed the crumpled paper to Lee Edward.

LEE EDWARD HOLT DEPOSIT $50,000 TO ACCOUNT OF BILL SMITH IN SAN ANTONIO WELLS FARGO BANK. HAVE ONE WEEK FROM TODAY.

"Damn," Lee Edward said as he handed the note to Abe. "I guess this shows us what we're up against."

"Who do you think could have done this?" Abe asked.

"The first person I would go after is Ruben Pugh," Lee Edward said.

"I knew you'd say that," the marshal said. "But Mr. Pugh wouldn't do a thing like this. I think it would more'n likely be one of these flimflam men hangin' around for the fair. We've been runnin' in all kinds of scams. Just yesterday, Opie Sadler lost five thousand dollars in a shell game. Can you believe that?"

"I don't think kidnapping a person can compare with losing money in a shell game," Lee Edward said in exasperation.

"I'll start askin' around and see what I can find out," the marshal said, "but if I was you, I'd start puttin' the money together if you want to see Mary Beth alive."

"How do you expect us to come up with fifty thousand dollars?" Abe asked.

"I don't know," Lee Edward said. "But we've got to. We'll go to the bank as soon as it opens and see what we can do."

For the next hour, Lee Edward, Abe, Marshal Wallace and Deputy Carr spread out, telling everyone they met what had happened to Mary Beth and describing her to those who didn't know her. Lee Edward and Abe met in front of the bank when it opened.

* * *

"I just saw Deputy Carr, and he told me about Mary Beth. Who would have thought something like this could happen in our little town?" Burt Rowe asked. "I tried to tell the town council something like this could happen when they planned this fair. Too much riffraff coming in." He unlocked the door and stepped inside. "Now what can I do for you?"

"We need to talk to you," Lee Edward said.

"All right, come on into my office." Rowe took off his hat and hung it on a rack. "Let me get a pot of coffee going."

"Mr. Rowe, we don't have time for that," Lee Edward said. He handed the ransom note to Burt as he sat behind his desk.

"Oh my, this makes this very serious," he said as he put on his spectacles. "What are you going to do?"

"We were hoping you could help us. We want to take out a loan," Lee Edward said.

Rowe was quiet for a long time. Then he spoke.

"Unfortunately, I know all the troubles Long Trail has been in since Jake's passing, and I also know you had to sell off some of your stock to pay off Ruben Pugh. Knowing this, I would be hard-pressed to lend—" He looked at the paper in his hand. "Fifty thousand dollars. I'm sorry, but I have a responsibility to Mr. Schreiner."

"Well, could you lend us anything?" Abe asked. "Five thousand? Ten thousand?"

"And where would you get the rest?"

"Everyone we've seen on the street has been telling us they want to help. Let's ask for help," Abe said.

Burt looked down. "I know you don't want to consider this, but you could raise this kind of money this afternoon."

"How?" Lee Edward asked.

Raising his head, he began to speak. "After Charles Schreiner, Ruben Pugh has the biggest account in this bank. If you were to sell Long Trail to him, with the combined acreage of all his properties, I would be happy to lend Pugh the money."

"Absolutely not," Lee Edward said as he rose quickly, knocking over the chair behind him. "Abe, let's go. We've got to find your sister."

Abe followed Lee Edward out of the bank three or four steps behind him.

"What are we going to do now," Abe asked when he finally caught up with Lee Edward.

"We have no choice. We're going to find her."

TWENTY-EIGHT

WHEN THEY LEFT THE BANK, LEE EDWARD AND ABE
headed back to the marshal's office. Just coming out of
the door was Linus Walker and another man.

"Lee Edward, I've been lookin' for you. This is Curley
Logan, and he's got something to tell you."

"I hope it's about Mary Beth."

"It is."

"Well, let's hear it. We don't have time to waste."

"I used to work at Long Trail until..." He stopped and
looked at Abe. "It's just that Abe and I had a
disagreement."

"Go on," Lee Edward urged.

"Now I work at the Double Diamond and I know
where they took Miss Hunter."

"Then it is Pugh who did this," Abe said. "I knew it!"

"Well, from what I hear, it was Bull Travers who actually took her. A couple of boys in the bunkhouse were a
talkin'."

"You said you know where she is. Tell us," Lee
Edward continued, cutting off the conversation.

"Scooter Condon said a bunch of 'em took some vittles up to that old trapper's cabin 'bout halfway up Twins Sisters Mountain. Said they needed to stay there about a week or so. Seems like that would be a good place to stash Miss Hunter."

"Then you don't know she's there for sure?" Abe asked.

"He doesn't, but it makes a hell of a lot of sense to think that's where Mary Beth is," Linus said.

"Which side of the slope is this cabin?" Lee Edward asked.

"This side. Abe, you might recollect it. We seen it once when we was makin' a cow gather for Mr. Austin."

"I know where it is," Abe said.

"Then let's get started," Lee Edward said, heading toward the livery.

"Wait a minute, Lee Edward. Twin Sisters is right there," Abe said, pointing to a nearby summit. "It's about fifteen miles east of here. The problem is this old cabin is about halfway up the slope. If there was a lookout posted, he'd have a view of anybody coming in their direction for miles."

"We're just going to have to take that chance," Lee Edward said, "because I don't intend to leave her up there, and I don't think you are either."

"If we got to the other side of the mountain, they wouldn't see us coming," Abe said.

"All right, we get to the other side of the mountain," Lee Edward said. "How long would that take us?"

"If you go straight toward it, like Abe said, it would only be about fifteen miles," Linus said. "But to get around it, it'd be almost forty miles."

"I don't see as we have any choice," Lee Edward said. "Curley, I appreciate you bringing this to us, and if you ever want to come back to Long Trail, you're welcome."

"I don't know about that." He looked at Abe.

Linus laughed. "You don't have to worry about him. It's like Abe's a new man."

Logan smiled. "Then I'd love to come back to Long Trail. If you want me to, I'll come with you to get Miss Hunter back."

"Then let's head out," Lee Edward said.

The four started toward the livery but on the way, a dust devil formed on the road in front of them.

"Wind!" Lee Edward said excitedly. "Yes, wind! That's what we need!"

Abe frowned in confusion. "Are you all right, Lee Edward? You're not making much sense."

"I'm making a lot of sense, my soon-to-be brother-in-law. We need to go back to the bank."

"Why? Mr. Rowe already told us he won't lend us any money." Abe said.

"I'm thinking five hundred dollars is about all I'll need."

"Now I'm getting a little worried about you," Abe said.

"Just hold on, you'll see," Lee Edward said with a huge smile.

After drawing five hundred dollars from the Long Trail account, Lee Edward started out at a very brisk walk. Abe, Linus, and Curley still didn't know what was going on, but they almost ran to keep up with him. Then, as they approached the open field behind the fairgrounds, it dawned on Abe what was in Lee Edward's mind.

"You want to go up in a balloon," Abe said.

"Yes."

"But we don't need to see where the cabin is. Curley already told us, and I know where it is."

"The wind," Lee Edward said.

"What about the wind?"

"You'll see."

When they reached the park, Lee Edward saw Professor Koch sitting on a folding chair. He was trying to read the newspaper, but he was having a hard time hanging on to it.

"Professor," Lee Edward said. "I would like to make use of your balloon."

"Really? Didn't I take you and a young lady up the other day? I don't think you'll want to go up, because with this breeze, you'll be bouncing around a lot—liable to lose your breakfast." The professor laughed. "There'll be all kinds of air boxes around here."

"I don't want it to stay tethered. I need to get to the other side of that mountain." He pointed to Twin Sisters. "And I'll give you five hundred dollars to put me on the ground over there."

"Five hundred dollars?" Koch said with a huge smile. "Gentlemen, you are about to make a balloon flight."

"Oh, no, I'm not getting' in that thing," Linus said as he backed off.

"Me neither," Curley said.

"All right, Abe, it's just you and me and the professor."

* * *

LEE EDWARD and Abe climbed into the balloon, Koch dropped the tether, and the balloon started up. The wind, just as Lee Edward had predicted, carried the balloon east toward Twin Sisters Mountain. Because the wind was as brisk as it was, they were going at a rapid pace.

"How fast do you think we're going?" Lee Edward asked.

"I'd say about thirty miles an hour," Koch said.

Lee Edward smiled. "Good. We'll be there within half an hour."

"I see the cabin," Abe said. He was using the binoculars. "There are two men on lookout about two hundred yards away. Do you think they'll see us coming?"

"If they looked up, they could see us," the professor said, "but they sure can't hear us, so I don't think they'll know we're here."

"I'd like you to set us down as soon as we get on the other side," Lee Edward said. "Can you do that?"

"Easily enough."

"Oh," Lee Edward said. "I wasn't thinking about you. What will you do after you drop us off?"

"No problem, I'll just fly on to the next town I see. When I land, I'll hire a wagon to take me and my balloon back to Kerrville."

* * *

JUST AFTER THEY passed over the summit of Twin Sisters, Koch made the gas adjustment that enabled the balloon to descend. It touched down no more than a hundred yards below the peak.

Lee Edward and Abe jumped down from the basket, then Lee Edward gave Koch a wave as he pushed enough gas into the envelope to allow the balloon to ascend once more. Catching the same westerly wind that had brought them, the balloon began to move off to the east.

"I wish I had thought for us to get our rifles," Lee Edward said.

"We'll make up with surprise what we lack in rifles," Abe said.

Lee Edward chuckled. "I have no doubt."

A few minutes later, the two of them were at the top of the peak, looking down toward the little cabin. They picked out the two men they had seen from the balloon who were down the slope. Though the lookouts thought they were well-covered, they were so exposed to Abe and Lee Edward that Lee Edward felt almost guilty for having such an advantageous position.

"Are we just going to start shooting or give them a chance to surrender?" Abe asked.

"Your call," Lee Edward replied.

"Let's start shooting."

"Wait. Mary Beth must be in the cabin, and that means someone will be with her. If he hears shooting outside, he might..." Lee Edward started.

"You don't have to go any further," Abe said. "It looks to me like what we have to do is get into the house before we do anything."

"Exactly," Lee Edward agreed.

Lee Edward and Abe approached the cabin from the rear. It wasn't necessary that they sneak down, because none of Mary Beth's guards expected anyone to be coming from that direction.

They made it to the back of the house, then looked in through the window. They saw Mary Beth sitting on the floor by the wall. It looked like her feet were tied, but Lee Edward couldn't tell for sure. There were two men with her, but they were sitting at a table on the opposite side of the cabin from Mary Beth. They were playing a game of cards.

"The big one's Bull Travers," Lee Edward whispered. "But I don't know the other one."

"That's Jim Grayson. He works for Pugh," Abe said.

"Travers and Grayson, well, that certainly backs up Logan's report," Lee Edward said. "There's no question who's behind this then, is there?"

"How do we get inside?"

Lee Edward pointed to the back door. "I doubt that it's locked, because they won't be expecting anybody approaching from this side. If it is locked, we'll have to kick the door in."

Abe tried the door, then smiled when he discovered that it was indeed unlocked. Abe opened the door, then with guns in hand, he and Lee Edward stepped into the cabin.

* * *

MARY BETH WAS uncomfortable because of the way she was tied and the way she was forced to sit. She was also frightened, because she was sure nobody knew where she was.

When she heard the back door open, she looked up, expecting to see one of the other men. Instead, it was Lee Edward and Abe.

Mary Beth felt a surge of joy and excitement that was almost too much to contain.

Travers saw the two at about the same time Mary Beth had, and his reaction was just as unexpected but there was no joy.

"Grayson!" Travers shouted as he drew his pistol and pointed it toward Lee Edward.

Grayson, reacting to the shout, drew his own pistol. For the next few seconds, the cabin was filled with the sound of gunshots. When the shooting finished, Travers and Grayson lay under a cloud of gun smoke, dead on the floor.

"Keep an eye out front," Lee Edward said as he hurried to free Mary Beth.

"Here they come," Abe said. He chuckled. "They haven't even drawn their guns; they just look like the gunshots have confused them."

The front door opened, and the two men came in.

"What the hell were you two shooting at?" one of the two men asked.

"Howdy, Ron," Abe said with a broad smile. "They were shooting at us. How about you two dropping your pistol belts?"

"What the hell?" Ron Ferrell shouted. "Where'd you two come from? How the hell did you get here?"

"You might say we flew in," Abe answered with a chuckle.

The two men, Ron Ferrell and Leon Bentley, were even more confused by Abe's answer.

"How about you two dragging Travis and Grayson out of here and drape them across their horses?" Lee Edward said. "We'll be taking them and you with us when we go back to town."

* * *

IT WAS ALMOST dark when the attention of the citizens of Kerrville was drawn to the macabre little parade moving down Goat Creek Road. It was a wagon followed by two horses, but it wasn't the size of the parade that drew everyone's attention. The wagon was being driven by Lee Edward Holt, and sitting beside him was Mary Beth Hunter. In the back of the wagon, Abe Hunter was guarding two prisoners, and the horses following the wagon each had a body draped across the saddle.

"Look, it's Mary Beth Hunter! Holt and her brother found her!" someone shouted as he ran toward the wagon.

"And that's Bull Travers," one of the townspeople said, pointing to one of the bodies lying belly down over a horse.

"And the other one's Jim Grayson," another said.

"Them two that's tied up in the back of the wagon is Ron Ferrell 'n Leon Bentley."

"All four o' them boys works for Pugh," another said.

"Damn, you reckon Pugh was behind takin' that girl like they done?"

"I say there ain't no doubt."

They stopped in front of the marshal's office, but they didn't have to go inside, because both Marshal Wallace and Deputy Carr had been drawn outside by curiosity.

"I didn't think you could pull this off," Marshal Wallace said. "When they told me what fool-thing you was a tryin', I thought for sure I'd be sending a search party out lookin' for three bodies."

"Well, we're back, and we have Mary Beth safe and sound," Lee Edward said. "But seeing as how all four of these men worked for the Double Diamond, what does that tell you?"

"Well, this could be a wild guess, you understand, but I'd have to say that makes Pugh guilty of conspiracy to kidnap," Marshal Wallace replied with a smile.

* * *

THE TRIAL WAS two weeks later. The prosecution tried to make the case that Angus Pugh was responsible for Jacob

Austin's death, but he was unable to connect the two cases. The best they could do was sentence Pugh, along with Ferrell and Bentley, to thirty years in prison for the kidnapping of Mary Beth Hunter.

After the trial, Lee Edward, Mary Beth, Abe, Hannah, Linus, and several others of the Long Trail hands were at the Hill Country Inn. Conrad Barnet had baked a chocolate cake, and he carried it out to the table.

"Why, thank you, Conrad," Mary Beth said. "You didn't have to do this."

"I wanted to," Conrad said. "You should see the wedding cake I'm going to bake for you two."

"What?" Hannah exclaimed. "Are you getting married?"

"Yes, are we getting married?" Lee Edward asked.

Mary Beth smiled. "I said Christmas, but I think a fall wedding would be better."

"Then a fall wedding it will be," Lee Edward said.

"Uhhh, boss, you'd better make that after the round-up," Linus said.

Mary Beth laughed. "Yes, after the round-up."

If you like this, you may also enjoy: A Rambling Man
Lucas Cain Book One

Bestselling author Robert Vaughan is back with another riveting adventure sure to please fans of all ages.

Captured in the last year of the Civil War, Lucas Cain becomes a POW in the infamous Andersonville prison. There he learns how to survive the cruelty of the Confederate guards, and the perfidy of a few who are prisoners themselves.

When the war ends, Lucas and almost 1,500 others crowd aboard the riverboat *Sultana*, which has a capacity of just under 400 passengers. After an unforeseen event occurs, Lucas finds himself further adrift.

Returning home to Cape Girardeau, Missouri, Lucas becomes a police officer. At the time, Cape Girardeau policemen received no salary, but were paid for specific tasks, including receiving bounties for prisoners captured. Lucas also finds an unexpected love interest in a journalist who works for the Cape Girardeau newspaper.

Tragedy strikes, and Lucas finds himself no longer able to remain in Cape Girardeau. He begins a western drift, rambling without a specific destination. He becomes a bounty hunter, and is very successful at it, eventually finding an opportunity to settle accounts with an old enemy.

AVAILABLE NOW

About the Author

Robert Vaughan sold his first book when he was nineteen. That was several years and nearly five-hundred books ago. Since then, he has written the novelization for the mini-series Andersonville, as well as wrote, produced, and appeared in the History Channel documentary Vietnam Homecoming.

Vaughan's books have hit the NYT bestseller list seven times. He has won the Spur Award, the Porgie Award in Best Paperback Original, the Western Fictioneers Lifetime Achievement Award, the Readwest President's Award for Excellence in Western Fiction, and is a member of the American Writers Hall of Fame and a Pulitzer Prize nominee.

He is also a retired army officer, helicopter pilot with three tours in Vietnam, who has received the Distinguished Flying Cross, the Purple Heart, The Bronze Star with three oak leaf clusters, the Air Medal for valor with 35 oak leaf clusters, the Army Commendation Medal, the Meritorious Service Medal, and the Vietnamese Cross of Gallantry.